Akhenaten's Alibi

Text copyright 2014 Fiona Deal
All Rights Reserved

This is a work of fiction.
Names, characters, places and incidents
either are the product of the author's imagination
or are used fictitiously.

Chapter 1

Summertime 2013

Our good friend Walid Massri told us he was being blackmailed on the same day President Mohamed Morsi announced he was appointing a former Islamist terror leader as the new governor in Luxor.

'We may as well pack up and go home, Merry,' Adam said in disgust. He looked up from his iPad screen, where he was reading the BBC News online. 'Morsi has just appointed Adel el-Khayat, a former jihadi, as our new governor. He's the same man whose fundamentalist group committed the massacre at Hatshepsut's temple in 1997.'

I stared back at him in horror, and moved to stand behind him so I could read the news article over his shoulder. I whispered the words aloud as I read, *"Adel el-Khayat was a founding member of the fundamentalist group Al-Gamaa Al-Islamiya. During the 1990s Al-Gamaa Al-Islamiya carried out a wave of terrorist atrocities targeting civilians and Western tourists. Scores were murdered, leading many analysts to speculate that Egypt was succumbing to an 'Islamic revolution on the Nile'."*

Adam took over and voiced the next paragraph, *"In 1997 the group committed its most high profile operation. Over the course of 45 minutes, six gunmen systematically* murdered 58 tourists and four Egyptians inside the Temple of Hatshepsut in Luxor."

I felt my stomach shift as a wave of nausea hit me. Hatshepsut's temple is one of my favourite places on earth. I knew about the tragedy, of course. But hearing it described like that made me feel physically sick.

'If Morsi is trying to kill the tourist industry in Egypt stone dead, he's going the right way about it!' Adam bit out. 'I don't see how we can possibly hope to survive this. Tourism's already on its knees thanks to the 2011 uprising that removed Hosni Mubarak from office. This feels like the last nail in the coffin!'

His gloriously mixed metaphors told me much about his agitated state of mind. 'But, look!' I interjected, desperate to close my ears to the resounding death knell to all our hopes and dreams I could hear ringing from the wooden beams of our dahabeeyah. 'It says here that Al-Gamaa Al-Islamiya renounced violence ages ago.'

'Try telling that to holidaymakers weighing up the relative merits of a week on the Nile versus a week sunning themselves on a beach in the Canaries,' Adam said with a defeated air. 'It's no use, Merry. The writing's on the wall and we have no choice but to read it. Thinking we could set up in business offering luxury Nile cruises to discerning travellers in the aftermath of the Egyptian Revolution, and with an Islamist like President Morsi running the show was naïve at best, and sheer lunacy at its – probably more accurate – worst! Any traveller worthy of being described as 'discerning' will be giving Egypt a wide berth as a holiday destination for a good long while to come. Let's face it; we haven't had a sniff of a booking since Ben Hunter was here in April. We can't go on like this.'

'But, surely we shouldn't just give up and go home with our tail between our legs,' I argued. 'There's bound to be protest at this appointment. I don't believe the hoteliers and tour operators in Luxor will sit idly by while this Adel el-Khayat takes up his new office. And we know there's already a lot of bad feeling against President Morsi. All the talk on the street is of plans to hold nationwide anti-government rallies at the end of this month to mark the one-year anniversary of his election as president. If you ask me, we should just sit it out and wait to see what happens.'

'The Muslim Brotherhood will never allow Morsi to be ousted,' Adam said, shaking his head. 'They say the calls for his resignation are an illegitimate attempt to undermine democracy in Egypt.'

'But things can't go on as they are!' I protested. 'Every day we suffer power blackouts and read in the News about foreign investors pulling out. And we know how scarce fuel is. Just look how long we had to queue for bottled gas yesterday!'

'You're describing a nation in turmoil, Merry,' Adam said sadly, reaching out to take my hand and drawing me down to crouch alongside him so he could look into my eyes. 'And my feeling is it's going to get worse before it gets better. No, lovely; I think we have to face facts. Egypt's not the place for us right now, no matter how much we love it. And, let's face it; it's damnably hot here in June, July and August. Maybe we should head back to England for the summer and sit things out there, out of harm's way.'

And that's when we heard the shout from the causeway outside where our dahabeeyah is docked, announcing the arrival of our good friend from the Egyptian Antiquities Museum in Cairo, Walid Massri.

He'd called us last night to say he had business in Luxor and asked if we could put him up on board the *Queen Ahmes* for a couple of days. Of course we were delighted to have him come to stay.

But it was obvious something was badly wrong from the moment we clapped eyes on him as we leapt up to greet him and he stepped onto the gangplank to come aboard.

Walid wears a perpetually world-weary air. This may have something to do with being slight of stature, with sloping shoulders and a just discernible stoop; probably the result of years spent bending over the antiquities it's his duty to conserve. He also looks to be permanently coated in dust; with dry, flaky brown skin and wispy hair that he combs carefully forward but sadly fails to disguise his seriously receding hairline. Yet when he speaks he has an aura of quiet authority about him, which subdues many who might take it into their heads to debate any particular point. And he has a fearsome intellect; regarded as one of the foremost Egyptologists his nation has produced - whilst never actually having courted fame or the Discovery Channel cameras in quite the same way as his more famous ex-colleague and erstwhile director of the Cairo Museum, a certain Mr Zahi Hawass.

Looking at Walid now, I was struck by how particularly dejected he looked. I'd call it more defeated than world-weary. It was enough to have me worriedly reaching out to him as he stepped off the gangplank into our little wood-panelled reception area. 'Walid! You look exhausted! What's the matter? Are you ill?'

He attempted a smile and patted my hand where I'd reached out and grasped his. 'No, no; I am quite well, thank you Merry.'

'But you look as if you're carrying the weight of the world on your shoulders!'

Adam reached for Walid's overnight bag. 'Let the poor man get his feet over the threshold, Merry!' he chided. But I could see he shared my concern from the narrowed glance he quickly masked behind a broad smile of welcome. 'Let's deposit your bag in your cabin, Walid; then you can take a shower and join us up on deck in the shade for a nice refreshing drink.'

Walid seemed only too happy to put this plan into action and wash away the travel-fatigue of his flight down from Cairo, if not whatever was so clearly bothering him.

'He looks positively done in,' I murmured to Adam as we prepared a fruit cordial in our gleaming stainless steel kitchen, adding quantities of ice made from our specially purified water to the pitcher to counteract the aggressive Egyptian heat.

'Give him a chance to catch his breath before you pounce on him,' Adam admonished with a small smile to show his tolerance of my habitual impatience. 'I'm sure he'll tell us what's worrying him without you needing to wrest it from him in one great heave.'

I took his advice and sat fiddling with the braiding on my chair cushion when Walid joined us up on deck. I turned my attention to the felucca being hauled up the Nile by a motorised water taxi, against the flow of the water, and in the non-existent breeze. It was preferable to fixing my gaze on the hollowed cheeks and harried expression of our friend and waiting for him to speak.

'So, what business is it that brings you to Luxor?' Adam asked in jovial tones after a long pause during which Walid intermittently sipped his cordial and shredded the paper napkin he'd draped across his knees in readiness for the small finger sandwiches I'd prepared.

Walid sent him what I can only describe as a hunted look. Then his shoulders slumped. 'There's no point in putting it off any longer,' he said in his softly Arabic-accented English. 'I have come to share something with you both and to ask your advice. I thought about confiding in Shukura...' he gave a small shake of his head, '...but she is too volatile in her nature. And Ted ... well, Ted draws on in his years, and I have no wish to worry him if it should prove unnecessary...'

It's fair to say the towed-up-the-Nile felucca immediately ceased to hold my attention. My gaze snapped to Walid's face the moment he started speaking.

'Of course, Ahmed is probably the one whose help I should seek. I daresay this is a matter for the police. But ...' He let the sentence trail off.

To say I was impatient for him to get to the point would be putting it more than mildly. It felt as if someone had replaced the blood in my veins with Tabasco sauce. 'But...?' I prompted.

He looked at me squarely and I watched him draw a deep breath, steadying himself. 'But the find was yours, Merry; yours and Adam's. So it's only fair I should speak to both of you first.'

The breath left my body in a great collapse of air at the mention of the word 'find' as if someone had whacked me in the solar plexus with a cricket bat. There was only one thing he could be referring to.

'I was foolish to think we could keep it a secret ... such an overwhelming discovery ...'

'One of us has broken ranks?' I cried, jumping up from my recliner and sending the cushion spinning across the deck. 'I don't believe it! We promised never to breathe a word! Who...?'

'No, Merry; it's not what you think,' Walid entreated, sending a look of naked appeal across at Adam. I was clearly proving myself every bit as volatile as Shukura.

Frowning, Adam stood up, reached out for me and drew me back. I slumped onto my seat; aware I was gaping inelegantly at our guest.

'I received a ... *communication*,' Walid said, choosing the word with care. 'Enclosed with it was a photocopy of a letter; a letter I had every reason to recognise ... and curse ... Because of course it was my idea to write it, and to make sure it was replicated several times over so each of us had a copy...'

My racing brain was starting to grasp his meaning. But Adam beat me to it.

'You mean, the letters you asked each of us to copy and sign the morning after you first rescued Merry and me from the ...' He trailed off.

'...from the tomb...' I whispered. 'My God, Walid! Someone's got hold of one of the letters? But I thought we'd all agreed to keep them locked up in bank vaults or safe deposit boxes?'

'Well, yes...' he said, looking uncomfortable. 'But we were counting without one of our number meeting an untimely end and leaving behind his personal effects to be sorted through and cleared after his death.'

'Mustafa Mushhawrar,' Adam breathed.

I felt a chill go through me and shivered despite the blazing heat.

'Quite,' Walid said in grim tones.

I remembered the fastidious former official of the Ministry for the Preservation of Ancient Monuments here in Luxor with a shudder of distaste. His untimely end had been of his own doing. Realising he'd been caught in the act of robbing the tomb we'd made a solemn pact to keep secret and protect, he'd deliberately set off a rock fall, burying himself and his shady companion beneath tons of rubble.

I found it impossible to regret his passing, since that same rock fall had imprisoned Adam, together with our best-buddy-cum-police-chum Ahmed - and not forgetting me - within the dead-aired sepulchre. But it was clear Mustafa's death had left a dangerously loose end hanging.

'So, one of Mustafa's bereaved relatives has come into possession of Mustafa's copy of the letter,' Adam said, his brain slotting the pieces together. 'And ...what...?'

'And he knows about the tomb!' I cried on a rising note of panic. 'It's obvious, isn't it?'

'...And he's seeking to blackmail me,' Walid said rather more slowly, even though he started speaking at the same time as me. His tone was so heavy it seemed to have lead weights attached.

'*What?*' Adam and I spoke the single word in unison. It managed to convey our shock, outrage and alarm as eloquently as a good many more words might have done. I was still grappling with the revelation that some stranger was now party to our closely guarded secret. That he'd hit on the idea of using his newfound knowledge so callously was a body blow that left me reeling.

Walid ran a rather shaky hand over his forehead, brushing away beads of perspiration. Then he reached into the breast pocket of his shirt and drew out a folded sheet of paper. I could see as he smoothed it out that it had rows of words cut from Arabic newspapers pasted onto it.

'Hmm, that old chestnut,' I muttered. 'Not very original, is it?'

Adam's Arabic is less than fluent and mine, apart from a few spoken words, remains - to my shame - largely non-existent. So Walid cleared his throat and translated aloud for our benefit.

"*I know your secret. Here is the proof. You will pay me, or I will talk. If you value your job at the museum and your reputation, you will be quick to pay. I want LE 10,000,000. You have one month. Await my further instructions.*" Walid folded the paper and sat slumped in his chair, a picture of misery and fear.

Adam and I stared at him with bulging eyes, assimilating the stark contents of the letter.

'Ten million Egyptian pounds is around a million pounds sterling, give or take,' Adam calculated.

Walid dropped his head forward into his hands and sat holding it, 'Where am I supposed to get hold of that sort of money?'

'When was the letter dated?' I asked, my brain working frantically. 'How much time do we have?'

Walid looked up and rubbed his eyes. 'It was sent to me at the museum last week.' It didn't look as if he'd slept a wink since. 'We have until early July.'

'And he enclosed Mustafa's letter along with the blackmail note?' I frowned.

'A photocopy of it,' Walid nodded. 'I don't imagine he's going to let the original out of his grasp for love nor money.' He clearly realised what he'd said and was quick to rectify the error and rephrase it. 'That is to say, we can only hope ten million Egyptian pounds will be enough to prise it from his sticky fingers. The alternative doesn't bear thinking about.'

I didn't need to see the photocopied letter to remember its explosive contents. In simple terms it told the story of

13

perhaps the most earth-shattering archaeological discovery of all time.

I don't suppose there can be many discoveries that would make Howard Carter's of Tutankhamun's tomb seem little more than a warm-up act. But I think I can say without fear of contradiction that ours - once the world came to learn of it - would easily claim that distinction.

Astonishing, incredible, unbelievable as it may be ... and, take my word for it, I could go on with the superlatives all day ... we had the dubious honour of being the finders of a hidden tomb that remained unknown to the rest of the world. Our tomb – for that's how I thought of it - contained the mummified remains and spectacular treasures of two of the most iconic names to come down to us from the depths of antiquity. These were none other than the heretic pharaoh Akhenaten and the world-renowned beauty, his queen and great royal wife, Nefertiti.

It was almost too much to take in, even now; and I'd had quite a long time to come to terms with it. Adam and I made the discovery almost exactly a year ago.

You may well ask how two ordinary people such as Adam and me – who may share a love of Egypt's ancient history – but have no Egyptological or archaeological qualifications or credentials between us (apart from Adam's unfinished degree and more recent online studies) should come to make such a remarkable find. The briefest answer I can give is that it started when, on a tourist holiday in the spring of last year, I found myself locked inside the Howard Carter Museum. Trying to escape, I smashed a framed picture of an original Howard Carter watercolour. Inside I found a cryptic message from the great excavator himself. Suffice it to say the message led us to discover an ancient papyrus originally from Tutankhamun's tomb. And decipherment of the papyrus led us to discover the tomb.[1]

Your next question might be to ask why we failed to announce our discovery. Particularly pertinent this, since it quite clearly left us frighteningly exposed to the blackmail scenario it seemed we were unhappily embroiled in now.

It was no great comfort to recall the vow of secrecy had been Walid's idea. He'd been determined the world should learn of the tomb, but deemed the timing all wrong. Egypt was a country in crisis, he'd said. To be fair, it was starting to feel as if it had been so for a long time, certainly since the Revolution of the Arab Spring in 2011. And it was looking increasingly and distressingly as if this may remain the case for some considerable time to come.

In the immediate aftermath of our discovery a year ago, Walid decided we should wait for a cooling off period of six months. The presidential elections were in full swing. Egypt was taking its first tentative steps towards real democracy.

---

[1] *Carter's Conundrums* and *Tutankhamun's Triumph* – Books 1 and 2 of Meredith Pink's Adventures in Egypt

Walid decreed we should say nothing before December to allow time for things to settle down and then take a view on the merits of coming clean.

But by the time December arrived the decision to maintain our vow of silence was coloured by a couple of weighty considerations.

Firstly, the new democratically elected president Mohamed Morsi had ceded himself what some described as 'almost Pharaonic powers' enabling him to legislate without judicial oversight or review of his actions. Whilst he rescinded the extremities of this position under pressure, his new constitution stirred up huge political unrest. Fully-fledged street battles broke out in Cairo between his opponents and supporters.

Secondly, one of the small band of conspirators bound by our solemnly sworn oath of silence broke ranks in quite spectacular fashion. Unlike the rest of us, Mustafa Mushhawrar was forced by the nature of his job as a member of Luxor's Ministry for the Preservation of Ancient Monuments to report for duty every day at Hatshepsut's mortuary temple on the west bank.

I don't recall if I've mentioned that our tomb lies hidden behind the walls of the Hathor Chapel on the first elevation of Hatshepsut's magnificent temple. This is where Tutankhamun and his chief vizier Ay decided to bring their 'precious jewels' Akhenaten and Nefertiti for reburial from Amarna (ancient

Akhet-Aten). They reckoned nobody would think to look there since Hatshepsut's temple was dedicated to the god Amun, whom Akhenaten sought to destroy when he elevated the Aten for sole worship.

They were right. They reburied Akhenaten, Nefertiti and a glittering selection of their treasures in something like 1333BC. We discovered them in June AD2012. In all the millennia in between, nobody thought to look for any trace of an Amarnan royal burial in the Deir el-Bahri cliffs. The controversial pharaoh and his glorious queen lay undisturbed all the while, just as Tutankhamun and Ay intended.

Undisturbed, that is, until Adam and I sleuthed our way inside. Our plan was to lock up and leave their tomb as we found it until Walid deemed the time was right to announce the discovery. Sadly we counted without Mustafa and his surrender to temptation.

It turned his head to report for work every day, draw his meagre salary, and know he was within a stone's throw of riches beyond his wildest dreams. Over the course of a few months he single-handedly dug his way through the rock of the cliff face behind the temple. His calculations proved unswervingly accurate, and he broke through into the burial chamber, shoring up the crumbling walls of his tunnel as he went. Who knows what riches he might have spirited away had we not caught him in the act.[2]

---

[2] *Hatsheput's Hideaway* – Book 3 of Meredith Pink's Adventures

Caught red-handed, perhaps he felt he had no choice but to set off the avalanche of rock that trapped Adam, Ahmed and me inside the tomb. It sent clouds of dust and loose chippings billowing into the tomb, smothering everything in a thick coating of filth, and successfully cutting off our escape route. I flatter myself I'd been making pretty impressive progress towards setting us free after Ahmed managed to impale himself on a stake. But my efforts proved unnecessary when our stalwart friends arrived in the nick of time to rescue us.

Perhaps you'll think I'm stretching credulity to the limit when I tell you there were nine of us who'd signed up to Walid's vow of silence before Mustafa went to the bad.

There was Ted, of course – Adam's old university lecturer, an Egyptologist specialising in philology. He retired out to Cairo a few years ago. He'd helped us decipher the hieroglyphic message I found inside Howard Carter's smashed picture frame. He also painstakingly translated the papyrus that led us to discover the secret location of the tomb. So it's fair to say he was in it with us up to his neck. Then there was Ted's daughter Jessica. She'd entered into a disastrous marriage with a smooth-tongued Egyptian who turned out to be a double-dyed criminal guilty of breaking into the Cairo museum during the 2011 Revolution. He and his villainous brothers made off with priceless artefacts, which

---

in Egypt

they were gleefully selling onto the black market before we intervened and put a stop to their shenanigans. This proved a happy outcome for Jessica as it not only released her from the bonds of her ill-judged marriage, but also introduced her to a certain ex-boyfriend of mine, Dan, with whom she was now happily co-habiting in the suburbs of south London.

It also provided a once-in-a-lifetime opportunity for Shukura al-Busir, a colleague of Walid's from the Egyptian Antiquities Museum in Cairo, to hog the limelight, featuring prominently in Egyptian newspapers as the local heroine credited with foiling the villainous brothers' thievery.

Then there was Walid himself. He was involved up to his eyeballs for permitting the "loan" of genuine Tutankhamun treasures, needed to free us from entrapment within the tomb.

Which left just Adam, myself, our police buddy Ahmed; and of course the dearly departed Mustafa Mushhawrar to make up the numbers. Nine people was quite a large cohort to swear to secrecy. But we'd each taken the oath with all due solemnity, never thinking this could happen.

I stared wild-eyed at Walid. 'We've got to find this blackmailer and we've got to stop him!'

Walid met my gaze, 'Yes, or else he'll pick us off one by one or simply blow the whistle and destroy us all. I was mad to think we should wait.'

'But with the political situation as it is, and with the tomb needing a few solid days' worth of effort with a dustpan and brush, honestly what choice did you have?' Adam asked. 'You couldn't possibly have foreseen this!'

'So, what are our options?' I demanded, thinking frantically. 'Surely the only way to call his bluff is to announce the discovery of the tomb now.'

'But how do we account for the delay?' Walid moaned, shaking his head. 'No, the authorities would lock us – or at least me – up and throw away the key. I'd lose my job for sure. And you two would be flung out of Egypt and have your visas rescinded. You'd lose this beautiful dahabeeyah and never be allowed back into the country. I can't have that on my conscience.'

I agreed these outcomes were too horrific to contemplate, but my brain was still whirring madly. 'Ok, so maybe we need to somehow 'stage' the discovery, so it looks as if we've only just stumbled across the tomb now. You've still got the papyrus safely locked away in a vault at the museum, haven't you?'

'Well yes,' Walid said slowly, looking doubtful. 'But all the reasons for keeping the tomb secret are still valid... perhaps even more so considering the planned protests against President Morsi.'

'Which will only get worse now he's appointed an ex-terrorist as the new Governor of Luxor,' Adam added darkly.

'Law and order broke down during the 2011 Revolution,' Walid reminded us. 'Even now, security at our archaeological sites is woefully lacking. Stories of unauthorised digging are reported to me at the museum almost daily. The tanks on our streets and the armed militia seem ill-equipped to protect our precious heritage. If there is a full-scale military coup to remove President Morsi from office as some predict, things will only get worse. Our country is breaking apart. I repeat what I said last year. I cannot even contemplate revealing the tomb at a time like this. I would hold no jurisdiction over what might happen to it. I cannot and I will not allow that magnificent tomb to become a pawn in a political or nationalistic power struggle.' He broke off and mopped at his perspiring brow with the remains of his shredded napkin. 'No, my friends, our tomb must remain protected. Staging its discovery is not the right thing to do.'

'And besides, it would still leave our friendly blackmailer in possession of Mustafa's copy of the letter,' Adam pointed out. 'Staging the discovery now wouldn't necessarily stop him blowing the whistle on us and making it clear we've known about the tomb for a year.'

'But there must be something we can do!' I cried, raging at the sweeping sense of impotence.

Walid slumped back in his chair and swung his despairing gaze from me to Adam and back again. 'I have only two choices. I fear I must become either a thief or a murderer.'

Chapter 2

'Walid! What on earth do you mean?' I cried, jumping up again in my agitation.

Walid looked as if he might throw up at any moment. His brown skin took on a definite greenish tinge as he contemplated his options. I watched him make a couple of attempts to swallow as if choking back bile in his throat.

'It seems to me either I must find this man and I must… I must silence him,' he croaked hoarsely, forcing the words out. 'Or else… or else…' He trailed off, looking desperately at Adam, almost in the way of a drowning man pleading silently for someone to throw him a lifeline.

'…Or else you need to steal an artefact from the museum and sell it, probably illegally, in order to raise the ten million Egyptian pounds,' Adam provided in the flat tones of one who'd hoped he might be able to throw a lifeline but had reached out to find there was none there.

'Exactly.' Walid dropped his head forward into his hands again and sat there with his narrow shoulders heaving. That he relished neither of these prospects was obvious to anyone with eyes in their head and half a brain. But it was equally clear to me that of the two choices before him, he found the prospect of murder by far the least repellent. To

Walid, the thought of stealing one of the treasures it was his job to conserve at the museum was akin to slitting his own throat.

I darted forward and squeezed his shoulder. 'We'll find this blackmailer!' I vowed passionately. 'We'll find him and we'll get the letter back from him!'

Walid lifted his head slowly and turned his haggard face upwards towards mine. 'But how?'

'I don't know yet,' I admitted with a very slight deflation of the passion. 'But we'll do it, even if we have to steal it back from him. We'll enlist Ahmed's help. He knows just about everyone in Luxor. Tracking down Mustafa Mushhawrar's bereaved relatives, certainly those who might posthumously have come into possession of his personal effects surely shouldn't prove too difficult for an officer of the law, even if he is strictly speaking tourist police. And then we need to lay some sort of trap!'

Enlisting Ahmed's help proved easier than we might have imagined since he dropped by the dahabeeyah before reporting for his evening shift to tell us about the meeting being hastily convened by the city's tourism chiefs, hoteliers and tour operators to rally against the appointment of a former Islamist terrorist as our new governor.

'Protests will be held outside de governor's office on Monday afternoon!' he announced grandly. 'De tourist industry is beginning to mobilise against President Morsi!' He looked impossibly proud at using such a fine English word. I wondered briefly who he'd heard say it first. But I didn't dwell on this unkind thought since I was delighted to hear the news. And besides, Ahmed's command of English improves by the day. If only he could get the hang of his 'ths', he'd be there. 'De president's decision is completely wrong,' he went on, puffing out his chest and pacing up and down the deck. 'To appoint dis man who was a terror leader is a very bad omen for bringing back de tourists to our beloved Egypt! You will attend dis meeting, yes? De authorities, dey will listen to you I think.' He swung his trusting gaze from Adam's face to mine. Faced with this towering confidence in our powers of persuasion, I couldn't help but think fleetingly of my first meeting with him. It had been a rather different story back then. I'd thought he might arrest me, mistakenly believing me guilty of breaking and entering into Howard Carter's house, now turned into a museum on the west bank. His English on that occasion had been execrable, I recalled fondly. But everything had been smoothed over and I'd escaped with my freedom intact. And also with the little scrap of paper on which Howard Carter had drawn his hieroglyphic message. Looking at him, standing there like a great big bear dressed in a white uniform with black belt and boots, and with black and gold epaulets, my fondness magnified tenfold. The simple fact was I had a lot to thank our police pal for. If Ahmed hadn't set

Adam the task of trailing me back then, believing me to be some kind of con-artist-cum-antiquities-thief, I might not be leading the life I was today. In Adam, I've found my soulmate. Our life as owners of the *Queen Ahmes*, our restored Victorian dahabeeyah, is a dream come true. At least, it would be, if the tourist trade would just pick up so we could start running our Nile cruises… and if we could avoid being flung out of Egypt never to return thanks to Walid's blackmailer. Neither of which prospect looked particularly promising given the current turn of events.

Ahmed's reaction to Walid's story was predictable. He behaved much as an angry bear might, terrorized by a vicious hornet intent on landing a sting. Put it this way, he jumped up and down a bit and there was a lot of teeth gnashing. In Ahmed's case this was a sight to behold. Ahmed's teeth are not his strongest point in the looks department. Every time Ahmed smiles or, as was the case now, bares his teeth, I'm reminded he sorely needs the attentions of a good dentist. This is a shame since otherwise he's a good-looking man, if you happen to like them large. He has fine deeply brown eyes, which snap and flash with whatever emotion has a hold on him in any given moment, and a seal-like cap of black hair.

'I will investigate,' he swore solemnly, his eyes gleaming darkly. 'I will discover all de relatives of dat bad man Mustafa Mushhawrar, and I will interrogate dem!'

I suddenly had uncomfortable visions of the Spanish Inquisition. Ahmed is fiercely loyal, and his devotion might just get the better of him. Besides, I didn't suppose for a moment he'd forgotten the agony of being impaled on a stake at the bottom of the deadly pit shaft in the entrance corridor to our tomb. I had a feeling Ahmed might approach the hunting down of our unfriendly blackmailer as something of a personal crusade.

'Just give us a list of names,' I entreated. 'We'll decide how to tackle things once we know how many suspects we have.'

It was a strange thing to have been reminded by Ahmed's improving command of English of those first days of what I've now come to think of as my adventures in Egypt. Back then I was on a post-redundancy time-out trip with my boyfriend of ten years, Dan Fletcher. I couldn't possibly have imagined how much my life was about to change. Or how I'd come to realise that those ten years were a decade in which I'd been treading water.

It was another strange thing to be reminded that bad things tend to come in threes. This rather stark remembrance was delivered in the form of an email, arriving in the early evening of the same day we learned of President Morsi's disastrous decision and Walid's beastly blackmailer.

"I know what the Egyptian postal system is like," Dan started rather abruptly after the *"Dear Merry and Adam"* opener. *"So I thought I'd better email you rather than stick an invitation in the post box, since it might arrive this year, next year, sometime or never.*

Jessica and I are engaged. We're planning to tie the knot at Christmas and we'd like to invite you both to the wedding. I have no doubt Jessica will email you separately with all the fluffy details. Suffice it to say I can barely find an inch of free sofa space to sit down on since she's already littered the place with magazines and fabric swatches! So I'll sign off for now. Just wanted to give you as much notice as possible in the hope you won't have to cancel a boat-load of holidaymakers to attend …"

'Fat chance,' I muttered, wondering if this was Dan's pitiful attempt at a joke. He's never subscribed to the view that sarcasm is the lowest form of wit.

He signed off with just his name and one of those little smiley faces made up of a colon and a closed brackets sign that I find so irritating.

'So now we have a wretched wedding to contend with,' I grumped, slamming down the lid on my laptop. Even the thought of Dan's usually pristine bachelor pad disappearing under piles of girly wedding paraphernalia didn't cheer me up. In actual fact in made me feel worse. I stomped through to the kitchen, poured myself a large glass of Obelisk wine and took

27

it up on deck to watch the sunset in the hope the combination of alcohol and the glowing hothouse colours in the sky might lift my mood. But as I brooded on the appointment of the grisly governor, the threats from the beastly blackmailer and the invitation to the wretched wedding, I decided this had turned out to be one of the most unpleasant days I could remember having in a long time.

'Are you ok Merry? You've been awfully quiet since Dan's email arrived.'

We were lying in bed in our cabin. Very unusually for me, I'd failed to turn into Adam's arms when he joined me under the covers and reached across to kiss me. Instead I'd lain staring up at the panelled ceiling noticing a tiny cobweb shivering in the lamplight and in the nighttime breeze drifting in through the wooden shutters.

'Do you wish it was you he was marrying?' Adam asked quietly.

'No, it's not that.' I turned against him and his arm immediately came around me pulling me against him so I could lie with my head tucked against his shoulder. 'It's just, I've been thinking if we're not successful in getting the letter back from Walid's blackmailer, there are a lot of lives he could ruin. I mean, what if Walid somehow raises the money to pay the ransom but the blackmailer wants more and refuses to hand over the letter? Walid said earlier he might try to pick us off one by one. That means we could lose everything we're starting to build here, for all that it's taking an age to get things off the ground. Dan and Jessica might have to call off their wedding plans. And I don't even dare to think about what it might mean for Ahmed, or Ted, or Shukura.'

Adam turned his head and kissed my temple. 'I don't think you need worry too much about the risk to Dan and Jessica's nuptials. If Walid doesn't give our blackmailer what he wants, he's far more likely to set his sights on those of us easily within reach in Egypt, rather than cast his net as far afield as England. Besides, Ahmed's on the case now. Once we have an idea about who the villain's likely to be, I'm sure we can come up with a way of stopping him. C'mon Merry, you're the one with the fertile imagination – we'll think of something.'

I was rather glad he couldn't see my face. The fact of the matter was, while everything I'd just said was genuinely worrying me, Adam had actually struck closer to the truth than he might have imagined by asking if I wished it was me Dan had asked to marry him.

It wasn't that deep down I wanted to marry Dan or secretly burned any metaphorical candles for him. Far from it. I was Adam's, heart, body and soul, forever and ever. And yet I was finding it hard to quash the disquieting little voice whispering to me that in all of the ten years Dan and I had been together I don't think it ever occurred to him to try to put

29

a ring of any sort on my finger. And yet he'd been with Jessica for barely twelve months and, hey presto, here he was signing up for a lifetime commitment. I didn't want Dan, but I had a deep, dark suspicion I might want what Dan was offering Jessica, and had never offered me. It was this I didn't quite know how to put into words, and wouldn't admit to Adam even if I did. I was singingly happy with Adam, and yet … and yet … I'd not been aware of the silent longing for something more, not until Dan's dratted email pinged into my Inbox.

I knew Adam loved me. The simple fact of him having the sensitivity to even ask the question about Dan was proof of how in tune with me he was. If the roles had been reversed it would never have entered Dan's head to ask me a question like that. I doubt he'd even have noticed I was a bit withdrawn.

I was being stupid. I decided I should count my blessings instead of lying here wishing vaguely for more. Let's face it; I'm the luckiest woman on the planet. I'm in love with a wonderful man and loved by him in return. Adam is kind, warm, generous, funny, brave and clever. He shares my passion for Egypt. Oh, and he happens to be drop dead gorgeous with deep blue eyes that always have laughter lurking in them, and glossy dark brown hair that's always full of sunshine. He's lean and fit and tanned … and …and…

…And I turned into his arms, lifted my head from his shoulder and kissed him with a rather determined conviction that commitment was a feeling not a sparkling diamond, a band of gold or a piece of paper with a couple of signatures scrawled on it.

'Please don't worry, Merry,' he whispered against my lips. 'I'm not going to let anyone take this away from us. This is our dream, and nothing and nobody is going to stop us living it.'

It was all the commitment I needed.

The hastily convened meeting of all those with an interest in the tourist trade in Luxor was crowded and volatile. There were hoteliers and tour operators, tourism chiefs, taxi drivers and shop owners. Ahmed was there with a couple of his superiors, representing the tourist and antiquities police department. The discussion was held in a curious mixture of Arabic and English, depending on who was doing the talking. No one appeared to have any trouble understanding everything said. And while things became heated on occasions, the general vibe was one of accord and a shared view that President Morsi was asking for trouble.

'This new governor, this Adel el-Khayat, is not a suitable man for Luxor at all,' protested Mohamed Adel Samir, the manager of Viking Travel.

'But his terrorist group Al-Gamaa Al-Islamiya long ago renounced violence,' our friend Saleh the taxi driver piped up a bit uncertainly, as if he desperately wanted to believe this made the crucial difference.

His pronouncement was met with a furious grumbling and he subsided, bowing his head as if in apology for his naiveté. It didn't take a genius to work out that those who depended on tourism for their livelihoods – already feeling the pinch of an industry crippled by the 2011 revolt – were incensed that a man whose group did so much harm in Luxor had now been appointed the city's governor. Not for the first time, I wondered about how deep was the level of naiveté Adam and I were exhibiting, trying to get started in the tourist business in such troubled times, when those who were already well established were suffering such a catastrophic downturn.

'Luxor is a tourist town,' said Sameh Roshdy, a local travel agent. 'And now the new governor is one of those linked with the 1997 attack? We are not going to stand for this!'

Unlike Saleh's tentative assertion, this bold statement was met with shouts of approval and a forward thrust of momentum as the small crowd surged towards the speaker in support.

'Even if he has renounced his terrorist associations, this appointment is a disaster,' piped up Abdul el-Saiyyid, Ahmed's commanding officer in the police force. 'Adel el Khayat's party attacked not just tourists, but also the Coptic Church and the police. He has enemies in many parts of our society. Even now, his party calls for strict implementation of Islamic Shariah law. This includes imposing an Islamic dress code for women, banning alcohol, and preventing the mixing of the sexes. For those of us who work in a city as heavily dependant on tourism as Luxor, I can only worry that these intolerant policies will further hurt our businesses.'

'So what can we do?' shouted voices from the crowd.

'We must join the protests against President Morsi being held in Cairo on the one year anniversary of his election on 30th June,' called Yasser Samir, another taxi driver, whom Adam and I knew vaguely. 'Morsi is ruining our country! Look at the petrol queues every day. Today I joined a queue that stretched for nearly a mile. There's no water, no electricity!'

'Salaries are low, food prices are high!' one of the hoteliers added loudly. 'We must act now to protect our livelihoods from total annihilation!'

'Every day more and more Egyptians are losing faith with the Brotherhood,' a bearded man offered, announcing himself as Mohammed Khalifa, a local tour guide and opponent of the Morsi regime.

'We must picket the governor's office and prevent Adel el-Khayat from taking up his appointment,' said Sarwat el-Agamy, chairman of the Travel Agents Association in Luxor.

'Or maybe we should block his arrival at Luxor airport,' someone else shouted.

Adam stood up and I sucked in a deep breath of nervous anticipation. 'My friends, I am new to the tourist trade in Luxor,' he started. 'But I love this country and, more importantly, this city, and, together with my partner Meredith...' he put his arm around my shoulder in a gesture of solidarity and I stood up so I could be counted as agreeing from within the circle of his arm with whatever he might be about to say, '...I consider this my home from home. I want only the best for this wonderful city, which can lay claim to some of the country's most famous and glorious Pharaonic ruins. I agree we must protest the disastrous appointment of this former terrorist as our new governor. But we must do so peaceably. To do otherwise would reduce us to the worst kind of copycat cowards. We must resist the temptation to fight fire with fire. That only results in everyone getting burned ... or, what was your word...?' he turned respectfully towards the hotelier who'd spoken earlier, '...annihilated? We all agree any reminder of the 1997 attack on tourists at Hatshepsut's Temple will further deter holidaymakers already put off Egypt as a holiday destination by the uprising in 2011. But any hint of violence on our streets will only make things worse. If Egypt is truly taking its first steps towards a real and lasting democracy then it will welcome our protests as a positive and legitimate part of that journey. After all, freedom of speech is one of the tenets upon which true democracy is founded. So, I entreat you, my friends, let's make our collective voice heard but do it democratically. So, by all means let's picket outside the governor's office to show our disapproval, but we must resist any attempt to prevent Adel el-Khayat taking up his appointment by more direct methods.'

I think it may have been Ahmed who started the clapping. It was a little hesitant to gain momentum, but after a few moments every pair of hands in the crowd was joined in a rhythmic and rather overwhelmingly noisy affirmation of Adam's speech.

A couple of days later Adam glanced up from his laptop with a look of grim satisfaction. 'We have support in high places,' he said. 'Egypt's tourism minister, Hisham Zaazou has resigned his position in protest over the appointment of Adel el-Khayat. Morsi has yet to accept his resignation but it's pretty much a formality. Listen …'

And he proceeded to read aloud from the News website he was scanning. *"The appointment of Khayat, who denies personal involvement in the 1997 massacre, has enraged not just Zaazou, but the tourism industry in Luxor, which fears the symbolism of the appointment will put off potential visitors."*

'And listen to this,' he went on. *"One of 17 governors appointed by Morsi this week, Khayat was not the only appointee to have been greeted with outrage. One new governor was allegedly forced to go to work disguised in a niqab while another was hit by a shoe as protesters in at least eight provinces demonstrated against President Mohamed Morsi's controversial inclusion of several Islamists among the new crop of state administrators."*

He looked up at me briefly, and then kept on reading. *"Egypt is more polarised than at any point since 2011. Recent polls suggest Morsi's popularity has halved since his election a year ago, while opposition activists claim to have secured 15 million signatures on a petition calling on him to resign."*

I bit my lip. 'Morsi's going down on 30th,' I prophesied. 'I don't see how he can possibly hope to survive this. It's almost as if he's thrown a grenade at his own administration.'

'And potentially at democracy in Egypt,' Adam said grimly. 'Unless he can make a conciliatory gesture of some sort I really fear this will erupt into violence. And that could be the worst possible outcome for all concerned.'

Despite these promising signs, it didn't stop us picketing outside the governor's office in central Luxor with our comrades, or joining in with the blockade on the Nile. Everyone with a boat, be it a felucca, river taxi, skiff or, in our case, dahabeeyah, turned out in force to form a 'bridge of watercraft' spanning the width of the mighty river from the west bank to the east. It was quite a sight, testament to the strength of feeling and unity of spirit among Luxor's tourism workers and inhabitants.

A couple of days later the news came through that Adel el-Khayat, Luxor's new governor had resigned in response to the uproar in Luxor over his appointment.

I read the headline over Adam's shoulder and felt a slow grin spread across my face. 'Amen to that,' I breathed as my eyes took in the words, *"The new governor of Egypt's Luxor province has resigned amid controversy over his links to an Islamist group that carried out a deadly attack on tourists there in 1997."*

I plopped down alongside Adam on the sofa in our lounge-bar. 'It says Khayat denied any involvement in Al-Gamaa Al-Islamiya's militant past and resigned because he will not accept one drop of blood be spilt because of a position that he did not personally aspire to at any time! Can you believe that?'

Adam grunted an acknowledgement and reached for my hand. 'Well, Merry, at least we can feel a modicum of satisfaction knowing the voice of the people has been heard. Maybe there's hope for democracy in Egypt after all.'

I squeezed his hand back. But inwardly I was reserving judgement. After all, the planned protests against the Morsi regime in Cairo were still a couple of weeks away. And experience had taught me a lot could happen in a couple of weeks. We had a blackmailer to unmask. And if only things could stabilise politically, it might mean we could take a definite decision about our tomb. Egypt's bigger picture was just the backdrop to a much more personal set of dilemmas.

Things were looking up on the blackmail front too. Ahmed dropped by the dahabeeyah on the same day we learned Adel el-Khayat had resigned his governorship of Luxor.

Walid was still our guest on board the *Queen Ahmes*. It was almost as if he couldn't face going back to the museum until he knew what our prospects were of catching the villain who was making his life such a misery. I could well imagine how badly he wanted to go back and resume his duties free from the stain of needing to look at all the artefacts within his care and decide which of them to flog to raise the ransom money, and how to go about it. The stress of being in this limbo while we waited for the result of Ahmed's investigations continued to take its toll. He'd lost so much weight it looked as if a strong puff of wind would blow him away. His cheeks were sunken, his eyes hollow. Poor Walid was a thoroughly honest man who'd lived his whole life staunchly upholding the laws of Islam. I couldn't help but feel a stab of guilt every time I looked at his drawn features, knowing Adam and I were responsible for embroiling him in this whole mess. If he hadn't been the keeper of the genuine Tutankhamun treasures needed to access the tomb perhaps we could have spared him. It made me more determined than ever that Adam and I should also be the ones to release him from the purgatory he was living.

The look of mingled hopefulness and terror with which he greeted Ahmed's arrival was almost unbearable to observe.

'I have done my researches!' Ahmed announced self-importantly once he'd joined us up on the sundeck and wedged his oversized frame into one of our cushioned steamer recliners in the shade cast by the canvas awning strung from one side of the deck to the other. 'It was a simple matter in de end to discover de next of kin of dat scoundrel Mustafa Mushhawrar ...' His eyes gleamed brightly as he looked around at us.

Ahmed loves nothing more than to tell a story or to play a role. It struck me suddenly watching the way his hand lifted to his mouth as if to twirl a non-existent moustache that for this particular conversation he'd cast himself in the role of an Arabic version of Agatha Christie's Hercule Poirot unveiling his deductions. He was certainly portly enough, if a little on the tall and dark side. And, of course, there were the teeth to contend with. It was always difficult to overlook Ahmed's teeth.

It made me smile to rumble him - all the more so wondering where he'd come by the word *scoundrel*. Ahmed loves colourful English almost as much as he loves storytelling. But it was clear Walid was a bundle of nervous

39

energy so I felt I had no choice but to curtail our police pal's performance. Left to his own devices, Ahmed could stay in character indefinitely. 'And …?' I prompted.

He snapped a frown at me. I let it glance off me. On this occasion I really was much more in sympathy with Walid's nervous anticipation. '…And all of Mustafa Mushhawrar's worldly possessions were handed over to his elderly mother after his body was released for burial. Dere is no one else. So mother Mushhawrar, she must be de one …!'

I couldn't help but cover a smile and wonder what the redoubtable Ms Christie would make of our would-be detective and the simplicity of his deductions.

But sometimes simple is best.

'Well, it's a good place to start,' Adam said smoothly, catching my eye briefly so I knew we were thinking in tune as always. 'But it does rather leave me wondering about the cousin with a jewellery shop in the Souk and the young – er – scoundrel… who played stowaway on board the *SS Misr* last year, trying to steal back the necklace that was inadvertently sold to my ex-sister-in-law.'

'But I'm sure mother Mushhawrar is a good place to start,' I jumped in quickly, injecting bucketfuls of enthusiasm to make up for Adam's deceptively mild tones.

Poor Ahmed couldn't have looked more confused if we'd turned him in circles then presented him with a shedful of shovels and told him to take his pick.

Walid, by contrast, looked almost pathetically grateful to have somewhere to start. I don't suppose he really believed any more than we did that an elderly Egyptian lady who'd recently lost her son could really be our blackmailer. But one never knew. I daresay stranger things have happened. 'Does she live in Luxor?' Walid asked rather desperately.

'Yes; in New Gurna on de west bank,' Ahmed announced, puffing out his cheeks in a way that suggested he was trying to recover some lost ground. I daresay this scene had played out rather differently in his head while he'd been behind the wheel of his police car, driving over here to the stone causeway where our dahabeeyah is moored.

'Perhaps you should come with us when we go to interview her,' I invited in conciliatory tones, smiling at Ahmed to reinforce the genuineness of this request, and to be clear we were thankful in all seriousness for the lead he'd given us.

'Yes,' Adam agreed. 'An interview with mother Mushhawrar under police caution seems like something we should expedite as quickly as possible.'

I don't suppose for a moment Ahmed was familiar with the word *expedite* but it didn't matter since Adam had provided an immediate translation.

'I have time tomorrow afternoon,' Ahmed supplied. 'We will go den, yes?'

Chapter 3

The modern village of New Gurna lies on the west bank of the Nile, further along the tourist road that branches left and right close to Howard Carter's old house. The left-hand intersection leads to the Valley of the Kings, whilst on the right is the road to the mortuary temple of Seti I. It was purpose built to relocate the locals from their homes built atop the rabbit warren of tombs once belonging to ancient noblemen who served under successive pharaohs. These are carved deep into the Theban hills and there are upwards of a hundred of them.

The original village of Gurna from whence the villagers had now been unceremoniously evicted dated back at least a couple of hundred years, and was still occupied during my first visits to Egypt a few years back. This scramble of tumbledown homes was a rather mysterious place full of intriguing histories of tomb robbers and rogues who built their mud brick dwellings right on top of some of the world's most treasured and ancient tombs. The problems this presented to the authorities were many and varied. For starters, the stories of tomb robbery were true. Our police chum Ahmed may be a fine upstanding pillar of the community nowadays but his ancestry is not of such unblemished character. His forefathers the Abd el-Rassuls were notorious back in Victorian times for having discovered - and systematically plundered - a hillside cache containing the mummified remains (and certain of the treasures) of some of the most famous Pharaonic names to have survived antiquity etched on temple walls the length and breadth of the land. While the mummy cache may not literally have been found under the Gurnawis floorboards so to speak, a good many ancient tombs of high-ranking officials who'd served the pharaohs were. Not only did the thriving village community living atop the ancient burial site prevent proper archaeological excavation, but; as the twentieth century turned into the twenty-first, it became clear the ramshackle dwellings of the inhabitants were leaking sewage onto the ancient tombs carved into the bedrock beneath them. Something had to be done. The Mubarak regime resettled or, perhaps more accurately, forced the eviction of scores of families from the hillside atop the tombs to the new village of purpose built modern homes with running water and telephones. (Both these modern luxuries were notably absent in Old Gurna.)

It struck me as something of a swan song for an authoritarian government that for decades had imposed its will on the people, keeping them poor but fed, underemployed but employed. I had a feeling the forced relocation, changing the way of life of a whole community, was possibly only accepted because it came for free, the new houses given to the villagers as a broad attempt to keep the peace. Even so, I suspect timing was everything. In these post-revolutionary days I doubted the residents could have been persuaded to move with such apparent good grace.

The trouble was the enforced resettlement rather robbed them of their livelihoods. Whilst the opportunity to earn a living looting the tombs that served as cellars for so many of their homes may have dried out when the underground treasure troves emptied, there was still an income to be had from tourists. Old Gurna was ideally located for travellers visiting the tombs and temples of the west bank, situated slap bang in the middle of the tour itinerary. The villagers set up workshops selling handmade crafts from simple mud-brick-and-plaster buildings painted with cartoonish characters of Pharaonic times. They sold mostly alabaster pots and rather crude ceramic statues of various pharaohs and animal-headed gods and goddesses from the ancient Egyptian pantheon.

But the new location beyond the beaten tourist track where the villagers now lived lacked the advantages of passing trade. Those still seeking to scratch a living from Egypt's dwindling tourist traffic were forced to compete for one of the market stalls clustered in narrow alleyways at the entranceways to all the main west bank sites. The trouble was visitors viewed these as something of a gauntlet to be run. All but the very unwary approached them with heads down, shoulders squared and at a determined pace. The locals have never really learned that Westerners don't appreciate hassle. Egypt has a reputation as the hassle epicentre of the world – even more so since the Revolution as the scarcity of tourists has added desperation to the mix.

In spite or possibly because of all of this, the new village seemed unusually quiet as we drove along the main street in Ahmed's police car. New Gurna has straight roads and row after row of identical one-storey villas. Each has a small, gravel-covered back yard, space enough for one donkey, or maybe a sheep or goat and a few pigeons. It is clean, suburban and, to my way of looking at it, quite alien to the normal way of Egyptian village life. This might be ramshackle, higgledy-piggledy and decidedly grubby to our Western eyes, the people walking barefoot on earthen floors rather than on linoleum, but it has a warmth and honesty about it that New Gurna lacks. Sleepy-eyed old women swamped in enveloping black robes observed us from benches placed outside their doorways, and a few raggedy children halted a ball game in the street to turn sombre dark gazes on us as we passed. But otherwise, except for the usual mangy dogs and slinky feral cats, our arrival went largely unremarked.

Apart from the hammering heat and small black flies swarming around a melon left to rot on the roadside I rather felt we might have altogether stepped outside of the Egypt I knew and loved. The flies and stomach-turning smell of decomposing fruit were oddly reassuring as we pulled up at the kerbside and stepped out of the car.

'Dis one here is de house of Mother Mushhawrar,' Ahmed announced, striding across the pavement.

Adam, Walid and I followed at a rather less purposeful pace. Walid hung back, with his rather habitual air of fearfulness and uncertainty.

Mrs Mushhawrar's small square villa was exactly the same as all the others on both sides of the street, with shutters at the front window to block out the harsh Egyptian sunlight. Despite the sound of four car doors slamming outside, there was no suggestion of movement from within as we approached the front door and Ahmed reached out to rat-tat our arrival.

The age it took for Mustafa's mother to come to the door was explained away in a moment when finally she opened it and we spied the Zimmer frame that helped her walk.

I immediately scratched her off our list of potential blackmail suspects. I'm not quite sure what it is about advancing age and disability that somehow don't fit with criminality in my mind. Perhaps it's some kind of positive prejudice of my own. But I took one look at Mother Mushhawrar gripping her walking device and decided she couldn't possibly be our villain.

If I'd been in any doubt, the way she laid into Ahmed almost certainly would have dispelled it.

It's fair to say Mrs Mushhawrar was not what I'd expected. Yes, she was the epitome of an Egyptian-lady-of-a-certain-age on one hand, decked out in the voluminous black niqab with hijab headscarf that denotes the status of a respectably married woman or, as I knew to be the case for her, widow. Yet despite years spent in the dehydrating Egyptian sun and her evident difficulty walking, she had a more youthful appearance than I'd have anticipated. I reckoned her son Mustafa to have been in his early middle age. Surely that must make his mother in her sixties at the very least. Yet her face was smooth and unlined, with bright, alert eyes and she had good teeth.

The second thing to strike me as I caught a glimpse of the living room behind her as she opened the door was the quantity of photographs on display. I couldn't exactly describe them as adorning every surface because in fairness there were very few surfaces available on which to display pictures. No windowsill, mantelpiece or sideboard and not a picture frame in sight either. Instead the photographs were stuck to the bare walls with sticky tape turning brown at the edges. And there were seemingly hundreds of them, leaving very little in the way of blank wall-space. I narrowed my glance and realised I recognised every single one of them as being of her dead son Mustafa.

It was impossible to do any more than glance over her shoulder into her modest living space since one look at Ahmed in his police uniform was enough to have her launching into a voluble diatribe of impassioned Arabic. Her loud tirade was punctuated with much stabbing of her forefinger at his chest. I'm not sure she even so much as glanced at the rest of us standing around Ahmed's bulk on her doorstep. The shrill volume and evident invective was enough to have us all stepping back a pace, especially poor Ahmed at whom her furious rant was directed. Walid positively cowered.

Adam, whose Arabic is more functional than fluent, looked shocked then perplexed and managed to murmur a quick translation for my benefit.

'She's demanding to know why it's taken this long for the police to show up when she reported the robbery weeks ago.'

'Robbery?' I frowned.

He shot a confused look back at me and shrugged while Mrs Mushhawrar continued to lay into poor Ahmed at the top of her voice in full throttled Arabic.

I was aware of doors opening across the street. The clutch of grubby children ceased their ball game altogether and came to stand at the kerbside and stare, more dark-eyed and solemn than ever. Even the flies seemed to stop buzzing blackly around the rotting melon for a moment to see what the fuss was all about.

These silly small details I noticed in the heartbeat of self-conscious embarrassment apparently ingrained in we Brits when we find ourselves unwittingly involved in anything resembling *a scene*. And it was difficult to imagine one more unexpected or ear-splitting than this one.

Finally Ahmed mastered himself. Throwing back his very broad shoulders and puffing out his very round stomach (I daresay it was meant to be his chest, which rather resembles a barrel – so now I know where the expression comes from – except sadly, in Ahmed's case his stomach is larger), he took a decisive step forwards and barked out an order for Mrs Mushhawrar to *stop* talking. Even *I* understood that much!

She obeyed, but continued to stare at him mutinously. If a competition were to be had in flashing dark eyes, I'm not sure I could have confidently laid a wager on who would win. The standoff seemed as if it might go on forever.

Eventually, of course, a modicum of order was restored and we were awarded a grudging admission across the threshold. This took a fair bit of to-ing and fro-ing between Ahmed and Mrs Mushhawrar. But since I didn't understand a word of it and neither Adam (who may have understood some of it) nor Walid (who self-evidently understood all of it) seemed inclined to help me out with a translation, I might as well just cut to the chase. We found ourselves crowded inside her small and sparely furnished living room. We were not offered tea. This spoke volumes. All Egyptians of my experience, when inviting one into their homes – and Adam and I have made the acquaintance of a good number of local taxi drivers and Caleche (horse-drawn-carriage) drivers, not to mention tour guides, who have extended us this courtesy – routinely offer tea. It's served black in small glasses rather than china cups or mugs; hot and sweet, and often with mint leaves left infusing in the water. This was a clear signal from Mrs Mushhawrar that we were not welcome.

I'm not sure if she asked who the rest of us were or why we were accompanying Ahmed. Perhaps she assumed we were some sort of plain-clothes division of the local police, if such a thing exists in Egypt; and I've not checked if it does. Whatever, her attention – no less hostile – remained fixed on our police pal, which allowed me time to inspect the photographs stuck to the walls, since I was unable to follow a word of the heated conversation that batted back and forth.

It was hard not to cringe visibly looking at the images of the man who'd cold bloodedly left Adam, Ahmed and me to a long lingering death in the choking confines of the tomb, having almost brought a rock fall down on our heads.

Mustafa Mushhawrar had been a decent looking sort of chap. One might even call him debonair. He was slim, with the lovely coffee-coloured skin of Egyptians from middle-Egypt and finely chiselled features. He'd sported a nicely trimmed narrow moustache and always smelled of what I'd usually call aftershave, but what, in his case, I'd call Cologne. My abiding memory was of his fastidiousness. He always carried a cotton handkerchief, and used it frequently and habitually to wipe his hands (when most of us have progressed to hand sanitizer). He wore crocodile skin shoes, always polished to within an inch of their lives – which was a minor miracle since Egypt is a land covered in more dust than just about anywhere else on earth. The short sleeves on his shirts were always pressed with a needle-sharp crease down the middle, as were the fronts and backs of his trousers. Perhaps that sort of precision should have served as a dire warning of some sort, but the truth is I didn't see any of it coming. I took him completely at face value, as an upstanding member of the Ministry for the Preservation of the Ancient Monuments in Luxor, who yearned to be an Egyptologist. And perhaps my benign assessment of his character wasn't so ill judged until the Akhenaten and Nefertiti treasures turned him.

I don't quite know whether I'm ashamed or proud to admit that I cursed him. Yes, when I realised he was plundering our tomb – and just after the moment when he'd held a knife to my throat – I entreated all the gods and goddesses of all the ages, past present and future to train their sights on Mustafa Mushhawrar that night and curse him with all the collective divine power they had at their disposal.

I daresay I'm lucky Mustafa didn't shoot me where I stood since he'd replaced the knife with a gun, which he was holding trained on me. Who knows, perhaps the gods intervened on my behalf. Anyway, it was Mustafa and his vile sidekick who lost their lives that night, thankfully not Adam, Ahmed or me. The fool used the gun, not on us, but to shoot down the rafters he'd used to shore up the tunnel he'd burrowed into the burial chamber. Whether he'd intended merely to block up the passageway behind him and make good his escape, leaving us entombed, we will never know. The simple fact is he brought half the mountainside crashing down, crushing and burying himself and his vile accomplice beneath tonnes of rock.

I may think twice before cursing someone quite so energetically in future. It's very slightly alarming to wonder if the gods were listening. I've tried to tell myself Mustafa realised he'd crossed to the dark side and his actions were a deliberate attempt to redeem himself. But who knows.

Whatever, it made my inspection of the gallery of photographs stuck to the otherwise bare walls all around me an unsettling experience. This turned into downright discomfort when I realised Mrs Mushhawrar also was pointing at the pictures of her dead son and crying. It wasn't the soft, snuffling, tearful-but-trying-to-hold-it-back sorrow of a bereaved mother in the Western world. It was a no-holds-barred keening wail of Middle-Eastern grief, and it was terrible to watch. Her face was contorted with pain and I had a horrible feeling if the place hadn't been swept clean, she'd be reaching down to scoop up handfuls of dust to throw onto her head in the age-old custom of female mourning.

Ahmed was desperately gabbling something, looking as if he'd very much like the ground to open up and swallow him. He was sweating profusely, big damp patches visible on the back and under the armpits of his white shirt.

It was Walid who stood up and motioned for Adam and me to do the same. As we preceded him to the door and out, even I, with my limited Arabic, could tell he was apologising profusely, almost bowing and scraping in a parody of mortification.

Ahmed gathered up the tatters of his dignity and followed us out. The front door slammed behind us, although the wailing didn't stop. I could hear her even once we were back inside the car with the windows rolled down until the air conditioning kicked in.

'Why do I have a feeling that didn't go as planned?' I asked as Ahmed, breathing heavily, turned the ignition key and started up the engine.

Walid looked quite overcome with humiliation. 'She is not our blackmailer,' he whispered dejectedly from the front seat alongside Ahmed.

'We never seriously thought she was,' Adam pointed out. 'But I get a sense that whole debacle was less about us interviewing her to find out what might have happened to

53

Mustafa's belongings and more about her haranguing poor Ahmed here about the failings of the local police.'

'But I am de tourist and antiquities police,' Ahmed said mournfully. 'I am not even de right department.'

'What was the wailing all about?' I asked as we pulled away from the kerbside, our departure observed by the solemn black-eyed stares of the children who seemed disinclined to return to their ball game until we'd gone. I had a feeling the echoes of Mrs Mushhawrar's keening might reverberate inside my head for some time to come.

'It was not a good idea to say we believed Mustafa may have had information that could help us with a serious police investigation,' Walid said, turning around in his seat so he could look at Adam and me in the back. 'It rather implied we were suspicious of him. We should have remembered the story we put about back at Christmas. If you recall, we let it be known that Mustafa was a fine member of Luxor's Ministry for the Preservation of Ancient Monuments, caught tragically in one of the recent rock falls around Hatshepsut's temple while pursuing an escaped antiquities thief.'

'Mrs Mushhawrar believes her son died a hero,' I breathed.

'Exactly,' Walid nodded looking shame-faced.

I thought back to the days after our friends released us from the tomb. It was true there'd been numerous rock falls in the Theban hills behind the temple over recent months. Adam and I had been unlucky enough to get caught up in one of them. Walid had used his clout as someone who could call on authority from the Ministry of State for Antiquities to close Hatshepsut's temple for a few days for reasons of health and safety to ensure the manmade barrier protecting the monument and tourists was intact. This was actually a foil for a bit of swift excavation work that revealed the two bodies crushed under the avalanche of rock and enabled us to recover the magnificent items they'd stolen from the tomb, which, I hasten to add, we immediately returned to it.

The truth of course was that far from pursuing the escaped antiquities thief, Mustafa was actually the one who'd sprung him from custody. His plan had been to use the hideous Hussein as both accomplice and access to the black market, where he hoped to sell the stolen tomb treasures without too many awkward questions being asked about provenance. Hussein was an old nemesis of ours and I could only applaud his passing.

But poor Mrs Mushhawrar didn't know any of this. She was simply a grieving mother. I suddenly felt quite sick for the pain we'd caused her, turning up unannounced like that. The need to unmask Walid's blackmailer was blinding us to the finer points of civilised behaviour. 'We should send her some flowers,' I muttered.

'Yes, and we should find de villain dat robbed her,' Ahmed declared from behind the steering wheel.

'Ah yes, the robbery,' Adam said, shooting out a hand to steady himself as Ahmed swerved around a deep sand-filled pot hole in the middle of the road. 'I think I followed a bit of what she was saying. It was some of Mustafa's possessions that were stolen. Did I understand that correctly?'

Walid turned to face us again. 'Yes, after Mustafa was laid to rest there was the usual procedure of packaging up his worldly goods from his workplace and clearing his personal effects from his bank vault. As he'd moved back home to live with his mother after his father died, she'd already sorted through his clothes and the few bits and pieces he had at home and shared them out in the village, as is the local custom. What was stolen was the small box she collected from his bank. It was taken on the evening of the same day she picked it up. She left it in the living room while she was in the kitchen preparing a meal. She meant to look through the contents that night, believing there might be some money and perhaps a couple of small items of jewellery Mustafa had bought for an English girlfriend he once had, who'd returned to the UK before he could give them to her. But the thief got there first. As you can imagine, Mrs Mushhawrar was distraught. She used a neighbour's telephone to immediately report the theft to the police in Luxor, believing an officer would be dispatched to interview her and investigate. That was two weeks ago.'

'So I can quite see why she treated you to that volley of abuse, Ahmed,' I sympathised, catching his eye in the rear view mirror as he drove. 'I wonder why the police have done nothing.'

'It is all de talk about riots against President Morsi,' Ahmed explained. 'De restlessness in de streets and de worries about de appointment of dat former terrorist. Dese are de matters dat have been concerning de police.'

'So poor Mrs Mushhawrar and the theft of some money, which the thief had probably already made off with or spent got shoved to the bottom of the pile,' Adam said with a slow nod.

'Except I'll bet that box from the bank vault also contained the envelope with Mustafa's copy of the letter inside it,' I surmised.

Adam turned his head to look at me sitting alongside him on the back seat of Ahmed's police car and reached for my hand. 'I'll bet you're right. Which rather begs the question of whether the thief was opportunistic, got more than he bargained for and then hatched a plan about how to turn this stroke of luck to his advantage…'

'…Or whether the thief was someone who suspected Mustafa may have had a secret stored in that bank vault and pounced the moment he knew Mrs Mushhawrar had gone to collect it,' I finished for him.

'Exactly.' He nodded, squeezing my hand to acknowledge our thoughts and deductions running along the same track as usual.

Walid's skin had that unhealthy, greenish tinge to it again. Whether this was a result of our hypothesis regarding the theft, or Ahmed's driving it was impossible to say. The roads on both banks of the Nile in and around Luxor are mini assault-courses; littered with abandoned chunks of masonry and rock, pitted with potholes and frequently traversed by donkeys, stray cats and feral dogs. Among these hazards, a driver is forced to negotiate around countless chickens, not to mention the small herds of sheep or goats often to be found being ushered along by their herdsman.

'Well, if my colleagues in de police will not investigate, den we must take de matter into our own hands,' Ahmed announced grandly. He loves the opportunity to make important statements like this, usually pulling himself up to his full impressive height, and adding a sweeping flourish of his arms for emphasis. The effect wasn't quite so majestic from his position wedged into the driver's seat with his back to us. And I'm pleased to report he kept his hands on the steering wheel. But he managed to make up for it moments later as we reached the spot on the riverbank where the *Queen Ahmes* was docked, turning the simple task of pulling up and parking on the bank above the stone causeway into a piece of almost cinematic theatre. There was much wheel spinning, sending stone chippings spraying in all directions as we screeched to a skidding halt and he wrenched up the handbrake. I noted a solitary donkey cowering between the palm trees the poor creature was using as scanty cover from this onslaught.

Poor Walid looked greener than ever as he emerged from the front seat and willingly accepted the arm Adam proffered to help him down the steep crumbling steps onto the small jetty where the dahabeeyah was moored. Walid is not an old man – only in his mid-fifties at a guess – but his small wiry body and habitual air of nervousness make him seem unsteady. Strange this, when I've seen him issue directives with an air of quiet authority that demands – and gets – immediate compliance.

But there was no time to ponder the contradictions of Walid's person and personality. Ahmed positively swept us onto the gangplank much in the way of a mother hen rounding up her chicks. That he felt the wrong we'd done to Mrs Mushhawrar most keenly of all of us was perhaps not surprising since her volley of abuse had been directed at him. And Ahmed's solid exterior and bluff, exuberant manner hide a heart of pure gold and a softness towards those who've been wronged that might go unremarked by those who know him less well. If he'd been keen to help us catch the blackmailer before, I sensed now he was on a personal crusade to do so.

We regrouped up on the sundeck under the shade of the wide canvas awning. I dispensed cold drinks and everyone looked much refreshed for having the opportunity to use the facilities to wash away dust-and-sweat stains and take a quick breather. A gentle breeze blew across the deck taking the ferocious heat out of the late afternoon sun. The Nile lapped against the starboard side of the dahabeeyah and a couple of grey-and-black kingfishers darted in and out of the tall reeds on the riverbank.

'Well, if it was an opportunistic theft, we've stalled in the starting blocks,' Adam pronounced after taking a long swallow of his iced lemon drink. I make it myself to a recipe I cadged from one of the wonderful waiting staff at the Jolie Ville hotel. (I was staying there when I started out on my adventures in Egypt.) It's sweetened but still with enough acidity to cut through the thirst-inducing effects of the bone dry Egyptian climate. The ice of course we make from specially purified water.

'Not a bad bit of opportunistic robbery to choose the very day Mrs Mushhawrar collected the box from the bank to decide to break into her living room while she was cooking,' I remarked archly.

'Unless someone observed her leave the bank with the box and guessed it must contain money, probably the cash-in equivalent of whatever Mustafa had in his bank account when he died,' Adam conjectured.

We all stared at each other knowing, if this were the case, we had about as much chance of identifying and catching our villain as pulling out a random stone block in the great pyramid and finding a cache of treasure stashed behind it.

'So we have to pin our hopes on someone who knew Mustafa guessing, heaven knows how, at something secreted inside that bank vault,' I advanced.

'Yes!' Ahmed pounced on the suggestion. 'Dat scoundrel Mustafa, he must have let something slip!' He beamed around at us, whether in delight at this possibility or at his own use of this piece of colloquial English, I couldn't say for sure.

Adam was frowning. 'I'd be very surprised if he let something slip,' he said. 'Mustafa struck me as a rather solitary and secretive sort. I doubt he had many friends. He was too finicky for all of that. I sense someone who didn't let many people close.'

'You're right,' I piped up as a sudden thought struck me. 'If you think of all those photographs his mother had stuck up all over the room, he appeared alone in every single one of them; no group shots or anything like that.'

'But how else would someone know to rob Mother Mushhawrar of de safe deposit box?' Ahmed asked in confusion.

'I can think of someone who might have had a very good idea that Mustafa had something he wanted to keep safely hidden away from prying eyes,' Walid said slowly, leaning forward to put his empty glass on the stripped and varnished floorboards at his feet. 'That cousin of his must have suspected something when Mustafa kicked up such a fuss about retrieving the necklace he'd innocently sold to a tourist.'

'Yes,' I nodded, cottoning onto his train of thought. The necklace had once belonged to Nefertiti. Mustafa had stolen it from the tomb and, for reasons best known to himself; asked his cousin to store it in his safe. Not realising its provenance, this enterprising cousin had sold the necklace. The tourist in question just happened to be Adam's ex-sister-in-law. And, of course, I recognised it the moment I clapped eyes on it having spent hours entombed with it during our first entrapment. All this came flooding back as Walid spoke. Mustafa had gone to some lengths to try to get it back. 'And after Mustafa's untimely end supposedly in pursuit of a runaway antiquities thief, you scoured the Souk in the company of the local police chief, Walid, confiscating the few items you knew to be from the tomb.'

'You made a lot of noise about the break-in to the Cairo museum during the Revolution, remember?' Adam added, nodding at Walid. 'And let them believe you thought they were trading in stolen goods, and should consider themselves lucky to get off so lightly with just a reprimand and repossession of the stolen items.'

'But it might not have taken a genius to work out there was more to it than all that,' I speculated seeing where this was leading us. 'Mustafa's cousin must have smelt a rat. Maybe he suspected Mustafa was somehow involved in the thefts from the museum and perhaps had some other stolen treasures stashed securely in the bank vault. Or it's possible he thought Mustafa had been selling things off and had a stack of cash in the bank.'

'Either way,' Adam nodded, showing his agreement with my deductions so far, 'It places Mustafa's cousin right at the top of our hit list. He'd be close enough to Mrs Mushhawrar that she possibly even told him when she was planning to collect the box from the bank.'

Ahmed leapt up. 'Dis cousin … Dis shop owner from de Souk … we must interview him immediately! Perhaps even arrest him!'

He looked as if he gleefully might march off into Luxor right now to do just that. But Adam reached out a restraining hand and stalled him. 'I think we need to learn from this afternoon's experience and be a bit cleverer than that, my friend,' he smiled. 'Besides, it will be getting dark soon. The Souk owners will be shutting up shop and heading home as the sun sets. There aren't enough tourists around to encourage them to keep long hours. I think we need to hatch a plan.'

Walid looked at us gloomily. 'But I need to head back to Cairo in the morning,' he reminded us. 'I promised to be at the museum to welcome Nabil Zaal when he arrives at the start of his Egyptian lecture tour.'

I sat forward with a start. 'God, I'd forgotten all about Nabil Zaal coming!'

'He's not exactly chosen the most opportune of moments,' Adam commented. 'Arriving just as the people are about to take to the streets around Tahrir Square to protest against President Morsi. The museum will be slap bang in the middle of the riot zone again.'

'Hmm, and just as we're embroiled up to our necks in a blackmail scenario,' I added.

'But it is too late to put him off,' Walid said wringing his hands with worry.

'Dis Nabil Zaal, why does he come again so soon?' Ahmed demanded. 'He was here to give de lectures in April, and now he returns again?'

I'd wondered this myself. Nabil Zaal was a native Egyptian who'd made his home in America, and made his name (and no doubt a small fortune) writing what Adam had once unkindly referred to as 'pseudo-historical psychobabble'. His premise was that some of the patriarchs of the Bible were in fact ancient Egyptian Pharaohs. He'd put forward an intriguing hypothesis that the Great Pyramid of Khufu was in fact built for Noah of the Bible. He'd also claimed that the pyramid of Khafre, guarded by the Sphinx was actually the memorial temple of Biblical Adam. And he'd said he hoped soon to be able to demonstrate that the smaller pyramid of Menkaure was in reality the funerary temple of Abraham. It's fair to say, to date, he'd produced not a shred of historical or archaeological evidence to back up these wild assertions. Hence Adam's scathing dismissal of his books.

But I wasn't quite so sure his claims could be so easily shot down in flames. Adam and I had come to know him as a result of the curious set of circumstances surrounding his recent lecture tour in the spring. We'd attended the presentation he'd given at the Winter Palace Hotel in Luxor in April. There he'd claimed King David of the Bible was none other than the mighty warrior pharaoh Thutmosis III, and that King Solomon was the self same individual as the pharaoh who'd presided peaceably over Egypt's golden age of empire, Amenhotep III (grandfather to the more famous Tutankhamun).

It's fair to say Adam and I had been quite ready to thoroughly pooh-pooh his fantastical hypotheses. That was until we came into possession of an ancient faience scarab that seemed to prove pretty conclusively that Joseph of the Bible (he of the coat of many colours) was a Vizier at the court of Thutmosis IV, a chap by the name of Yuya.[3] As this had

65

long been another of Nabil Zaal contentions, it did rather cause our objections to shrivel a little.

The scarab was now on display in the Museum of Antiquities in Cairo, under Walid's watchful eye, and had proved quite a draw to those intrepid visitors still braving Egypt as a tourist destination.

'That scarab seems to have put a new fire in his belly,' Walid said, addressing Ahmed since he was the one who'd asked the question. 'He's now taken it into his head that Moses and the heretic pharaoh Akhenaten were one and the same person, and that it was Akhenaten who led the Israelites out of Egypt in the Exodus.'

'But that can't possibly be true!' I exclaimed. 'As we all have cause to know, Akhenaten is right this very minute lying mummified inside his sarcophagus in a hidden tomb not five miles from here!'

'True,' Walid agreed, with an odd little glint in his eyes. 'But Nabil Zaal does not know this. It seems he has spent the couple of months since he left Egypt pulling together a portfolio of evidence to support his belief. It is this he plans to present at his lecture at the museum later this week.

'I've got to be there to see that!' I vowed.

Adam nodded. 'Me too. But first we've got to see what we can learn about the theft of Mustafa Mushhawrar's bank

---

[3] *Farouk's Fancies* Book 4 of Meredith Pink's Adventures in Egypt

box. I suggest Merry, Ahmed and I hatch a plan and then we can travel up to join you in Cairo in a day or two Walid. Hopefully by then we'll be a step closer to unmasking your vile blackmailer, so you can play host to Nabil Zaal without the threat of exposure stalking your footsteps.'

'Amen to that,' our devout Muslim friend said vehemently.

Chapter 4

'So, what does Cousin Mushhawrar have conveniently at his disposal as part of the fixtures and fittings of his jewellery shop in the Souk that would prove a pretty secure place to keep Mustafa's copy of the letter should he happen to be our blackmailer?' Adam asked.

He and I were in bed in the darkness of our cabin. Earlier we'd prepared a simple meal for our friends, which we'd eaten under the starlight up on deck in the balmy heat of an Egyptian summer's night, listening to the black waters of the Nile lapping gently against the dahabeeyah. Then we'd waved goodbye to Ahmed as he strode off along the causeway in the moonlight towards his car, and, a little later after a nightcap, wished Walid a good night's sleep for his last night aboard the *Queen Ahmes* before his early morning flight back to Cairo tomorrow.

'I'd hazard a single guess at a safe,' I murmured against Adam's shoulder, planting a kiss there at the same time. It was a small habit I'd formed to punctuate any conversation that happened to take place between the sheets, pressing little kisses against whichever part of his anatomy happened to be closest. This could lead to quite interesting developments I'd discovered.

'That's my reckoning,' he agreed, squeezing me a bit closer to acknowledge the kiss but not seeming inclined on this occasion to stray from the point. 'So it strikes me we need to find a way of getting to see what's inside that safe.'

'And I don't suppose from the way you've phrased that you're planning on asking him to give us the code so we can have a little look-see.'

He levered himself up on one elbow so he could lean over me and I decided maybe the kiss had made more of an impression than I'd thought. 'I'm sure we can come up with more inventive ways of getting a glimpse inside,' he murmured. 'You'll just have to help me to get my creative juices flowing, Merry.'

He shook me awake before it was light. 'Merry, I've had an idea!'

I blinked and rubbed the sleep from my eyes, groaning to see the room still in darkness. Reaching out for the bedside clock I blinked blearily at the little illuminated dials. 'Adam, it's the middle of the night. This had better be good.'

'I need to be inside the back room of Cousin Mushhawrar's shop when he opens the safe,' he explained. 'It's the only way to take him by surprise. We need to spring a trap!'

Usually I loved it when the spirit of Boy's Own adventure descended over Adam. It made him reckless, a bit devil-may-care, and incredibly attractive. But since it was pitch black inside our cabin, and I'd been wrenched unexpectedly from a rather nice sleep I was feeling less inclined than usual to be swept along. And, in the dark, without the impact of his deep blue eyes gazing into mine, the effect wasn't nearly so dizzying as I'd known it before. 'Wouldn't it be easier just to get Ahmed to caution him and order an inspection of the safe?' I murmured, preparing to roll over and allow sleep to reclaim me.

'We came over all heavy handed with the police when we went to visit Mustafa's mother, and just look where that got us,' Adam persisted. 'No, Merry; I think this one should be down to us. Maybe we can let Ahmed play a bit-part if he agrees not to over-do it, but let's not offer him the starring role.'

It was clear Adam had no intention of allowing me to slip peaceably back to sleep so I rubbed my eyes again and tried to drag myself into more of a state of alertness. 'So what do you propose?'

An hour later we were approaching the Souk in Luxor. It was still dark. Adam was using the little built-in torch on his mobile phone to guide our footsteps. This was a sensible precaution against a severely twisted ankle since the paving was cracked and somewhat uneven along the Corniche.

The Corniche is the main promenade, which borders the east bank of the Nile in central Luxor. Usually it's alive with the sound of Caleche drivers clip-clopping along hawking their horse-and-carriage rides at the tops of their lungs. Their shouts are always accompanied by a frantic tinkling of the jingle-bells they use to adorn their carriages, and the light cracking of their whips as they encourage their horses to keep pace with their intended victims (I mean, passengers). It felt truly odd to be walking along in the dark without the persistent cries of 'taxi, taxi, or 'caleche, caleche,' ringing in our ears, and without street traders running up to us every few paces entreating us to buy boxes of dodgy cigarettes or fake designer sunglasses.

The Souk in Luxor during the daytime is bursting with colour, bustling with people and redolent with the aromatic scent of spices. It's a single arcade, linking the Corniche with one of the back streets running parallel to it. Shops and market stalls are crammed alongside each other on both sides, their contents spilling forward higgledy-piggledy into what's meant to be the walkway down the middle. This makes it virtually impossible to stroll from one end to the other in a straight line. Instead, one is forced to skip around huge baskets of brightly coloured and pungent spices and skirt trestle tables piled high with all manner of replica Pharaonic artefacts. Some are quite tasteful, like the carved alabaster vases, which make nice tourist souvenirs. Others are bright, gaudy replicas of Tutankhamun's mask or Nefertiti's bust wrought in tacky plastic or glow-in-the-dark wax. There are the ubiquitous postcard carousels to negotiate, and tables groaning under the weight of mini obelisks, pyramids and all manner of animal-headed deities made from resin or - if you're lucky, prepared to pay the price and can take the weight in your luggage - granite or sandstone. Rolled carpets abound, as do shelves laden with painted papyrus in protective cellophane sheaths. The Souk is a positive Aladdin's cave of tourist trinkets.

But it wasn't daytime. So none of this tumult of exotic colour or clamour for the attention of each of one's senses was in evidence. The Souk, with its riotous wares shut up for the night, was an eerie place, shadowed and silent, patrolled by a veritable army of stray cats.

Whilst it was dark, it most certainly was not cold. Luxor in June is a breathless oven of a place, even at night. Admittedly without the ferocious glare of the sun, it was more blanket-like than blistering, but I could still understand why so many of the townsfolk chose to sleep on the square, flat roofs of their plastered mud brick homes in the summer months. Very few of the locals could afford the luxury of air conditioning.

'There's a narrow alleyway that runs behind the Souk. The entranceway's over there,' Adam motioned; shining the narrow beam of light from his mobile in the general direction we were headed. 'My flat used to overlook it.'

When I first met him Adam was renting a tiny flat overlooking this place. He handed the keys back when got together since it was in no way spacious enough to accommodate both of us. Given our current nocturnal wanderings, this struck me as a shame. Adam's flat had been ideally located for the skulduggery we had in mind tonight. And we wouldn't have needed to leave our scooters parked in a side street a bit further back along the Corniche. 'We'll have to watch our step. It's used as a bit of a refuse tip and the local dogs tend to do their business there too.'

The malodorous stench that rose up to fill my nostrils confirmed his assessment as I followed him cautiously into the narrow passageway. I was heartily glad I'd laced my feet into solid-soled trainers rather than slipping on my more habitual flip-flops. Even so, I decided my footwear would need a complete cycle through the washing machine once we were back on board the *Queen Ahmes* to remove the various nasties I could feel myself squelching through.

The darkness was almost as oppressive as the effluvium. There was no moon and the pale starlight was unequal to the task of filtering into the alley. We knew whereabouts in the Souk Cousin Mushhawrar's jewellery shop was located, since we'd had a full report on its position (and most of its contents) from Adam's ex-sister-in-law Eleanor, she who'd been the unwitting purchaser of the magnificent Nefertiti necklace. We'd also been hovering in the background at Christmas when Walid, in the company of the local police chief, made his tour of inspection and confiscated the few other items that had somehow (thanks to Mustafa and the heinous Hussein) found their way from our tomb into the Souk. Unfortunately for us, our destination was right at the other end of the alleyway, being one of the shops located closest to the main entrance from the Corniche and furthest from the way into the back alley.

'Careful, Merry, there's a load of broken glass here,' Adam cautioned, reaching back for my hand as we edged forward through the disgusting litter-strewn passage. The torchlight from his mobile phone revealed a smashed Coca-Cola bottle resting amid various bits of rotting detritus I didn't care to identify.

'I don't understand why people can't use proper refuse sacks, rather than just chuck their rubbish out here,' I complained. 'It doesn't look as if this alleyway's been cleared for months.'

'We just have to hope they're a bit lapse with their security for the same reason,' he replied. 'I doubt anyone's actually attempted to walk along this alleyway for the same amount of time. Fingers crossed it's made the shop owners complacent.'

'And if it hasn't?'

'Then I may just have to pick the lock,' he said cheerfully. 'I'll consider it payback for all the nights I had to try to get to sleep with this revolting smell permeating in through the window of my flat.'

A few more stomach-turning and footwear-ruining moments later and we were squeezed up against the back entrance to Cousin Mushhawrar's jewellery shop. I say squeezed because the space directly outside his back door was almost fully occupied by a rotting mattress propped against the wall. That this served as board-and-lodging for communities of rodents and insects alike was immediately apparent by the frantic scuttling and buzzing we set off as we shoved it aside. I shrieked as a rat the size of a remote-controlled car bolted across my foot, and shuddered shrinkingly at the flesh crawling evidence of all manner of creepy crawlies disturbed from their slumber. The secondary usage of the mattress as a drop-in toileting convenience for countless passing canines and felines was obvious from the truly sickening smell that rose from the disintegrating fibres.

'Dammit, Adam; this is not my idea of fun!'

'Try to hold your breath,' he advised. 'You just need to help get me inside, then you can get the hell out of here.'

'I won't just need a shower when I get home,' I muttered. 'I'll need fumigating.'

'Remind me to call pest control,' he agreed grimly, gripping the back door handle and giving it a violent yank.

Puffed with the exertion of his second attempt, he let go in frustration. 'Stuck fast,' he grunted.

'More likely locked and bolted on the inside,' I croaked, trying not to inhale.

'It'll have to be the window then. You'll need to give me a leg up, Merry.'

The window was small and square, positioned just above head height, and held closed on a latch. I took his mobile phone-cum-torch while Adam, on tiptoes, reached up and, frowning with concentration, worked his penknife into the fastening. He wiggled it around until with a soft crunch the mechanism gave way. 'I'm in!' he exhaled.

Trying to share his enthusiasm I made the mistake of taking a deep breath. My stomach heaved and I had to force back the bile that rose in my throat.

But if I'd thought the experience couldn't get worse I was wrong.

'Ok, give me a leg-up, Merry, can you?'

Attempting to hoist Adam upwards, my right foot slipped on something unmentionable. I wasn't quick enough to let go of Adam and shoot out a hand to steady myself. My balance went and with a horrified yelp I fell face first into the revolting squelchy mush I'd slipped on.

The look on Adam's face came nowhere close to relieving my distress, although I suspect the memory of it may stay with me for some time to come. If the speed with which he hauled me back upright was anything to judge by, the only thing that could have traumatised him more was if I'd dragged him down with me. 'My God, Merry; are you *alright*?'

'No!' I spat. 'I think I'm just about as far away from alright as it's possible to get. You have precisely five seconds to get through that window before I start dreaming up terrible ways to punish you for bringing me here. And you can forget the idea of a leg up. I'm done!'

He wasted three precious seconds staring at me to see if I meant it. My expression was clearly enough to convince him if my tone of voice left any room for doubt. In the two seconds he had left, he used the mattress as a bolster and heaved himself upwards, diving at the window space. I had to grab his legs and shove him the rest of the way, hearing him fall with a crash and a stifled shout into the darkened room beyond.

'Ok, mission accomplished.' He called back out to me a moment later. 'I'm in. Pass me my phone can you please, Merry?'

I reached up and handed his mobile through the window opening into his outstretched hand. 'Can you see the safe?'

Muffled sounds of movement followed and I fixed my gaze on the faint glow from Adam's mobile-cum-torch, which vaguely illuminated the window space above me. The sickening smell of the rotting god-knows-what all around me made me gag. But there was no point holding my nose since I was now coated in the stuff. 'I can completely see why Cousin Mushhawrar keeps his window closed and his back door bolted,' I muttered to myself.

'Yes! It's here with a blanket thrown over it!' Adam called out.

'No chance you can break into it, I suppose?' I called back.

'Nope. It's one of those metal stronghold types with a round number dial and a three-pronged handle. I think we'll need to stick with Plan A, Merry. So you get out of here and I'll hole up and try to make myself comfortable and inconspicuous. Tell Walid I'm sorry not to be there to say goodbye in person. Hopefully he'll agree the chance to unmask his blackmailer over-rides my lack of manners. Fingers crossed we'll have good news for him in Cairo. And remember to make sure Ahmed's completely clear what's expected of him. We don't want his love of theatrics to get the better of him.'

I've never been so delighted and relieved to get away from somewhere. And that's saying something considering some of the sticky situations I've been in. That alleyway took stickiness to a whole new level.

Dawn was just starting to break as I got back to the *Queen Ahmes*. Deciding the washing machine was unequal to the task of cleaning my soiled clothes, I stripped them off and dumped them, underwear included, straight into the rubbish bin. My trainers went in too.

Getting myself back into a state I could consider somewhere approaching human was another matter. Short of presenting myself at a local paint-strippers workshop and asking to be doused in various chemicals, I decided I had no choice but to entrust myself to the shower. Of course a jet-hose would have been preferable to blast the various stains from my body. But I could only hope the shower would wash away the worst of them while the steam from the scalding water cleared the smell that seemed to be trapped inside my nose.

Walid was gracious and forgiving about Adam's absence. The hopefulness in his expression as I explained what we had in mind was almost unbearable to observe. 'Let us hope he is our man and you and Adam can recover the letter from him,' he prayed as I hugged him goodbye. Then I waved him out of sight as the taxi whisked him away to the airport for his flight back to Cairo.

Ahmed sounded thrilled to be offered a role in our scheme. The chance to expose Cousin Mushhawrar as the thief of his aunt's strongbox and Walid's malicious blackmailer was more excitement than he knew how to contain. 'Yes, yes,' he shouted down the telephone, almost deafening me. 'Dis is a most excellent plan! It will be my honour to assist you.'

'*Assist* being the operative word,' I murmured under my breath as I hung up.

It didn't take me long to get myself ready. Knowing Adam had his mobile set on vibrate mode I pinged him a quick text to let him know I was on my way. His reply bounced back quickly. Cousin Mushhawrar had arrived to open up for the day. Adam was holed up behind some boxes under a table in the back storeroom. He was suffering with cramp but otherwise ok. I texted back to say I'd let him know when I was outside the shop as his cue to move. I'm not always the world's biggest fan of modern technology. But it does have its uses.

The temperature was already soaring as I turned the key to start up my scooter and steered it out of the deep shade where I always parked up on the riverbank above the stone jetty. It's a pleasant drive into Luxor from our mooring platform on the west bank. The road skirts the irrigation canal that runs parallel to the Nile some way inland. I skimmed past vast fields of okra and sugarcane dotted with clusters of dusty palm trees, and then turned left to cross the bridge that spans the great river. Once on the east bank I steered left again and followed the main road into Luxor. The scenery as I entered the more built-up areas was a multi-coloured blur of pink, yellow, orange and lilac bougainvillea growing riotously along the central reservations.

Usually I take time to appreciate all the sights of rural and semi-suburban Egypt as I travel along these now-familiar roads. But this morning I was too keyed up to properly enjoy the ride. I kept imagining all sorts of misfortune befalling Adam while he waited tensely hidden in the back room of Cousin Mushhawrar's shop. It would only take a curious cat to follow him in through the broken window and start hissing to bring our carefully hatched plans crashing around our ears. Adam was a quick thinker but I doubted he could talk his way out of this one if he happened to be caught.

I'd arranged to meet Ahmed in one of the side streets behind Luxor Temple in the centre of the city. He was already there when I arrived. I paid a scrawny-looking little kid a generous tip to stand guard by my scooter. He assured me in a gabble of high-pitched Arabic – almost none of which I understood – that it would be safe with him. I didn't need to follow his words. His expansive hand gestures, wide gap-toothed smile and earnest nods were enough to convince me he'd protect it against all comers and be there waiting patiently for the top-up tip I promised him when I got back. Of course the fierce look Ahmed gave him may have had something to do with the excessive nature of his assurances.

'He's a little Ahmed in the making,' I smiled, falling into step with my police pal as we walked back towards the main road. This was no easy feat since Ahmed tends to stride out as if he's marching in a parade to the accompaniment of a big brass band.

'You gave him too much, Mereditd,' he lectured me. He's never quite mastered the pronunciation of my name. It's not helpful that it has a 'th' at the end. 'It will make him greedy for more.'

'Well, so long as my scooter's there safe and sound when I get back he can have more with my blessing,' I said cheerfully. I did a quick exchange-rate conversion in my head. 'Really, Ahmed, I've only given him a few coppers.'

He frowned at me and I decided to change the subject. 'So, you know what we've got to do when we get there. Timing is everything. We have to give Adam the best chance possible of a proper look inside that safe.'

'I will know exactly de right moment to move,' he assured me.

Approaching the Souk I was struck by the contrast a few hours could make. Shadowed, silent and a bit creepy as it had been in the darkness before dawn, it was now ablaze with colour and alive with the shouting that passes as conversation between Egyptians. The stray cats that had patrolled so stealthily at night were nowhere to be seen. But a few scruffy dogs were lying in the shade cast by the closely clipped bushes near the roadside trying to escape the heat.

A couple of the shopkeepers broke off from their voluble exchange to look at me hopefully as I approached.

But seeing me in the company of a member of the local tourist and antiquities police they dropped their gazes in disappointment and returned to their discussion.

I hadn't been sure it was a good idea to turn up with Ahmed. But Adam had felt it might make Cousin Mushhawrar both nervous and especially eager to please. We could only hope it might also encourage him to lower his guard when it came to the crucial moment of opening the safe.

I made sure to look purposeful as we entered the Souk. Pausing only to fire off a quick text to Adam saying we'd arrived, I made a beeline for Cousin Mushhawrar's jewellery shop. As was typical of all the traders, he was slouching in the open doorway. But I wasn't fooled by his relaxed stance. In reality I knew he was ready to leap forward to waylay passers-by and entice – or rather bully – them to step inside to sample his wares. A hand-written sign pasted in the window announced 'NO HASSLE' in big letters. But this was just a formality. Hassle was a way of life here. How else were the shopkeepers supposed to compete for the business of the few tourists on offer? The sign above the shop read 'Jamal's Jewels'. Nicely alliterative, I noted.

'Jamal Mushhawrar,' I muttered under my breath as we approached. 'Are you our villainous blackmailer?'

There's no way he could have heard me. But it was a disconcerting moment all the same when his gaze lifted and crashed into mine. Actually I think it was a carbon copy of the hopeful glance the other traders had cast me. I was just hypersensitive since he was our quarry. His reaction on seeing me in company with Ahmed was exactly the same as his fellow storeowners too: a puff of deflation and a loss of interest. I clearly wasn't worth the energetic sales pitch launched like a missile at most Westerners.

His manner changed though when I approached the window of his shop and made a great show of studying the dazzle of items on display. The dull gleam of gold, the glitter of semi-precious stones and the soft patina of turquoise and jasper vied for my attention. Quantities of chunky rings crowded against scarabs of all sizes from those little bigger than a fingernail up to those the size of my fist. There were golden pendants cast in the shape of lotus flowers and the ubiquitous Tutankhamun and Nefertiti busts, together with several charms intricately wrought to depict the Eye of Horus. Gold necklaces, bracelets, collars and cuffs in all shapes and sizes jostled for position set off against the black cloth they were displayed on. I could see why Adam's ex-sister-in-law Eleanor had chosen this as the place to buy a special gift to take home.

Casting Ahmed in his police uniform a rather uncomfortable glance, Jamal Mushhawrar plastered a welcoming grin onto his face and stepped towards me. 'I can help you with somezing today, Mizz?' You look for somezing in particular?'

I smiled up at him; surreptitiously crossing my fingers behind my back in the way my school friends once told me took the wickedness out of telling a bare faced lie. 'Yes, a wedding present; I have some close friends getting married.'

'You want jewellery?' He looked a little confused, clearly thinking it an odd choice of wedding gift.

'I was thinking maybe something like one of these scarabs,' I offered. 'Something special to remind them of Egypt. But I don't really see one here I like.'

'I have others inside my shop,' he announced proudly. 'You wish to come inside and see?'

I smiled and nodded. 'Thank you.'

He cast another uncertain glance at Ahmed.

'I want to buy something very special,' I hastened to assure him. 'My friend is here to help me choose and to make sure I get a good price.'

The reference to Ahmed as my friend seemed to reassure Jamal Mushhawrar we weren't here on police business. I daresay he recognised Ahmed. Most of the people in Luxor seem to know each other on one level or another, however distantly.

He bustled us inside his shop where display cabinets crowded the small space, each overloaded with gold glinting gaudily under the spotlights hung on wires from the ceiling. The glass cabinets were dusty. This was normal. Everything in Egypt is dusty.

Jamal moved to stand behind the main counter. 'You would like tea while you consider, yes?'

I should have anticipated this. Tea drinking is a little ritual the shopkeepers enact to make the experience of browsing more akin to a social occasion. They've clearly cottoned on that it's much more difficult to walk away without buying something once you've accepted their hospitality. But of course it meant he'd need to go into his back room where I had every expectation Adam was easing himself out from the boxes he'd been hidden behind since before sunrise.

'Thank you,' I said in a loud voice. 'Tea would be lovely.'

If my unnecessary volume surprised him he didn't show it. Getting a nod from Ahmed to also accept the offer of tea, Jamal slipped though the hanging screen of coloured plastic ribbons separating the front of his shop from the storeroom behind. I held my breath, half expecting a shocked shout of discovery. But none came so I slowly released it.

It wasn't as trusting of him as it may at first have appeared to leave us alone in his shop since all the cabinets were locked and the front window was barred with a padlocked screen.

I made a great play of studying everything on display, keeping up an inconsequential chatter to Ahmed all the while until Jamal returned carrying small glasses of tea on a round tray. I accepted mine with a smile and took a sip. As always it was hot, minty and very sweet. I acquired the taste long ago so managed not to grimace at the excessively syrupy flavour.

'You see somezing you like, Mizz? Zese scarabs, zey are better, yes?'

'I like these ones made of alabaster and those over there, which I take to be silver?' I pointed as I spoke, and he nodded eagerly. Can you give me an idea of the price of that one there ... the one in gold decorated with turquoise, carnelian and mother of pearl...?'

I saw the avaricious glint flash in his eyes, quickly masked. I'd deliberately chosen what I took to be the most expensive item on display. It was closely modelled on a scarab-shaped pectoral found in Tutankhamun's tomb, with patterned wings circling out on both sides of the beetle body shape.

'Ah, zis one it is very beautiful, yes?' he said, drawing a cluster of keys from the pocket of his galabeya, sorting through them and inserting one into the lock. His choice was unerring and he lifted the glass a moment later, reaching in for the scarab. He handed it to me with a sorrowful look. 'But zis one, it iz my most high-priced.'

Haggling is a game in Egypt, and I recognised his opening gambit as a small test to see if I was serious. Bingo, I thought. He handed it across to me and I let its warm weight settle in my palm. It was a beautiful piece, patterned with onyx, jasper and obsidian as well as the other stones I'd already mentioned. I studied it closely waiting for him to name his opening price.

'Zis one I could not let go for less zan 10,000 Egyptian pounds.'

I immediately knocked four fifths off this in my mind. The truth was; if I decided to proceed with a purchase, we'd end up at a figure between quarter and half of his opening price. At somewhere between two-hundred-and-fifty and five hundred quid, it made for an expensive wedding gift.

Ahmed choked on his tea alongside me, but I ignored him and tilted my head on one side as if I were seriously considering it. I needed to up the stakes. 'It is lovely,' I agreed slowly, crossing the fingers of my other hand even harder. 'But these are very special friends and I want my gift to be something they will keep and treasure forever. Is this the very best you have to offer? Ideally I would like one that is a little bigger, but still has the same exquisite workmanship and mixture of inlaid stones.'

This was my big roll of the dice, the gamble I'd come here at Adam's behest to play. If this were indeed the finest example he possessed, I'd have to think on my feet and change tack to persuade him to open up his safe.

'Don't you have a few items in reserve set aside for special customers?' I appealed. I placed my canvas bag with great deliberation onto the counter-top. I hoped he'd take this as an indication I was very serious indeed about making a costly purchase, and was willing to stay as long as it might take us to agree a price.

He cast a quick, suspicious glance at Ahmed. It wouldn't surprise me to learn that some of the traders in Luxor acted as a foil for antiquities dealers. I'm sure it skittered through his mind that we might be springing a trap, especially in view of how recently he'd had items confiscated.

Ahmed caught the glance too and fired out a few short sentences in Arabic. I had no idea what he said, but whatever it was made the jeweller laugh and visibly relax. He looked back at me and reached out for the scarab, securing it back in the display cabinet. Then he straightened. 'Yes, I believe I have somezing else you will like to see. If you will wait here for one moment, I will get it from my safe, yes?'

At the mention of his safe I felt my knees buckle. I could only hope Adam had heard it too and was able to move into a position, still hidden, from where he could act quickly.

Jamal slipped through the ribboned screen again. But this time Ahmed followed him; not all the way; just far enough that he could peak between the ribbons into the back room and give me the signal the moment he saw the safe was open.

It came quicker than I was expecting. Jamal was evidently eager to make a profitable sale. Gathering my wits, I let out an ear-piercing shriek. 'Stop! Thief! My bag!'

As we'd agreed, Ahmed leapt back across the room and sped past me, scooping up my canvas holdall from the

89

top of the cabinet on his way. He flung open the door, while I kept on screaming, watching him bound out of the shop.

The plan was for him to make off as if in pursuit of some opportunistic thief who'd spied my bag sitting unattended on the counter top and slipped into the store behind me while my attention was diverted to surreptitiously steal it. The idea was for Ahmed to leg it through the Souk and then present himself back here with my rescued bag held aloft, admitting the imaginary thief had seen him in pursuit so dropped the bag and escaped Ahmed's clutches. It might even have worked if my screams hadn't roused the attention of the other shopkeepers who had little to distract them with so few tourists to target. As Ahmed darted through the doorway with my bag pinned under his right arm, one of the enterprising shopkeepers appeared quick as a flash with a foot outstretched to trip him up.

Ahmed went sprawling like a felled tree and the contents of my holdall spilled in all directions. My scream stuck in my throat, almost choking me. I stared paralyzed in horror.

'What is it? What has happened?' Jamal Mushhawrar was at my side in a heartbeat. It was of little comfort to see the truly glorious scarab he was clutching in one hand. 'Did zis man ze policeman try to rob you? But I thought he was your friend?'

It was the only conclusion on offer in the circumstances as they presented themselves.

'I … no … well, yes… well, I …' I trailed off. This wasn't in the script and I had no idea what to say. The commotion in the doorway arrested my attention as shopkeepers came to stand guard over poor Ahmed, who was looking at the scattered contents of my bag as if he'd never seen a hairbrush, compact mirror or lipstick before. I nearly fainted clean away when I saw them all stand back for the military officer bearing down on Ahmed with his gun unslung and held loosely between his hands. The military police and those of the pre-revolutionary force vied for supremacy in these troubled times. It didn't bode well for Ahmed.

Chapter 5

'Next time you wake me in the middle of the night to tell me you've had an idea, remind me to ignore you and go back to sleep, would you please?' I grumped at Adam. 'I've had to throw away an entire set of clothes, not to mention a perfectly good pair of trainers. I feel as if I've got the smell of that awful place imprinted on my senses. And if we've come close to losing poor Ahmed here his job on previous occasions, I should think we've well and truly nailed it this time!'

Adam had the grace to look mortified. 'Things didn't go exactly according to plan,' he conceded. 'And since it seems pretty certain Jamal Mushhawrar is not our blackmailer, I'm willing to admit the whole thing was a bit of a disaster.'

The only mildly good thing to have come out of the whole debacle was the ample time it had given Adam to conduct a thorough search of the jewellery shop safe while all attention was diverted by the farce being enacted front of house. He'd reported it revealed some rather wonderful gold and silver pieces too precious to keep on display in the shop, legal documents, a pile of banknotes - but no letter. Leaving the safe standing open, as Jamal had abandoned it when I screamed, Adam had made good his escape through the broken window. We could only hope, since nothing had been stolen, that Jamal wouldn't view the damaged latch as suspicious and choose to investigate further. It was a simple fact it hadn't occurred to Adam to wear gloves. I had no doubt a thorough dusting of the storeroom with the right powder would reveal fingerprints we'd struggle to explain. I felt some remorse that for all his trouble Jamal Mushhawrar had not made the hoped-for sale. Once all the pandemonium had died down, I'd cast him an apologetic look and made good my escape, with my Egyptian pound notes secure and untouched in the purse that had been restored to my canvas holdall and handed back to me.

Ahmed was inconsolable. Not only had he suffered the indignity of narrowly avoiding arrest in front of an avid crowd of Souk shopkeepers, but when finally he returned to the police station it was to find Mrs Mushhawrar had made a complaint against him. She'd described his behaviour on the visit to her home of the previous day as high-handed and insensitive.

'I'm so sorry, Ahmed.' Adam apologised. 'I thought you'd be able to slip out of the shop with Merry's bag without anyone noticing you. Merry, you screamed too soon. And perhaps if your bag were a bit smaller...'

'Don't start blaming me!' I retorted, riled. 'You told me to scream the moment the safe door was open so Jamal Mushhawrar didn't have time to close it again. You said we needed to startle him into leaving it wide open.'

'And now I am thought of as a thief,' mourned Ahmed. He had some trouble with the word, since the 'th' followed by the 'f' seemed to tie his tongue in knots, especially coming so soon after the word 'thought'. 'A robber,' he added, just in case we hadn't caught his meaning.

'I think we managed to convince the military officer it was all a big misunderstanding,' I sought to mollify him.

'You said Ahmed grabbed your bag from the real thief just as he slipped through the door,' Adam reminded me. But he was grinning with that quick return to good humour that's such a mercurial part of his personality. 'I'm not sure you convinced anyone since no one was to be seen running off.' I knew he was teasing me. Adam and I can never stay mad at each other for long. 'But since I think he fancied you, he was inclined to accept your story at face value. Luckily for Ahmed.'

'It was all I could think of in the heat of the moment,' I snapped, feeling a strong need to defend myself. 'After all, the idea was for Ahmed to be the hero of the moment not the villain.' My guilt over Ahmed's close shave brought me out in a cold sweat.

Adam mock frowned at me, his eyes twinkling. 'Hmm, your imagination is clearly not as vivid as it once was.'

But Ahmed was not yet of a mind to see the funny side. 'And now I have been reprimanded for wasting time on duty and suspended while Mother Mushhawrar's complaint is investigated.' Our big friend looked as if he might burst into tears at the injustice of it all.

'We know Ahmed, and its all our fault,' I soothed, racked with regret. 'But it will blow over in a few days, I'm sure. Mrs Mushhawrar is just looking for someone to take her seriously. You happened to be the first officer to turn up. So you got both barrels. We'll think of a good reason to account for our visit to her yesterday. In the meantime, I think it might be a good idea to get you out of Luxor for a few days to let the dust settle. Besides, I have a suggestion for how we can make it up to you.'

It was not at all gratifying to see the look he gave me laden with misgivings. That Adam's glance was equally full of qualms nearly halted me in my tracks... nearly, but not quite.

'Come to Cairo with Adam and me,' I entreated. 'We're joining Walid to hear the lecture Nabil Zaal's giving at the museum later in the week. That promises to be fun. He always manages to set the cat among the pigeons with his wild claims. Besides, I was speaking to Selim on the telephone recently and he said he'd be more than happy to take a look at your teeth. He doesn't want payment. His only stipulation was to say you need to come to Cairo so he can see you at his practice there.' Selim, Shukura's husband, was a dentist and a good one.

Ahmed stared at me doubtfully for what I'd swear was a full minute. I could almost feel the seconds ticking off. Then his face broke into wreaths of smiles. Sadly, these served only to reinforce quite how badly in need of a skilful dentist's attention Ahmed's teeth were. Ahmed is a good-looking man and, I suspect, a vain one. In the just-over-a-year I'd known him I'd detected no hint of a love interest in his life. Yet I was pretty sure this was a situation Ahmed, in his mid-to-late-thirties, if I was any judge, might secretly yearn to rectify. 'I will come,' he announced grandly, rather in the manner of *him* being the one doing *me* an enormous favour. Then his expression clouded again. 'But I will not fly. We travel by train, yes?'

* * *

The first time Adam and I travelled on the overnight sleeper train from Luxor to Cairo, we had separate compartments since we'd only just met and officially I was still in a relationship with Dan. This time around we shared one. But the romantic potential of this development was seriously hampered by the knowledge of Ahmed ensconced in his own compartment butted up right next door to ours. Our accommodation was more comfortable than lavish. The Orient Express this was not – although since I've never travelled on the iconic train so beloved of Agatha Christie aficionados, perhaps comparisons are unfair.

Our beds were of the bunk variety. Our cabin attendant pulled each one down from its place discreetly hidden in the bulkhead before he wished us a good night. The pillows were soft and everything was spotlessly clean.

Before turning in for the night, we ate a tasty supper in the dining car, refusing wine in deference to Ahmed's Muslim observances. Instead we washed down our meals with a bottle of Coke each. The sun was setting as we journeyed north. We sat back with coffee and enjoyed the view skimming past the window. As the track ran alongside the Nile on its northward route, this was of the huge glowing ball of the sun making its fiery descent over the hills beyond the river on the west bank, sending a flaming reflection like a burning highway back towards us across the inky water. Through the opposite window of the narrow dining carriage the sinking sun softly illuminated rural scenes; huge cultivated fields of sugarcane bordered by knots of waving palm trees. Farmers dressed in long white galabeyas, with turbans wound around their heads, encouraged their donkeys homewards for the night after a long day toiling in the fields.

Soon it became too dark to enjoy the scenery. It's a long held joke that nightfall in Egypt comes with a thud. There's no lingering twilight in the way of an English summer's evening. So bidding each other goodnight, we headed back to our tiny compartments and made ourselves comfortable for the night.

'It was a good idea to ask Ahmed to join us,' Adam said, kissing me goodnight and climbing onto the upper bunk. 'It'll take his mind off things for a few days, and we can help him get it all sorted out when we get back. I'm just sorry we're not bringing good news for Walid.'

There really didn't seem to be much left to say on either subject, so I kissed him back and pulled the sheet up to my chin.

I slept surprisingly well. Perhaps it was the rocking motion of the train chuntering along the tracks. I am, after all, used to sleeping on a boat with the soft swell of the Nile current underneath.

Our cabin attendant brought us breakfast boxes at first light and Adam and I sat alongside each other once the lower bunk was converted back into a settee, observing the view through the window while we ate. Agricultural land had given way to shadowy stretches of pale desert rock overnight. But the barren landscape reverted to a more rural one as we sped closer to our destination. Wide green fields stretched into the distance; interspersed with single storey mud brick huts surrounded by livestock. Gradually this pastoral view yielded to one of grimy suburbs blurring past. Cairo welcomed us to its grey-smudged metropolis. Everything, including the illuminated neon signs and huge poster boards set atop high-rise apartment blocks, looked slightly out-of-focus in the smog of pollution hanging in the air. Cairo is one of the most densely populated cities in the world. If the traffic-clogged flyovers snaking across the city were anything to judge by, I reckoned most of its fifteen-million-or-so inhabitants were on the move this morning.

It was little more than a year since I'd last been in Cairo. But as soon as we got off the train on the long platform at Ramses station it felt different. A palpable air of nervous tension hung heavy over the city.

Adam took my hand as Ahmed busied himself finding a trolley for our luggage and hefted our three bags onto it. He probably needn't have bothered since my case and Adam's both had wheels and pull-out handles. But it clearly made him feel useful. And it served as a distraction from the armoured tank sitting like a great big squat frog square in the middle of the concourse as we emerged through the ticket barrier.

'Let's hope it's just a precaution ready for the anti-Morsi protests next weekend,' Adam murmured. 'Nobody wants more violence on the streets of Cairo.'

'I'd say it's a bit late for that.' I snatched up an English-language newspaper from a stand as we passed, pressing some coins into the seller's outstretched hand. 'Look, the front page is full of the mob attack on those Shia Muslims a couple of days ago in Giza.' I scanned the copy. 'Four men were killed when the mob stormed the house where they'd been worshipping with Molotov cocktails!'

Ahmed was shaking his head, looking at the horrifying picture of a badly injured, possibly dead, man being dragged along the street. 'Dis is very bad,' he said.

'Carried out by a gang led by Salafist preachers.' Adam was reading the first paragraph over my shoulder. 'And Morsi hasn't helped matters by failing to speak out against the sectarianism that's going on right under his nose.'

I've known Adam long enough now to know he doesn't hold much truck with religion, organised or otherwise, blaming it for many of the world's ills. And it was hard to disagree with him when I held the evidence in my hands that religious intolerance was causing blood to be spilled in the streets of the country I love.

'His enemies will just see it as more fuel on the fire,' Adam prophesied.

'Morsi's due to address the nation tonight,' I reminded them both, trying to sound hopeful. 'Perhaps he'll be more conciliatory so things don't degenerate into a standoff between him and the military.'

But in this wish I was destined to be disappointed.

We caught a cab directly to Ted's flat after leaving the station. We'd made arrangements for Ahmed to stay with Shukura and Selim for the duration of our stay in the capital, which made sense since Selim could then keep an eye on his dental patient. Adam and I were booked into the Mena House hotel, near the pyramids. This was another nod both to nostalgia and the progression of our relationship, since the last time we'd stayed there we'd had separate rooms. I had high hopes the potential for romance and nocturnal activity might be somewhat higher than we'd experienced on the train up from Luxor. Adam and I had never actually had what one might describe as a holiday together. So to say I was pinning high hopes on this trip to Cairo might not be putting too fine a point on things.

But Ted's apartment was our first port of call. Professor Edward – Ted – Kincaid had been Adam's university tutor back in the day. He'd retired out here to Cairo a decade or so ago, deciding to spend his twilight years in the land whose history he'd studied so avidly all his life. His professional Egyptological credentials still had the power to kick some considerable ass. But to Adam and me he was like a mentor and favourite uncle all rolled into one.

'Adam, my boy! Merry, dearest! And Ahmed, my fine fellow! What a sight you all are for my sore old eyes! Come in, come in...' He ushered us into his compact apartment.

I'd describe everything about Ted's home as neat... and not in the American or adolescent sense of the word. Let's just say it's compact. The word might be *bijou* in the French, with everything tidily stored away. A place for everything and everything in its place... that was until it came to Ted's books. The place was littered with them. Bookshelves lined every wall. Each shelf groaned under the weight of volumes not just jammed alongside each other, but also squeezed horizontally into the space between one shelf and the next. Every available worktop, from the kitchen counter to the windowsill and desk in the lounge was similarly adorned with paperbacks and hardbacks alike. Often open at seemingly random pages, their spines bent back, revealing Ted's squiggled notes in the margins or paragraphs coloured in with a bright yellow highlighter.

Ted himself was less like his books and more like his apartment: a small, neat man, impeccably attired in a crisp shirt with a perfectly knotted tie set off with a beautiful golden tiepin crafted in the shape of a sphinx. And I happened to know that underneath his shirt, Ted sported a neat white vest. I knew this because on one never-to-be-forgotten occasion he'd stripped down to the said undergarment so we could rip up his shirt to use as bandages. But with his shirt firmly on, his tie knotted and his tiepin in place, Ted's only personal nod to the chaos his books suggested was his gold-rimmed glasses. They seemed to remain connected to his nose by a sheer force of will, certainly not their fit. Or perhaps it was the habit of his forefinger constantly reaching up to slide them back into place. Ted's constantly slip-sliding glasses had been a source of fascination to me for as long as I'd known him – as with Ahmed, this was a little over a year now. And yet, as with Ahmed, I felt as if I'd known Ted forever. He'd been our stalwart, a source of wise counsel and unimpeachable knowledge throughout our adventures in Egypt so far; not to mention the scrapes he'd rescued us from. Adam and I loved Ted like family, and knew he returned the sentiment.

'Make yourselves comfortable out here,' he invited, ushering us outside into the shade of the awning that stretched from above his balcony window. It afforded a somewhat obscured view of the pyramids. Ted's flat is in the Giza district, not far from the famous plateau as the crow flies. The sad truth of the matter though is that the crow's direct flight is interrupted by an urban sprawl that seems just a little out of control. The spread of modern suburbia strikes me as somewhat irreverent when the whole of history appears to stand as its backdrop. 'Now, what can I get you to drink? Iced tea? Something fizzy?'

We settled on the iced tea and Ted brought it out to us in tall glasses set on a tray. With drinks in our hands, it seemed our gazes were drawn by some unseen magnetic force to the ancient monuments obscured so cruelly by the ugly modern apartment blocks.

'And so, the pyramids stand witness to another chapter in Egypt's unfolding history,' Ted said.

He didn't need to clarify the statement for us all to know he was referring to President Morsi's precarious grip on supposedly democratic rule.

Adam sipped his iced tea. 'Revolutions pass like a ripple on the Nile,' he said, clearly in the mood to wax philosophical. 'In the – what? – five thousand years since the great pyramid was built, empires have risen and fallen; wars and natural disasters have wracked the land; civilizations have sprung up, developed and disappeared; major religions have come into being and faded away. It does rather make you wonder at the relative significance of what's going on today.'

'True,' Ted agreed. 'And yet we can each live but one life, the one we're born to. So, to those of us just a little younger than the pyramids, these events resonate with particular meaning.' He smiled to acknowledge the ironic nod to his own advancing years. He's in his mid-seventies after all.

'The army has said it will intervene next weekend if the mass rallies planned against the president descend into chaos,' I said, putting the newspaper I'd picked up at the station onto the coffee table in front of me.

'But the army has stopped short of endorsing either Morsi or his secular opponents,' Adam added, having read the article in the taxi on the way here.

'Their promised intervention is one of the strongest warnings the military has given since it handed over power to Morsi's civilian government a year ago,' Ted nodded, reaching for the folded newspaper and shaking it out so he could scan the front page. 'It was reported on the radio this morning that

Abdel Fattah el Sisi, the defence minister, said he would not allow Egypt to descend into what he called a "dark tunnel of conflict". He called on all political factions to reach consensus before the mass protests against President Morsi planned for Sunday-week.'

Ahmed nodded sagely. He was sitting straight-backed with his big hands resting on his knees. He always reminds me of the granite statues that line the Pharaonic temples in that pose, and it's a favourite one. 'Dere is a sad state of division in our society,' he announced in sonorous tones. 'De continuation of it is a danger to de Egyptian state. El Sisi is correct in what he says. Dere must be unity among all Egyptian peoples.'

Ted put the newspaper back down again, shaking his head at the chilling picture on the front page. 'I can't help but feel alarmed about the massive protests Morsi's opponents are planning for the anniversary of his election. Many claim they will not leave the streets until the fall of the Muslim Brotherhood. They argue that for all his talk of democratic legitimacy, Morsi has little respect for wider democratic values.'

'But surely his removal would be a bitter blow for democracy in Egypt,' Adam remarked. 'If the people can remove one democratically elected president, they can surely do so again.'

Ted sipped his iced tea, frowning slightly. He pushed his glasses up onto the bridge of his nose and looked across at Adam. 'I take your point, my boy. At home when we choose the wrong government – and when did we ever choose the right one? – we live with it. That's democracy.' He lifted an ironic eyebrow. 'As one reporter said on the News this morning, "When George W Bush had only 22% in the ratings, Americans didn't talk about early presidential elections; that's not the way democracies are run.'

'But some of the people on the streets of Luxor accuse Morsi of creating an almost fascist regime,' I frowned. 'That's not to be tolerated surely.'

'It seems a large proportion of the population agrees,' Ted concurred. 'More than fifteen million Egyptians have signed a petition calling for the president's downfall. You're right; they're furious at Morsi's unilateralism.'

'And also at de plummeting living standards,' Ahmed interjected. He sat up even straighter, looking as proud as punch to have used such a word.

'Exactly so,' Ted nodded. 'And they accuse him of prioritising his Islamist allies at the expense of national unity.'

'But Morsi can still rely on strong, if falling, support among Islamist sections of society,' Adam pointed out. 'On Friday more than 100,000 Egyptians gathered in support of his presidency at a mosque in East Cairo. They say they'll fight against him being forced from office three years before the scheduled end of his term.'

'Hmm, 100,000 supporters versus fifteen million opponents,' I commented. 'With odds like that, I don't fancy his chances.'

'Well, it seems to me Morsi has one last opportunity to redeem and maybe save himself,' Ted said, collecting up our empty glasses. 'He's giving a televised address to the nation tonight. It's billed as a reconciliatory speech. Let's hope he delivers on that promise.'

He didn't. We stayed and had lunch with Ted, sitting out on his balcony in the shade, with the wall mounted fan blowing. I was keen to find out how the professor had taken the news of his daughter's forthcoming marriage to a certain ex boyfriend of mine. It's fair to say Dan may not have made the most favourable of first impressions on his future father-in-law in their early encounters. But when I broached the subject, Ted smiled benevolently and said, 'I can only hope Jessica will be happier with her second husband than with her first.' I had to smile at this. Even Dan, for all his faults – a warped sense of humour being primary among them – couldn't be worse than Youssef Said, to whom Jessica had been disastrously wed the first time around. I was rather glad for Dan that Ted had this earlier benchmark to compare him against. I'm not sure Ted would necessarily have approached his only daughter's second plunge into matrimonial waters with such apparent good grace otherwise. 'But I have to say the prospect of a wedding in England in December does not fill me with the warmest of glad tidings,' Ted admitted. 'I've become accustomed to the heat and sunshine of Egypt.'

I shared these sentiments to a large extent. Although it would be lovely to be home for Christmas, the dreary December weather held little appeal – unless Dan and Jessica could somehow prevail upon the temperamental English weather to favour them with snow. A white wedding followed by a white Christmas might be nice.

After leaving Ted's, we saw Ahmed happily settled with Shukura and Selim and held a virtual re-run of the conversation we'd had with the professor. It seemed the unfolding political situation in Egypt was all any of us could talk about.

Shukura and Selim seemed to agree with the majority of Egyptians that President Morsi had made a pretty poor fist of the job gingerly handed to him, with so much misgiving, and a scraped 51% of the final tally in last year's elections.

'The need to avoid violence on our streets is not an argument, far less a justification, for his continued rule,' Shukura said. She said a lot more besides, as Shukura usually does. This was basically that the president had failed to build the inclusive administration he'd promised, with both Copts and women among the disappointed constituencies.

He'd pushed through a constitution that was too indulgent by far of the military, and too Islamist in character for the comfort of Egypt's secular or non-religious peoples; and attacked, or seemed to attack, the judiciary and independent media.

Escaping at last, Adam and I hailed another taxi to take us onwards to the hotel. After checking in at the Mena House and taking a quick shower in the rather luxurious bathroom, we donned our bathrobes, set the air conditioning to a comfortable setting, ordered a bottle of wine and some snacks from room service, and settled down for the evening to watch the televised presidential address. I was quite sure a similar scene was being played out up and down the length of Egypt, as televisions across the country were tuned to the correct channel. We chose the one with English subtitles.

Morsi's meandering speech lasted more than two-and-a-half hours. We stuck with it, hoping for a gesture of genuine conciliation. But none came.

'If you ask me, that speech leaves Egypt more dangerously divided than ever,' Adam said disgustedly when it was finally over, zapping the television off with the remote control. 'It wasn't exactly a peace offering to denounce unspecified "enemies of Egypt" for sabotaging the democratic system. He might have done himself more favours had he actually tried to address the substance of their arguments.'

'If those same enemies topple him from power next weekend, given the degree of polarisation in Egypt today, we won't have a stable government here for decades,' I agreed, disappointed. 'Walking on stage and effectively accusing the whole country of treason hardly seems the way to win over his dissenters. It seems to me the Muslim Brotherhood is unable to manage its transition from outlawed pressure group to governing authority.'

In truth, I considered Morsi had deliberately thrown away his last chance at achieving any sort of consensus between his Islamist supporters and the secular opposition in Egypt. He'd pledged radical reforms to state institutions and admitted to making mistakes during his first year in office. But he refused to offer serious concessions to the opposition. Instead he'd made a speech I viewed as provocative and full of threats and accusations. I found myself increasingly in agreement with Morsi's opponents that the president was both incompetent and autocratic.

'He seemed at pains to win over the army,' Adam said, putting our now-empty bottle of wine amid the few leftovers on the dinner tray and carrying it across the room to leave outside for collection. 'He pointedly praised the military.'

'That's because he knows his opponents hope the army will facilitate a transition of power in the coming weeks,' I said cynically. 'Let's face it; the intentions of the military are the subject of the most frenzied debate in all this. They've been quite guarded about showing their hand so far.'

'The army will make its strategic decisions based on what they perceive to be in the best national interest,' Adam said. 'They're unlikely to give Morsi their support based just on the contents of that speech. No, Merry; I think you're right. Morsi's days are numbered. What that might mean for Egypt I wouldn't like to say.'

'And it's hardly the most auspicious backdrop for trying to discover Walid's blackmailer,' I complained. 'Whoever he is, he holds all the aces. If he blows the whistle on the tomb at a time like this, Egypt will explode like a powder keg.'

Adam joined me on the bed and lifted my empty wine glass out of my hand, setting it on the bedside cabinet. 'I think we need to make it our first priority tomorrow to tell Walid the bad news that we've been unsuccessful in unmasking the villain so far,' he said, 'And think about what to do next. But, in the meantime, let's make the most of some time to ourselves, shall we? It strikes me this room has some facilities it might be fun to explore. The whirlpool bath seems particularly rich with possibilities.'

Chapter 6

'I feared as much,' Walid said sorrowfully when we gave him the bad news early the next day, shortly after our arrival at the museum. 'It was too much to hope for that we should reveal his identity so soon. And besides, I have received another communication from him.'

'You have?' I gulped, feeling my eyes bulge. 'What does it say?'

Walid felt in the pocket of the white laboratory coat he wears over his trousers, shirt and tie when on duty. He drew out a folded sheet of paper and handed it across to me. Adam moved to stand alongside me so we could take a look together.

The blackmailer had used the same device as before, cutting words from newspapers and pasting them onto a single sheet of paper. I wondered what Hercule Poirot might make of this rather clichéd approach. The message was crafted in Arabic, so Walid translated it for us. He'd evidently learned it by heart:

"Politics plunge Egypt into chaos. You will do what I say or I will act. My demand remains the same. But I want a gesture to show you take me seriously. All Egypt will be watching the demonstrations in Tahrir Square. You will use

this as a cover to deliver a token of goodwill. This will be a down-payment against the full amount. Ten percent is fair. LE one million. I will contact you again to say where to deliver the money. If you fail me, I will make life difficult for those who signed their names to your pledge. Then I will speak out."

'One million Egyptian is about a hundred thousand in sterling, give or take,' Adam calculated. 'That's a lot of money, Walid. There was a time I might have been able to help you out. But Merry and I have sunk the best part of our savings into the *Queen Ahmes*.'

'I would not take your money, Adam,' Walid frowned. 'Not under any circumstances, and most certainly not under these.'

I moved to stand at the window of Walid's office. It was in one corner of the upper storey of the Egyptian Museum, above the floors on which the nation's treasures were on display. It afforded a sideways view of the now world-famous Tahrir Square; cradle of the 2011 uprising that toppled the Mubarak regime. Even now, the square was filled with people. Most had been there since last night. They'd gathered to watch President Morsi deliver his speech on huge screens set up for the purpose. I'd seen the News reports of the crowds reacting furiously for the length of his address, many holding their shoes in the air as a sign of disrespect. I had no doubt they'd remain there now for the duration, making their presence felt ahead of next weekend's planned protests, when thousands more were predicted to surge into the square to swell their numbers. I wondered if our despicable blackmailer might happen to be out there somewhere, mingling among the masses, anonymous in the crowd, watching Walid come and go from the museum, much as a venomous snake might slink through the undergrowth and watch its prey. In which case, he'd doubtless observed Adam and me arrive just now. We were on his target list, those who'd signed their names to Walid's carefully composed letter. So, too, Ted, Shukura, Ahmed and, over in England, oblivious but as deeply threatened by this as the rest of us, Dan and Jessica, happily making their wedding plans.

'We have to stop him.' I declared, spinning back around to face Adam and Walid. I'd suddenly had a horrible vision of one of our blackmailer's nasty little cut-and-pasted notes arriving on Dan's desk at the KPMG offices in Canary Wharf where he works. Having Dan haring out here to glare at me for daring to embroil him and his intended in all this was almost more terrifying than the prospect of our blackmailer blowing the lid sky high on our tomb. Dan's repertoire in put-downs, with facial expressions to match, was nearly enough to have me contemplating bank robbery as a way of getting our unknown tormentor off our backs.

'I have no way of getting my hands on that sort of money without resorting to something criminal,' Walid said, looking sick, and seeming to read my thoughts.

'There must be some way we can find out who it is,' I said desperately. 'What about the envelope the letter came in? Was it post marked?'

'It was hand-delivered to the museum,' Walid said.

'So, we know he's in Cairo!' I pounced; 'And willing to risk approaching the museum directly. Perhaps we should post a guard on the gate so when he tries to deliver his next communication we can grab him!'

'I don't think he'll come anywhere near the place if he catches sight of one of us hanging around the entrance,' Adam said dampeningly. 'But I agree it would be good to keep a watch out from a distance. Sounds like a job for Ahmed.'

'But he's getting his teeth fixed!'

'You heard what Selim said; he'll have to fit Ahmed with a temporary plate of false teeth before he can screw in the permanent ones.'

I winced. This was a little too graphic for me.

Adam noted my reaction and went on, 'I'm sure Ahmed will have some time, and he'll be pleased to help out. You know how he lights up at any prospect of an arrest.'

'It relies too much on luck,' Walid interjected, wringing his hands. 'I fear I have no choice but to get all in readiness to deliver to this despicable individual the money he demands.'

Adam and I both stared at him and opened our mouths to say 'but' at the same time.

Walid continued before either of us could get the word out. 'I can only hope the demonstrations planned for next weekend will keep all eyes away from me. And if something should go missing from our beautiful museum, maybe I can point the finger at opportunistic looters once again.'

I felt as if my jaw might hit the floor to hear Walid speaking like this. 'Surely there must be another way,' I cried. I knew it would break his heart to steal from the museum he loved so much.

But he'd clearly spent some time hardening his heart against such an eventuality since receiving this second letter from his unknown blackmailer. 'You would be surprised, Merry and Adam, at how often I am approached by private collectors asking about the possibility of making a purchase for their personal collections of antiquities. These are not dealers; you understand, no, nothing so unscrupulous. Some of them are very wealthy men with state of the art facilities of their own in which to store and display their artefacts. Strictly speaking, it is still illegal, of course. But in these recent troubled times I have heard stories of looters selling precious artefacts on the Internet. Ebay, is it called? Some sort of online bring-and-buy sale? Surely to sell an object to a private collector who will treat it with the reverence it deserves and keep it safe cannot compare with such travesty?'

I wasn't sure whether it was us or himself Walid was trying to convince. Usually a man of few words, this verbal deluge was quite unlike him. And he wasn't finished.

'There are artefacts in the museum's storerooms that have not seen the light of day for years,' he went on. 'Some I doubt even to be catalogued on our inventory. It has been known for objects, even mummies would you believe, to go missing. I'm not sure a small item from the stores would be missed, and, if it were, probably not for many months. Within a couple of years we are due to open our new modern museum here in Cairo, you know. Yes, it will be situated near to the pyramids. All brand spanking new and featuring the latest thermostat-controlled display cases for preserving our ancient treasures while they are on show. It is a source of constant worry to me that something may go missing in the move. All of this makes me wonder if it is worth taking a small risk now in the hope it will not be discovered.' The pleading look he gave us was almost heart-breaking.

Adam spoke up. 'The alternative seems to be for our friends to be dragged into this sorry state of affairs. So its clear we can't sit by and do nothing. If our blackmailer suspects you may not be good for the money, Walid, he's likely to do as he says and set his sights on the rest of us, either individually or collectively. And I doubt we can lay our hands on a million quid even if we empty out all our combined piggy banks.'

'It's either that or let him announce the tomb to the world,' I added. 'And there's no way we're allowing that to happen.'

'So reluctantly we have to conclude my proposal is our only option,' Walid said quietly. 'I will stay here at the museum overnight tonight. I can tell the guards I am checking security arrangements in view of the planned street demonstrations. It will give me time when no one is around to decide on an appropriate artefact to offer for private sale.'

'But, Walid, if you're caught, either with the artefact, or in making the approach to a private collector…' I trailed off. The consequences were only too obvious to us all and really didn't bear thinking about.

'Then all bets are off,' he said sadly. 'And now, Merry and Adam, it is my duty to play host to our distinguished visitor from America, here to give his lecture this afternoon. Mr Nabil Zaal.'

* * *

The grand, columned halls of the Egyptian Museum in Cairo are usually dominated by giant stone statues and sarcophagi arranged to dramatic effect. But this afternoon all attention was focused on an unremarkable looking man of about fifty wearing a suit that appeared to be a size too large for him. Nabil Zaal had chosen the exhibition galleries on the first floor as the setting for his lecture, close to the magnificent Tutankhamun treasures. From where Adam and I were sitting squeezed at the back of the hall with Ahmed, Ted and Shukura, the author's head was just visible over a forest of microphones carrying the logos of the world's most recognisable TV companies. Since the planet's media were all here in Cairo anyway to cover the unfolding political events, it seemed they'd decided they might as well show up and report on the controversial author's lecture. Nabil Zaal had a reputation for setting hares running, writing what many called 'revisionist history'. He'd sold books by the shedload, mostly linking the patriarchs of the Old Testament with 18th Dynasty Pharaonic Egypt.

The lecture space was crammed with people. As well as the world's assorted press, Egyptologists and Biblical historians from far and wide had shown up to hear what he might be about to say this time.

We'd had time only for the briefest of hellos when Walid rushed us down from his office to welcome the author. Nabil was busy ensuring his notes were in order and testing that his lapel microphone was working. He'd invited us to enjoy his lecture with an odd little gleam in his eyes. It rather filled me with foreboding. 'Well, I guess Walid's already given us some inkling of the wild claim is he going to make this time,' I murmured as Adam and I left him to his preparations and went to find somewhere to sit for the lecture. 'I'll be interested to see the reaction he gets.'

From the platform at the front a discreet cough alerted us the talk was about to begin. This was Walid, who had the task of publically welcoming the Egyptian-American writer. He stumbled and stuttered his way through this opening address with excessive amounts of umming and erring. Despite the quiet aura of authority I'd seen him exude on more than one occasion, Walid was not a confident public speaker by any stretch of the imagination. His performance was frankly painful to witness. Thankfully it was soon over and Nabil Zaal stepped forward. In contrast to our friend the tongue-tied but otherwise quite brilliant curator of the museum, Nabil Zaal spoke for an audience as if born to it.

'My friends, fellow historians and ladies and gentlemen of the word's combined media,' he started, 'I hope I shall provide you with an absorbing distraction from the political events surrounding us here in Cairo this afternoon.' He smiled. 'Perhaps some of you may even spare me a few column inches as you go to press tonight for tomorrow's morning papers, amid the more important events you are duty bound to report. My aim is to make valuable use of the time you have generously given up to be here today. So, let us begin.'

Bright-eyed, he gazed at his assembled audience. I craned upwards in my seat, trying for a better view of him. But it was almost impossible given the number of people crammed between the display cabinets. I fanned myself with the small printed card, which advertised Nabil's latest book *The Pharaonic Bible.* Its very title was provocative.

'We are assembled here together in this wonderful old city of Cairo at an important crossroads in the modern history of this ancient land,' Nabil started. 'Some predict the military will lead a coup d'état next weekend and oust President Morsi from the office he has held for only a year. Many find this prospect shocking. And yet I say there is nothing new under the Egyptian sun. By my reckoning, the first military coup d'état took place in Egypt in perhaps 1336 BC. The army general responsible for leading the campaign to remove – not a democratically elected president, but a divinely anointed pharaoh – was called Horemheb. The pharaoh he ousted from power has come down to us through the millennia as a controversial and much maligned figure, often known as the heretical pharaoh. His name was Akhenaten.

'So, let me start by saying this. It is my belief that Akhenaten's rule over Egypt towards the end of the hitherto glorious 18th Dynasty was not brought to an end by his death. I contend he was the victim of a military coup that removed him, first in favour of his brother Smenkhkare, and then in favour of Tutankhamun, who some believe to have been been Akhenaten's son. Forced to abdicate his throne, it is my belief Akhenaten retreated to a place called Sarabit-el-Khadim in

Sinai. I can set a portfolio of evidence before you to suggest Akhenaten lived in this wilderness for upwards of perhaps thirty years. His time in the Sinai desert certainly spanned the reign of Tutankhamun, the short reign of Ay, and then the lengthy reign of Horemheb himself, when this upstart general finally had himself crowned Pharaoh.

'I believe Akhenaten returned to reclaim his throne during the one-year reign of Ramses I at the start of the 19th Dynasty. When this attempt failed, he led his followers out of Egypt. These followers, many of them descended from the same genealogical line as Akhenaten himself, have become known as the Israelites. Their departure, and the route they took out of Egypt across the Sinai Peninsular are better known as the Exodus. In short, my friends, I believe I can prove that the heretic pharaoh Akhenaten was none other than that towering figure of the Old Testament, the father of Judaism and the forefather of both Christianity and Islam... Moses.'

This pronouncement was greeted with a wall of sound as people started muttering to themselves or their companions, and a myriad of camera shutters clicked in unison around the room.

I turned and frowned at Adam. I was sure Nabil Zaal's ultimate claim was frankly ridiculous, since I happened to know where Akhenaten, quite dead at the time, had been safely buried. I was also party to the knowledge that Tutankhamun and Ay were the ones responsible for his burial, or reburial as was actually the case. Yet, to my certain knowledge, the author had struck incredibly close to home with his claims about the army general Horemheb and his campaign to topple the Amarnan rule.

Horemheb had indeed dealt a crushing blow to the throne. But only after Akhenaten was dead. I had no idea what evidence Nabil Zaal felt he could lay before us. In my experience, evidence was something he was generally pretty short of. But I knew there was proof sitting safely locked away in one of the vaults in this very museum to show that Horemheb had committed regicide in an attempt to set himself on the throne. His military onslaught was against the ephemeral pharaoh Smenkhkare and his queen Meritaten, who held the distinction of being both Akhenaten's eldest daughter and also Smenkhkare's Great Royal Wife. Smenkhkare was indeed Akhenaten's brother and it was he, not Akhenaten, who was Tutankhamun's father from an earlier marriage to his sister.

These were the secrets contained in the papyrus Adam and I had followed Howard Carter's trail of hieroglyphic clues to discover. The same papyrus had led us to find the tomb, secretly carved into the cliffs behind Hatshepsut's Temple, where Pharaoh Akhenaten lay mummified in his stone sarcophagus even now.

Adam opened his mouth to speak, but Nabil had only paused for dramatic effect. Tapping his lapel microphone to hook back our attention, he continued,

'You may have heard me speak before and claim there is no evidence to be found of a mass movement of people that might account for the Biblical Exodus. I stand by this assertion. Not because the Exodus did not take place but because, in my view, it was not a mass movement of people at all. I believe the people Moses led out of Egypt were the followers of Akhenaten's new religion, worship of the single God, the Aten. And among their number were descendants of the tribes the Biblical Joseph invited into Egypt when he brought his father Jacob and his brothers from Canaan. You see; Akhenaten was also descended from these same tribes.'

The buzzing of muttered conversation started up again. Nabil Zaal forestalled it by holding aloft a small object and waiting in silence until all eyes were once more upon him and the artefact he was holding in the air. The muttering died out. Nabil allowed the expectant silence to draw out before he spoke again.

'I have been criticised over the years for presenting overwhelming circumstantial evidence but nothing concrete to support my claims. If firm evidence is what you need to take me seriously, I invite you to take a closer look at this.' He held the object forward towards his audience in one outstretched hand. Around the room I could sense zoom lenses being focused.

'This small scarab made of turquoise faience was once owned by King Farouk in the last century. Its provenance before Farouk owned it is sadly unknown. As you may know, our last reigning monarch had an unfortunate reputation for kleptomania. That the scarab is genuine, however, can be in no doubt. It has been authenticated by some of the finest Egyptologists in the land.' Since one of these happened to be Ted, I knew he was telling the truth.

'This scarab,' Nabil went on proudly, 'was issued originally by the great pharaoh Amenhotep III to commemorate his marriage to the commoner who became his Great Royal Wife, Queen Tiye. Amenhotep III issued hundreds of these so-called 'Marriage Scarabs'. You'll find examples in museums around the globe. What sets this one apart is the inscription carved into its underside. It differs from others of its type in one quite remarkable way. I shall translate it for you, so you can understand the extreme historical significance of this unique artefact.'

He cleared his throat, swung his glance around the audience to ensure he had everyone rapt and attentive, then began his translation of the hieroglyphics inscribed on the scarab.

'It starts with the usual list of the pharaoh's royal titles: *"Strong bull who appears in the glory of Ma'at; he who establishes the laws and who pacifies the two lands; Horus of Gold, great of strength, who defeats the Asiatics; The King of Upper and Lower Egypt; Son of Ra, Amenhotep, which means Amun is pleased; the ruler of Waset, given everlasting life."* Nabil paused and looked around at us all again. 'The scarab goes on to detail Amenhotep's empire as stretching from modern Sudan to the Euphrates river in north-east Syria. So far, this scarab is almost identical in its text to others you will find displayed around the world. My friends, it is what comes next that sets this particular scarab apart from the rest. None other like it has been found to date. So I consider myself particularly fortunate to have come into possession of this one, which I have now bequeathed to this magnificent museum for all to see.' He smiled beatifically and continued with his translation:

"The great royal woman is Tiye, may she live forever. Her father's name is Yuya, great of praises; he who is Overseer of the Granaries and protected Egypt from mighty Set's displeasure during the great famine that afflicted the two lands. Her mother's name is Thuya, mistress of music. Tiye is the woman of a strong king and will reign in glory."

His translation was greeted by a profound silence. This made a nice change from the usual muttering. In truth, I'm pretty sure the significance of what they'd just heard was completely lost on the majority of his audience.

'Let me explain,' Nabil invited benevolently, clearly realising the same thing. His expression suggested he not only realised it but positively relished the opportunity it gave him to wax lyrical about the importance of this unique artefact.

'Many years ago I wrote a book about my belief that Joseph of the Bible, he of the coat of many colours, the interpreter of dreams, was a vizier at the court of Pharaoh Thutmosis IV. Thutmosis IV had a relatively short reign. On his death the throne of Egypt passed to his son Amenhotep III. It does not seem unreasonable to suppose that a trusted vizier should remain in office and transfer his allegiance from one pharaoh to the next, i.e. from father to son. This vizier went by the name of Yuya. It has long been my belief that Joseph of the Bible and the vizier Yuya were one and the same person. The circumstantial case is overwhelming. But I lacked hard proof.'

Somehow, he managed to lift his gaze across the packed throng so his eyes met mine as he said, 'That is, until a couple of months ago, when I came into possession of this ancient scarab.' He smiled at me before turning his attention back to his audience. In that smile was an acknowledgement of the part Adam and I had played in securing the scarab for him. 'This inscription proves that Yuya was in charge of Egypt's granaries during the years of famine that afflicted Egypt. What more evidence do we need that Yuya of the 18th

Dynasty Egyptian court and Joseph of the Bible were the same man?'

This was evidently a rhetorical question as he didn't pause long enough for anyone to answer him, but swept on

'Now, as many of you will know, the American dilettante and excavator Theodore Davis discovered the intact tomb of Yuya and Thuya in the Valley of the Kings in 1905. We know they were Queen Tiye's parents, which makes them the grandparents of Akhenaten and his brother Smenkhkare, and the great-grandparents of the boy king, near whose treasures we are assembled here today, Tutankhamun. If Amenhotep's marriage scarabs were not proof enough of this relationship, recent DNA testing on both Yuya's mummy and that of Tutankhamun has proved it beyond doubt.'

A murmur started to rise again from the audience but Nabil Zaal silenced it with a gesture. He was about to hammer home the significance of the inscription he'd just read aloud for us.

'This scarab takes matters a critical step forward,' he said in ringing tones. 'It *proves* Yuya was Joseph of the Bible. I can see you are now beginning to appreciate the importance of this evidence.' His bright gaze swept the room. A sort of electrical energy seemed to radiate from his listeners as his gaze touched them.

'It means both Akhenaten and Tutankhamun were descended from Biblical Jacob who brought his sons from

Canaan to settle in Egypt. Since Jacob was referred to in the Bible as 'Israel', this means his family were known as the 'Tribe of Israel'. In short, the Israelites.'

'I'm not sure it proves it beyond all reasonable doubt,' Adam whispered in my ear. 'Just because Yuya was in charge of Egypt's granaries during a famine, it doesn't necessarily mean he's Joseph.'

But I'd heard Nabil's body of evidence and was inclined to agree the circumstantial case was overwhelming.

Nabil Zaal swept on with his lecture, cutting off the possibility of further comment. 'Now, I think we have to ask ourselves a very simple question. And it is this: why did Amenhotep III feel the need to issue Marriage Scarabs in their hundreds?'

Once again, he left no room for response and continued in the next breath, 'The romantics among us might suppose it was because he was in love, happy and wanted to share his joy at his betrothal to Tiye with the whole of his empire. And yet, so far as we know, his action is unprecedented in Pharaonic history. So those of us more astute might look for a political as opposed to a personal motivation. To me, the proliferation of Marriage Scarabs in museums around the world smacks of Amenhotep's need to justify himself or, more accurately, his decision to marry Tiye. Why? Because not only was she a commoner, but she was also a Hebrew, an Israelite. He was proposing to taint the pure Egyptian royal house with foreign blood. Worse; the blood of a people whose belief was in a single god, not the pantheon worshipped by ancient Egyptians.'

He allowed another dramatic pause to draw out for a few seconds. This time the buzz of conversation was muted. Most of his audience appeared to be in thrall waiting for him to continue. I noticed a few journalists scribbling frantically in their notebooks. Others fiddled with the volume controls on their Dictaphones.

I glanced sideways at Ted. His pose was one of intent listening, his head cocked sideways. This was a helpful position, since it served to keep his glasses in place on the bridge of his nose. Ahmed, alongside him, was frowning with concentration. His English was better than ever before, but I wasn't sure exactly how much of the author's argument he was following. Shukura had her gaze fixed on our speaker with a rapt attention that might have passed as adoration in a different scenario. None of them noticed me looking at them.

'Now; let us fast-forward a little,' Nabil invited, speaking into the hush. 'Akhenaten, when he became Pharaoh, not only believed in a single god; he elevated his god, the Aten, to the status of the sole god of Egypt and eventually outlawed the worship of any other. So, let us make our first explicit link between Pharaoh Akhenaten and Moses of the Bible. The Hebrew word 'Adonai', meaning 'my Lord' is used in the Bible to refer to God. In 'Adonai' the 'ai' can be removed as these letters represent a Hebrew pronoun meaning 'my' or 'mine' and signify possession. We are then left with 'Adon' (Lord), which is the Hebrew word for the Egyptian 'Aten' as the Egyptian 't' becomes a 'd' in Hebrew and the vowel 'e' becomes an 'o'. The name of the God of Moses, Adon, is therefore the same in its many references in the Bible as the name of the God of Akhenaten, 'Aten'. The Jewish creed says, *"Schema Yisrael Adonai Elohenu Adonai Echod",* which translates as "Hear, O Israel the Lord God is one God". Using the same translation from Hebrew into Egyptian, the sentence from the Jewish creed could be translated, *"Hear, O Israel, our God Aten is the only God."*

I was about to turn to Adam to see what he made of this assertion, when a loud explosion sent me flying out of my seat with fright.

I heard someone close by me shout, 'The pharaohs were NOT Jewish!!' And then all Hell broke loose.

I felt Adam's weight fall on me to protect me from whatever attack was taking place. He pinned me to the floor, breathing heavily. 'Don't move, Merry,' he ordered. And then I felt his weight shift off of me. Alert to the shouting, scraping of chairs and general pandemonium all around me, I opened one eye, then both, and tried to get a sense of what was going on.

All my immediately watering eyes could see was billowing smoke. An acrid smell filled my nostrils as tentatively

I lifted my head. A smoke bomb, if I was any judge. Blinding, choking, but not deadly.

I felt a violent movement beside me and realised Ahmed had launched himself forward.

It took a long time for the smoke to clear. Never before have I heard so many people coughing in a confined space. When finally it was possible to see through the fug, it was to spy Ahmed pinning a man against a pillar with his forearm locked sideways against his victim's windpipe. All the men and women of the world's assembled press who happened to be within range had their camera lenses trained with precision accuracy on our police buddy.

I spun sideways. Adam was half way across the room. But he wasn't quick enough to reach Nabil. Even as I watched the author let out a strangled cry of horror. 'The scarab! It's gone! Someone literally snatched it out of my hand!'

Chapter 7

The military moved in quickly to secure the museum. Armed personnel swiftly manned all entry and exit points. We were evacuated from the building in an orderly, if rather officious manner.

The television crews dispersed, back to report on the mounting tension in Cairo. I stood with my companions on the museum forecourt, amid Pharaonic statues set there to whet the appetite for the riches displayed inside. We were waiting to be allowed back in.

'Bang goes my chance of scouting out the museum tonight for a potential artefact,' Walid mourned, rubbing his hands together, and sounding curiously British in his use of idiomatic English. 'Until the Ministry of State for Antiquities have satisfied themselves nothing else was stolen during the chaos caused by the smoke bomb, none of us will be allowed to return to our posts.'

'My face will appear on the evening News and in the newspapers tomorrow,' Ahmed whimpered. This was not the typical way our friend from the Luxor tourism and antiquities police department expressed himself. 'I will lose my job for sure.'

'I have lost my scarab,' Nabil Zaal wailed. 'I was assured it would be safe here at the museum.'

Hearing all these cries of defeat I felt the need to assert myself. 'The bold theft of the scarab is truly awful,' I agreed. The fact was, that scarab had been stolen more times than I cared to count. And that was just in its recent history. I wasn't sure its loss this time around was really such a tragedy for Nabil since he'd already used it to make his point, and pretty effectively in my view. I turned my attention to our police chum. 'Ahmed, you were a hero today. If the man who let off the smoke bomb can be persuaded to speak now he's in custody, he'll lead the police to his accomplice who snatched the scarab. And then we'll be able to celebrate your quick and decisive action in catching him. It also bodes well for us getting the scarab back.'

Ahmed looked less than convinced, and so did Nabil Zaal. As things were, I decided this was no bad thing since it meant they were so focused on their own misfortunes they failed to register the import of Walid's thoughtless statement.

But I heard it, and so did Adam. We drew him aside. And just in time. A small missile flew through the air falling onto the ground where Walid had been standing. 'What the...?' Adam started, spinning round. I turned too, just as several more small objects hurtled towards us. These turned out to be stones or, more accurately pebbles, tossed with frightening precision from beyond the gate. Adam pulled me behind him so he could shield me with his body. But we didn't appear to be the ones the stone throwers were aiming at. One hit its mark squarely, cracking Nabil on the forehead, just as the assailant shouted, 'Israel will NEVER claim our Pharaohs!'

Nabil let out a cry and dropped to the ground. Stones rained around him. Ted quickly pulled Shukura out of harm's way behind a giant sarcophagus. With a shout, Ahmed started to give chase. But the museum's security guards were ahead of him, running out of the gate. Our attackers – there were two of them as far as I could see – hurled a last handful of stones each, then turned and legged it.

I didn't much rate the security guards chances of catching them, since they ran in opposite directions. And, sure enough, a few minutes later both guards returned looking hot and puffed, but without our stone-throwing assailants in tow.

We'd regrouped, checking for injuries. Nabil had a nasty gash on his forehead, oozing blood. Some of the stones had sharp edges. Luckily Nabil was the only one of us to have suffered a direct hit. A pebble had glanced off my canvas holdall. Adam had managed to dodge the ones that had come his way.

'You don't seem to be very popular around here, Nabil,' Adam remarked.

'It is not me, it is the message I bring,' Nabil said sadly, dabbing at the blood on his forehead with a tissue Shukura handed him. 'The truth is hard for some people to accept. I understand. You see; there is no love lost between the states of Egypt and Israel. Let's face it; Egypt has waged several wars with Israel in recent history, and lost most of them. Egyptian territories in the Gaza Strip and the Sinai Peninsular have fallen under Tel Aviv's control. Israel even crossed the Suez Canal into the Egyptian mainland during the Yom Kippur War of 1973.'

Ted was nodding. He remembered these events. 'People are angry at your claims that Akhenaten and, perhaps more importantly, Tutankhamun, may have shared DNA with Jewish groups historically. I guess their concern is that this information could be used by Israel to argue that Egypt was part of the Promised Land, and to claim Tutankhamun as their own.'

'Well, they were certainly successful in bringing your lecture to an abrupt end,' I said, handing Nabil an antiseptic wipe I'd pulled from my bag.

'Which is a shame,' Nabil nodded, tearing it out of the packet and cleaning his wound. 'I had yet to lay out my most compelling evidence to show Akhenaten and Moses were one and the same man.'

I couldn't help but think maybe he'd gone far enough for one day. I glanced at my watch. 'It's gone five o'clock. I wonder if we shouldn't call it a day,' I suggested. 'I don't rate our chances of getting back inside the museum this afternoon. The military seem to have it pretty much secured and cordoned off. Nabil, it would seem a sensible idea for you to leave Cairo for a few days to let the dust settle.'

To my surprise Nabil leapt at this idea. I'd expected him to argue. After all, he was a famous author, here in Cairo to market his latest work and no doubt drive book sales.

'Akhenaten and Moses have only one chapter dedicated to them in *The Pharaonic Bible*,' he said, eyes gleaming. 'But I think with a little more research I could write a whole book to show they shared but a single body. I would like to go to Amarna. I want to see for myself the place where Akhenaten built his new city, The Horizon of the Sun. I want to visit his tomb to satisfy myself he was never buried there. I am sure I will find evidence others have missed in that ancient place, evidence that will further support my theories. Perhaps you could sail me there on your beautiful dahabeeyah, Merry and Adam. I will pay, of course. To my knowledge there are limited facilities in Amarna. If you agree, your *Queen Ahmes* can be my floating hotel on the Nile.'

I turned in dismay towards Adam, reluctant for our stay at the luxurious Mena House to be cut short. But he was already nodding. Opening my mouth to suggest we delayed our departure for a few days, I was forestalled by Ted. He too was nodding, with a strange air of excitement about him.

'I would love to revisit Amarna,' Ted remarked. 'It is many long years since I was last there on a winter excavation project. I am sure the ancient site of Akhet-Aten has many secrets it has not yet given up. I'd go so far as to suggest it might be the site of the buried treasure listed in the Copper Scroll.'

'The Copper Scroll, did you say?' Adam asked.

'Buried treasure was dat?' Ahmed queried.

Ted smiled. 'Let me explain. You remember all that hullaballoo about the Dead Sea Scrolls we got involved in back in April?'

Adam and I nodded in unison. It wasn't something we could easily forget. Ahmed let out a grunt of acknowledgement.

'Well, it got me interested in finding out more. So I started doing some research. You know, of all the Dead Sea Scrolls, none has baffled experts more than the Copper Scroll. It was discovered in 1952 by a team of Bedouin led by an historian from the École Biblique in Jerusalem. The Copper Scroll appears to be a list of buried treasure engraved on copper pieces. Like the Dead Sea Scrolls, it was considered to be the work of a devout, secretive Jewish sect, the Essenes, who lived in Qumran by the Dead Sea around the time of Jesus. But more recent analysis has shown that the weights and numbering systems used in the Copper Scroll are actually Egyptian in origin.' He turned to Nabil, addressing the author directly as he went on, 'And you'll be interested to know, Nabil, that this analysis further shows how Greek characters inserted into the text of the Copper Scroll make clear references to the Egyptian pharaoh Akhenaten. Some scholars have gone so far as to say the Copper Scroll will completely change our understanding of the relationship between Biblical Moses and historical Akhenaten.'

The author was staring back at the professor in a way that made it look as if his eyes were at risk of popping right out of his face.

'Buried treasure?' Ahmed repeated as if bringing us back to the point.

Ted smiled at him. 'The suggestion seems to be that followers of Akhenaten's monotheistic religion left Egypt after the pharaoh's downfall, taking with them quantities of his temple treasures, some of which they buried on their journey. The Copper Scroll appears to be a kind of treasure map to remind them where they stashed the booty. It seems these followers of Akhenaten were dedicated to keeping his beliefs alive. They handed them down through the generations until the Qumran Essenes seem to have hit upon the idea of putting everything down in writing in the Dead Sea Scrolls. If this turned out to be true, it would mean some of the earliest known Biblical writings could trace their origins back to Akhenaten. Quite what the church might make of that I wouldn't like to say.'

'Especially when the time comes that I am able to prove it was Akhenaten himself, not just his followers who left Egypt to keep the monotheistic beliefs alive,' Nabil finished for him.

Ted's words seemed to cast a spell over us. We all stared back at him in absolute silence for a moment. It was Walid who spoke first.

'I will speak to the Ministry of State for Antiquities,' he said. 'We must get permission for an authorised expedition to Amarna for the purpose of proper research.'

I opened my mouth to protest his need to stay in Cairo in order to carry through his plan at the museum. But he forestalled me before I'd spoken the first word. His eyes gleamed with purpose as he looked back at me,

'I have had an idea!'

* * *

Walid's official Egyptologist's visitors permit was granted almost immediately. I daresay it helped that Ted's name was on the application; so, too, Nabil Zaal's. These were famous names in the field of Egyptology. And Walid's position at the museum packed a punch. Or perhaps the Ministry of State for Antiquities was desperate for anything that might divert attention from Egypt's political situation. Whatever; it seemed we were destined for Amarna. The very name was enough to send a thrill through me.

This was where Akhenaten had built his new city of Akhet-Aten, The Horizon of the Sun, when he abandoned the religious capital, Thebes, in year five of his reign. Akhenaten relocated to his new city, with Nefertiti and their six daughters, worshipping their sole god, the Aten. To me, it was an almost mythological and strangely romantic place, situated on the Nile almost slap bang in the middle of the ancient cities of Memphis and Thebes, modern Cairo and Luxor.

'You know; contrary to the general view, the name Amarna was not derived from the Muslim Arab tribe which settled in the area,' Nabil said conversationally. 'No evidence exists to substantiate such a claim. The name is, however, derived from the name in the second cartouche of Akhenaten's god, namely *"Im-r-n"*.'

He paused to make sure we were all listening, and went on, 'Amran or Imran, was the name given in the Bible to Moses' father, and it is precisely the same name Akhenaten gave to the god he called his *father*, the Aten. It seems to me this is yet another reason to believe that Moses and Akhenaten were one and the same.'

We were on the train, speeding back towards Luxor. This conversation was taking place in the dining car, while we waited for our supper to be served. Walid, Ted, Adam and I were travelling south with the author. We'd left Ahmed in the care of Shukura while her husband Selim carried out the dental work on his teeth. Our police friend had strict instructions to keep an eye on the comings and goings at the museum. He'd been reluctant to stay behind, especially since Ted had mentioned buried treasure. But he was as keen as mustard to have his new smile and eager to keep a lookout for any suspicious-looking character hanging around the museum. So persuading him to stay in Cairo hadn't proved too difficult in the end. Walid had taken Shukura into his confidence about the blackmailer. He'd decided he had no choice since he would be away from Cairo for a few days, and would need someone he trusted to intercept any mail that may arrive for him. I hadn't been there for the conversation. But I had no difficulty imagining Shukura's reaction. The image that came forcibly to my mind was of a clucking hen swathed in a brightly patterned kaftan, with an equally bright headscarf and quantities of chunky gold jewellery.

Adam and I had made the most of our final night at the Mena House and checked out with some reluctance. But, as Adam explained, the chance to break the *Queen Ahmes* from her mooring at the crumbling stone jetty in Luxor, where she'd been tethered for months, was just too good to pass up. Nabil Zaal had offered us a generous fee for our services sailing him down the Nile to Amarna. We'd be mad to refuse. Heaven knows, we'd had little enough return on our investment so far. Besides, it gave us an opportunity to visit the site of Akhenaten's ancient city. I was bubbling with as much eager anticipation as everyone else.

'I've always wondered why Akhenaten upped sticks from Thebes and decided to build a new capital city miles from anywhere,' I mused. I wasn't quite ready yet to give Nabil an opportunity to vent the whole *Moses was Akhenaten* theory. I had a feeling once he started he may not stop. 'I read a novel once, which said he was sailing on the Nile and had something of an epiphany – or, if that's too Christian a word, let's call it a mystic vision – when he reached the spot on the river where he built his new city. Something about the Aten appearing to him at dawn...'

Adam grinned at me and said for the author's benefit, 'You'll have to forgive Merry, Nabil. She's learned most of what she knows about ancient Egypt from reading romantic fiction.'

Ted came quickly to my defence. 'Don't knock it, my boy. She's proved she knows just about as much as the rest of us. And I should say she's had far more fun in the process than we've had in years of academia.'

I beamed at him. I knew I had a stalwart supporter in the professor.

His pale blue eyes twinkled back at me from behind his glasses, and he picked up the thread of conversation I'd left hanging. 'Some say the reason Akhenaten chose that particular virgin site for his new city is because there's a cleft in the bay of cliffs that semi-circles the city. At sunrise the sun lifts into the sky directly behind that cleft every morning, bathing the city in light. Perhaps that's why Akhenaten named his city *The Horizon of the Sun*.'

'I think you'll find the reason Akhenaten left Thebes,' Nabil interjected, 'is because he was not accepted by the priests of Amun, and he and his followers wanted to be free to worship their monotheistic god in peace.'

It seemed we were in for another lecture, whether we liked it or not. Politely, we allowed him to continue.

'I believe Akhenaten suffered a form of persecution by the traditional priesthood of ancient Egypt throughout his early life. In my view, it had to do with his lineage. As I said in my lecture before I was so rudely forced to abort it, Queen Tiye, his mother, was not just a commoner, she was foreign; worse, a Hebrew. Her father, Joseph, was Canaanite. So Akhenaten was of mixed race.'

Ted's gaze caught mine across the table and he raised an eloquent eyebrow. I smothered a smile as the author went on, warming to his theme.

'I think it's distinctly possible the Establishment sought to get rid of Akhenaten when he was born. He had an elder brother, Thutmosis, who'd died in mysterious circumstances. In my view, the story of Moses and the bulrushes derives from Queen Tiye seeking to protect her baby from the hostility of the religious priests of Amun, who saw the threat posed to their authority of a half-Hebrew prince mounting the throne of Egypt. The historical record suggests Akhenaten grew up in

Memphis. It is my view he spent much of his childhood under the protection of Queen Tiye's Hebrew relatives in the border town of Zarw. Biblical scholars have identified Zarw as the city of Goshen, where the tribes of Jacob settled after their descent into Egypt. It is here I believe he formed his early religious views, which later developed into his monotheistic belief in Aten as the sole god.'

At the mention of the story of Moses and the bulrushes, I'd tilted my head to one side. 'You know, I can't help but notice the similarity between the name Moses and the name Thutmosis,' I remarked.

I was quite unprepared for the look of delight with which the author greeted this observation. 'You're right, Merry!' he exclaimed, treating me to a radiant smile. Clearly I'd offered him another opportunity to prove his case and he wasted no time in grabbing it.

'Biblical researchers have claimed the name Moses derives from the Hebrew word *moshe*, which means *to draw out*, presumably of the water. Perhaps that's because they did not wish to acknowledge the glaringly obvious derivation from the ancient Egyptian word *mos*, meaning *son of*. You've spotted the Egyptian convention of linking *mos* to the various deities.' He beamed at me again. 'So, Thutmosis, for example translates as *son of Thoth*, the ancient Egyptian god of knowledge and wisdom. Another popular ancient Egyptian name was *Ramose*, or *Son of Ra*. I think Moses has come down to us simply as *'the son'*. Akhenaten saw himself as the son of the one true god, the Aten.'

Ted nodded slowly. 'Hmm, I could see how perhaps after the campaign by the Ramesside dynasty to obliterate Akhenaten's rule from the historical record, his followers might refer back to him simply as 'the son'.'

Nabil Zaal was clearly delighted to have the opportunity to speak to an audience willing to treat his hypotheses with some genuine scholarly interest and even respect. I'd witnessed at first hand back in April the ridicule with which his 'wild claims' were more often than not greeted. The violent disruption of his lecture at the museum just served to demonstrate how easily ridicule could turn to anger and hostility, particularly where peoples' beliefs were threatened.

It was almost as if the author read my mind. But he wasn't thinking about himself. His thoughts remained rooted firmly on the case he wished to prove.

'Yes, Akhenaten suffered persecution in death as in life,' he agreed. 'There's evidence Amenhotep III went to some lengths to legitimise his son's right to rule. There is a Memphite Inscription dated to Amenhotep's reign, seeking to defend his action in placing *'the male offspring upon the throne'*. This certainly suggests to me there was opposition – undoubtedly from the Amun priesthood and probably the nobility – to his action in securing the inheritance for his son.'

'But I thought the pharaoh was all-powerful,' I interjected. 'Surely they couldn't challenge his decisions.'

'True,' Nabil agreed. 'The pharaoh was seen as semi-divine, head of the priesthood, head of the army and head of the administration of the Two Lands. And that's my point. This divine right to rule was precisely what was being threatened, allowing a mixed race pharaoh to mount the throne. It is my belief Amenhotep III had a lengthy co-regency with his son, continuing to rule from Thebes to pacify the Amun priesthood, while Akhenaten moved to his new city to worship his sole god in peace. But I'm not sure Akhenaten felt safe even at arm's length from his enemies. I believe he relied on the army's support for protection and, possibly, as a safeguard against the confrontation that would be inevitable once his father died and he became sole ruler. In temple and tomb inscriptions Akhenaten is shown wearing the king's military headdress rather than the traditional ceremonial crowns of Lower and Upper Egypt, almost as if he wanted to emphasise his military authority.'

Adam was nodding slowly. 'It makes a certain sort of sense. From what I've studied, it seems scenes of military soldiers and activity abound in both the private and royal art of Amarna. Taken at face value, the reliefs give the impression the city was practically an armed camp.'

Nabil was nodding. 'Yes, everywhere we see parades and processions of soldiers, infantry and chariotry with their massed standards.'

I jumped in at this point, frowning. 'But I thought critics of Akhenaten blamed him for not using the army to repel the enemies of Egypt conducting border raids and threatening the empire. I've read books describing him as a pacifist who refused to engage the army in active warfare, even when it threatened the security of Egypt.'

Nabil looked back at me with an odd little gleam in his eyes. 'Exactly right Meredith. And I think we may look no further for the reason than the necessity of keeping the king's person and his family safe from attack. The army was deployed in protection.'

'And yet you believe it was the army who led a military coup d'état to force his abdication,' Adam queried mildly.

'Ah, well, this is where things get interesting,' Nabil smiled, not in the least put out by Adam's tone.

He was forced to break off as the waiter served our meals and we wished each other *bon appetit*. But it didn't take him long to return to what he'd been saying.

'There were two very senior men in the army during the reign of Akhenaten. And I think it's fair to say they were in opposite religious camps. The first was Ay.'

I'd picked up my fork to start eating, but I put it down in favour of my wine glass at the mention of this name. I had a particular affinity with this particular character from antiquity, since he was the author of the papyrus we'd found.

'That the army in Akhet-Aten was loyal to the throne was almost assured by the person of its commander,' Nabil went on. 'Ay was Akhenaten's uncle, since he was Queen Tiye's brother.'

Adam nodded. We knew this relationship to be true. Since we happened to know Ay was also Nefertiti's father, this made him Akhenaten's father-in-law too. But Adam didn't give this away. 'You believe Ay was the son of Biblical Joseph,' he said.

Nabil nodded. 'And a Hebrew who worshipped a single god; yes. It's clear from the Amarnan inscriptions that Ay held posts among the highest in the infantry and chariotry. I believe it was the loyalty of the army under Ay that kept Akhenaten in power for the uneasy years that followed his coming to the throne as sole ruler in his Year Twelve upon the death of his father.'

'That's when his persecution of Amun started in earnest,' I said. 'He closed the temples and outlawed the worship of the Egyptian pantheon. The Aten was officially elevated to the status of the sole god in Egypt.'

'You're right,' Nabil approved. 'He dispersed the priests and gave orders that the names of other deities be hacked from the temple walls. He dispatched army units to ensure his wishes were carried out.'

'That can't have increased his popularity,' Adam remarked. 'I don't imagine every member of his armed forces necessarily subscribed to his monotheistic beliefs.'

'Precisely!' Nabil agreed. Adam had clearly led him exactly where he wanted to go. 'And that's where I think the general Horemheb made his presence felt. That he was a senior ranking officer in the Egyptian army at the time can be in no doubt. I think he was appalled at what he may have viewed as the desecration being carried out by Akhenaten's troops. And I think he was powerful enough to strike back.'

The author was confident enough in our attention to take a mouthful of his dinner and chew it thoughtfully before he continued,

'I suspect in the power struggle that ensued between the two army men, Ay saw the writing on the wall and, perhaps to avert a civil war, persuaded Akhenaten to cease the persecution and abdicate in favour of his brother Smenkhkare.'

Walid had been listening intently to the conversation as it batted back and forth. Walid knew, of course, as did the rest of us, that Akhenaten had a watertight alibi against Nabil Zaal's identification of him as Moses. The heretic pharaoh's residency even now in the secret tomb behind Hatshepsut's temple was the killer blow to the author's theory. In actual fact, I thought we'd all shown remarkable tolerance and restraint in giving Nabil and his conjectures so much airtime on this journey southward. The simple truth was we all thrived on this sort of Egyptological discussion. Whether the hypotheses had some basis in history or was a load of hokum didn't really matter. We relished the debate. The slowness of our food leaving our plates showed quite how much. It was certainly no indication of any lack of flavour or skill in preparation on the part of the chef.

Now the museum curator spoke for the first time. 'Whilst I think it follows that Akhenaten may have been part-Hebrew, which might explain the reluctance of the priests of Amun to accept him as pharaoh, I'm not sure I can take the mental leap necessary to identify him as Moses. After all, when Tutankhamun came to the throne he seems to have been accepted without concern, and yet you believe he was of the same mixed race.'

'Ah, yes; but Tutankhamun reverted to Amunism,' Nabil pointed out. 'He changed his name from Tutankh*aten* to Tutankh*amun* and very publically erected what's become known as the Restoration Stele in the Temple of Amun at Karnak denouncing the actions of his predecessor.'

'Perhaps the priesthood and nobility looked to the boy king as someone malleable,' Adam suggested. 'Maybe they felt a period of stability was needed.'

Nabil Zaal put down his fork. 'But was it all just a front?' he questioned. 'Ay was a wily old fox. He was also incredibly powerful. You know; It wouldn't surprise me to learn he made Tutankhamun pharaoh just to prevent Horemheb seizing the throne. Especially once Akhenaten's younger brother Smenkhkare was dead.'

Around the dining car table, I felt a certain stillness settle over our small party. The author was striking close now to what we knew to be the truth of the matter. Without a word or a gesture passing between us, I knew Walid, Ted, Adam and I had closed ranks. We'd protected our secret and would keep on doing so, even if it meant humouring the author and allowing him to pursue his fantasy about Akhenaten's alter ego.

Since none of us responded, Nabil carried on. 'It wouldn't take too much to convince me that Tutankhamun and his prime minister Ay reverted to the Egyptian pantheon for political expediency. Horemheb was a clever man, and perhaps after removing Smenkhkare he was willing to play a waiting game. Perhaps, that is, until the boy king reached maturity. If foul play was behind Tutankhamun's early death while he was still a teenager, it's not difficult to see Horemheb's hand at work.'

'But Horemheb didn't take the throne on Tutankhamun's death,' Ted pointed out quietly. 'Ay did.'

'Ah yes, but that may also have been a political masterstroke,' Nabil observed. 'Ay was an old man when he became pharaoh. And there's evidence to suggest Horemheb was married to Ay's daughter, a woman called Mutnodjmet. I think it's possible the only reason Horemheb let Ay mount the throne was to legitimise his own claim to the throne on Ay's death through his marriage to the old pharaoh's daughter. You see, Ay was a blood relation of all the Amarnan kings: Akhenaten, Smenkhkare and Tutankhamun, even if that blood was of the Hebrews. But Horemheb was just an army general. I think Horemheb needed Ay's daughter to cement his claim and enable him to mount the Horus throne in the absence of any remaining blood relation from the Thutmoside line.'

I could tell the rest of us were holding a collective breath. Nabil Zaal had hit the nail on the head with his supposition. The only link in the chain he'd missed was that Horemheb had kept Ay and, through him, Tutankhamun to heel throughout their reigns with threats to Mutnodjmet's life.

'I think it's possible Tutankhamun may have attempted to re-assert worship solely of the Aten on reaching his maturity,' Nabil said. 'Perhaps that explains his mysterious death so young.'

I reached for Adam's hand under the table and gave it a gentle squeeze. It was impossible not to wonder what else the author might be spot on with in view of the deadly accuracy of the suppositions he'd just made. Adam squeezed my hand back and I gave myself a mental shake. Nabil Zaal had struck lucky, that was all. I knew his wilder claims could not possibly be true.

Nabil Zaal smiled around the table at us, picked up his fork and resumed eating. 'I can tell by your silence you think I may be onto something,' he remarked benignly. Then his smiled widened. 'And if I'm not too far wide of the mark with my suggestion that Akhenaten's family remained loyal to the monotheistic belief he'd instilled in them, then maybe I'm not aiming too much into left field with my contention that Akhenaten inspired religious following in the same way Moses did. In short, they preached the same message because they were the same man.' He favoured Ted with what I could only describe as a smug look. 'Akhenaten/Moses will turn out to be the force behind your Copper Scroll, Professor; you mark my words.'

My grip on Adam's hand tightened. I couldn't help but think how disappointed the author would be as and when – *if* and when, I should say – our tomb became known to the world.

Spotting Ted's twinkly-eyed expression across the dining table – he wasn't in the least bit put out by the author's subtle jibe – I couldn't help but think our excursion to the remains of Akhenaten's capital city at Amarna was rich with all sorts of promise.

But first we had a few important matters to address in Luxor.

Chapter 8

We had two primary reasons for making Luxor our first port of call. First and foremost it was to get the *Queen Ahmes* ready for our voyage north, down the Nile to Amarna. I've never quite got my head around the fact that to journey northwards on the river is actually to sail *down* the Nile. It's all to do with the flow of the current, which runs from the mighty river's source in the hills of Ethiopia downriver until it spills into the Mediterranean at the end of its journey.

Our secondary – but no less important – purpose was to enable Walid to put into practice his *idea*. This had struck him while we were all standing on the museum forecourt after our evacuation from Nabil's lecture, when it had become apparent we weren't to be allowed back inside. He'd taken Adam and me into his confidence but no one else.

I suspected there might be a third reason when Nabil Zaal disappeared for a couple of hours during the morning of our arrival. That he was paying a visit to his brother Ashraf in jail was evident to me by his tight-lipped departure and his reluctance to talk about where he'd been upon his return.

Preparing to set sail on our dahabeeyah was easily accomplished. We keep the *Queen Ahmes* in top-notch condition. This might be because the novelty of owning her had not yet worn off for either Adam or for me. We'd only taken ownership of her a scant six months ago, at Christmas. It may also have something to do with the eternal optimism that's such a driving force in Adam's personality and my own. Whilst the tourist situation in Egypt since the Revolution meant we'd not yet hosted a proper Nile cruise, we lived in hope. We'd decided to pin our ambitions on the prospect of the return of visitors drawn by the allure of antiquity and the romanticism of visiting the historical and archaeological sites from a lovingly restored Victorian dahabeeyah. So the *Queen Ahmes* was ready to be pressed into action at a moment's notice.

We'd agreed on one added extra, much in the way of a bonus on our journey back from Cairo. This was that Adam should hire some help to actually sail the dahabeeyah so he could be free to join in with our exploration of Akhenaten's ancient city once we arrived there.

There was only one man we considered suitable for the job. And since his work at the boatyard restoring Nile cruise vessels had dried up, Khaled leapt at the chance of some paid employment when we approached him and offered him the opportunity to be at the helm as we set sail down the Nile. We could afford his services as Nabil was paying us so generously to make the trip.

Khaled had a special relationship with the *Queen Ahmes* since he was the man who'd restored her to her former glory from the rotting hulk of disrepair she'd become since the heady days of turn-of-the-century Nile travel.

So, task number one was easily accomplished. It was our second objective – the putting into practice of Walid's *idea* – that filled me with a strange mixture of terrified trepidation and exhilarated excitement.

The reason for my mixed emotions was simple. We were going to pay a visit to our tomb.

* * *

'It's just that I couldn't bring myself to steal from the museum,' Walid explained. 'I thought I could. But my overwhelming feeling when we were debarred from re-entry after Nabil's lecture was one of relief. I felt as if I'd been let off the hook, offered a reprieve. The museum has been my life for more years than I care to count. Taking something from it by theft would be like stabbing myself in the heart. I don't think I could live with myself afterwards. But I know I still have to come up with a down-payment to satisfy my blackmailer and keep him off my back until its time to meet his ultimate demand. When Nabil and the professor talked about making the trip to Amarna, I spotted my chance.'

'You're going to take something from the tomb instead,' Adam deduced.

Walid sent him a look of appeal. 'It doesn't feel like quite such a dastardly deed to take something small from a treasure trove that hasn't been officially discovered yet, as to take it from somewhere that's dedicated to preserving and displaying the public property of the world.'

'And the trip to Amarna?' I questioned, still not completely clear of the curator's intentions, although I felt I had a growing inkling.

'I thought I could claim to have discovered the object I take from the tomb among the ruins of Akhenaten's city. That's where the tomb's contents originated from, after all. And if I can select something small enough...'

'Yes, I see,' Adam nodded. 'It's possible it could have been overlooked all these years during the excavation work. New discoveries are being made all the time. Yes, you could just pull it off.'

'And then the problem of provenance would go away,' Walid added. 'Everyone would accept it was a genuine Amarnan artefact, since that's where I'd claim to have discovered it. Nobody would look any further for an explanation. So the tomb could remain our secret, at least for now.'

'You might have a hard time offering your discovery for sale to a private collector, rather than taking it back to the museum,' Adam frowned, looking for loopholes.

'I've thought of that,' Walid responded more calmly than I'd heard him speak in weeks. 'I've decided perhaps I should select two items from the tomb, so one can act as a cover for the other. What do you think?'

I looked at Adam. It still felt like sacrilege to me. But Walid was caught between the proverbial rock and a hard place. In the circumstances it seemed to be the only course of action open to him. Adam was nodding slowly.

'And the press associated with one can serve to both authenticate the sale of the other as well as hopefully drive up its price. Yes, Walid, I think you've hit upon a workable plan.'

* * *

We'd decided the only way to approach the tomb was under the cover of darkness. Visitors to Luxor might be few and far between. But that did not mean they were non-existent. Hatshepsut's Temple was a prime tourist site. We simply couldn't take the risk of attempting our visit during the daytime when a tour party might happen to be there.

Besides, we needed a key to gain entry. The secret entrance to the tomb was via the pillared Hathor shrine, carved into the rock behind the walls of the Hathor Chapel on the first elevation. The chapel was off-limits to the public for reasons of preservation of its remarkable wall reliefs. Visitors were permitted only to peek inside by way of the open top half of a locked stable door. This also meant it was off-limits to us.

So we hatched a plan necessitating a trip to the temple on the day before our planned nocturnal visit to the tomb. Luckily, Walid had the clout to request the key and the seniority to expect his request to be granted with no questions asked.

Even so, he made a point of explaining to the official in the Ministry building tucked behind the ticket office that he was here to make an inspection on behalf of the Antiquities Service in Cairo, and waving his identification papers under the young man's nose.

If I was rather put in mind of the famous Shakespearean quotation about protesting too much, I was courteous enough not to voice it.

It was from this small Ministry office that Mustafa Mushhawrar had worked every day. It afforded a clear view of Hatshepsut's temple through the small square window set into the white plastered wall. Since the desk was positioned directly in front of the window, I could well imagine how it had turned Mustafa's head to look out every day, knowing such treasures were hidden in the secret tomb carved into the cliffs behind the temple façade. I spared him a quick thought, a fleeting moment of regret, while Walid shook hands with his replacement and accepted the key from him.

As soon as we were back outside in the blinding sunlight, Walid passed the key to Adam who'd been loitering outside studying postcards on a carousel positioned by the ticket office. Adam immediately strode off back towards the car park where his scooter was parked. Walid had travelled here on the back of my scooter with me. Our plan was to make a slow tour of the temple while Adam darted back into Luxor to have a copy of the key made.

While Adam zipped away, Walid and I rode the long trolley bus, which snaked its way along the concourse stretched across the dusty desert basin in front of the temple. I'd loved Hatshepsut's temple even before our discovery of the tomb. It's a masterpiece in design and simplicity. Rising on three terraces and cut with graceful porticoes and long sloping ramps, it sits nestled against the tawny gold cliff-face of the Theban hills. I doubt there's another manmade structure on earth so much in harmony with its natural surroundings. Once deposited on the broad forecourt, perimetered by a low stone wall, we made our way slowly up the lower ramp onto the first terrace and headed left towards the pillared Hathor shrine. This was set against the backdrop of sheer terracotta-coloured rock rising sharply behind it, at the extreme southern boundary of the temple. Just in case Mustafa's replacement in the Ministry office happened to be watching through that small square window, we wanted to make it appear an inspection of the Hathor Chapel was indeed the primary purpose of our visit. The columned shrine set in front of the chapel had the advantage of offering some shade from the fierce intensity of the sun and respite from the suffocating heat.

We found a spot in deep shade to perch and shared the bottle of water I took from my canvas holdall.

'Well, that went remarkably smoothly,' Walid remarked. 'The young man handed over the key without a murmur.'

'Your seniority and credentials demand respect,' I smiled. 'Besides, you asked him nicely.'

We took our time resting among the shaded columns each topped by a Hathor-headed capital. Then, when we deemed enough time had gone by for a detailed inspection of the chapel, we headed back out into the sunshine to make a slow tour of the temple. Our real purpose was to look for scaffolding planks. We'd need these once inside the tomb tonight to use as a bridge to span the deadly pit shaft set into the ground half way along the entrance corridor designed to impale the unwary on its upturned spikes. But we didn't want to make our search obvious. So Walid and I ambled along the columned porticoes stretching on both sides of the central ramp, sticking to the shade and admiring the wall reliefs. These are some of the best preserved in all of Egypt, beautifully carved to depict the defining moments of Hatshepsut's life story. They include birth scenes where she claims divine conception from the god Amun, as well as the perhaps more famous scenes of the fabled expedition to the land of Punt and the raising of her obelisks at Karnak. They never cease to amaze and impress me, but today I was perhaps a little less inclined than usual to be awestruck.

Nervous knots were twisting inside my stomach as I tried to work out the distance between where we were standing and the secret tomb carved into the cliff behind the temple. The prospect of setting foot inside it tonight made the blood fizz in my veins.

'Are you alright, Merry?' Walid shot out an arm to steady me as I swayed.

'It's just the sun,' I assured him. 'I should have brought more water.'

'Let's go to the rest house,' he suggested. 'We've been here long enough to convince that young official we've made a thorough inspection. And look; that section of scaffolding over there looks to have some good sturdy planks attached.'

The scaffolding sectioned off a large square of the wall reliefs. Hatshepsut's temple had been undergoing restoration for most of the last century and it was clear the work remained on-going – luckily for us.

A text pinged through to my phone from Adam to confirm his success at having the key copied as we were sitting down next to a wall-mounted fan in the little refreshment area set off to the side of the temple. 'He's on his way back,' I confirmed. 'He'll meet us at the ticket office.'

With the original key safely returned to Mustafa's replacement in the Ministry office, there was really little to do but return to the *Queen Ahmes* and try to relax ahead of our planned night time excursion.

We'd confided our intentions in Ted as it seemed sensible to let him know where we were going, just in case something should go wrong. Ted helpfully suggested he and Nabil should have dinner in town at the historic 1886 restaurant in the Winter Palace Hotel. This would also give the author an opportunity to visit his elderly aunt who lived in a suite of rooms there.

'I expect we'll be in bed by the time you return,' Adam said untruthfully, waving them off. 'Enjoy yourselves.'

Walid, Adam and I shared a quiet meal under the stars up on the open deck as nightfall gathered her warm cloak around us. Our conversation was desultory. We were each anticipating the night ahead in our own way. Now we were set on what to do, there really wasn't very much to say. Instead we listened to the chorus of frogs along the riverbank and let the droning chant of the muezzin from the nearby mosque soothe our nerves.

We were forced to wait until eleven o'clock before setting off, since that's when the temple floodlights are switched off every night.

We packed a couple of rucksacks with the essentials we'd deemed necessary, then made the journey along the west bank in the dark on our scooters. Walid shared the ride with me, his arms circling my waist from behind me, his knees clamped against my outer thighs.

All was shadowed and dark as we left our scooters under a cluster of palm trees just outside the car park. We considered they were unlikely to be observed there by anyone who happened to pass by between now and morning. The temple was in complete darkness. There was no moon. But starlight bathed the scene in a pale silvery semi-light.

We didn't dare use our flashlights as we crept across the desert basin approaching the temple forecourt. It was a wide open space, something of a dustbowl in front of the long curve of the cliffs that served as the temple backdrop.

The crunching underfoot of the loose scree that covered the terrain was the only sound. We were all wearing tightly laced walking boots, the most sensible footwear for scrambling across uneven surfaces in the dark.

It remained infernally hot, even out here on the borders of the desert that stretched away beyond the Theban hills. It was a dry heat, somewhat like being wrapped in a blanket that had been recently removed from an oven.

Not a word passed between us as we crossed the open space at a semi-jog. That Adam's and Walid's ears were pricked for any sound that meant we'd been discovered, as were mine, I had no doubt. For all Walid's high-ranking status at the Egyptian Museum, I doubted his ability to explain the need for nocturnal inspection of Luxor's ancient monuments in a way that would satisfy any but the most credulous of security guards.

Once we reached the temple precinct we were able to stop being so furtive. The shadowed colonnades offered us some cover. We made a beeline for the section of scaffolding and worked free a long, sturdy-looking plank. With me at one end, Adam at the other, we transported this to the Hathor shrine, while Walid dug about in his pocket for the replica key to the chapel. It fit snugly into the lock. With a soft click as he turned it, we were in.

Finally, with the door closed firmly behind us, we dared to switch on our flashlights. I caught my breath as the shadows leapt to life. Life-size images of Hatshepsut before the deities of ancient Egypt crowded the walls. I took a moment to settle my senses as our triple beams of torchlight seemed to add movement to the reliefs. My heart felt like a kettledrum being beaten in my chest. I felt sure Adam and Walid must be able to hear it. But, stealing a glance at my companions, it was to see them similarly transfixed staring up at the walls.

'I'd forgotten how creepy this place is,' Adam murmured.

Walid was blinking, looking nervous. 'Let's just get it over and done with, can we?' he suggested. He was unable to disguise the slight tremor in his voice and my heart went out to him. He was more than nervous. He was terrified. 'I feel as if the gods are watching us,' he muttered.

I knew exactly what he meant. I, too, felt as if the eyes of eternity were upon us, and shivered despite the sweltering heat.

Adam was already rummaging in his rucksack. He pulled from it first one and then the other Aten disc. These were the replicas he'd made last year. We'd recovered them at the same time as rescuing Ahmed from the pit shaft last time we were here. The originals, from Tutankhamun's Mehet-Weret ritual couch, were safely back on display in the Cairo Museum. I was thankful Walid had at least been spared the hair-raising task of bringing them to Luxor, as he'd done twice before. I had no doubt both previous trips had taken years off his life.

We moved across the chapel until we were standing underneath a superb carved wall relief of Hatshepsut seated between the god Amun and a huge image of the goddess Hathor, depicted as a cow with long up-curved horns, between which the round disc of the Aten was set. Alongside it was a deep gash in the wall.

My heart was pounding loud enough to bring an avalanche of rock crashing about our ears as Adam fitted one of the Aten discs into the gash in the stone. The action was very much like pressing a gigantic penny into a slot. He pressed down hard on the disc, using all his weight. For a moment it seemed stuck fast, jutting proud of the wall. Then it was literally like a slot machine in action. The Aten disc disappeared inside the wall. There was a moment of stillness and silence. We all held our breath in an agony of anticipation. I counted five beats. Then we heard it: the rasping sound of ancient stone scraped against ancient stone. It sounded like a great sigh of exertion as the centuries-old stone responded to the hidden mechanism that worked it. As we watched, breathless with nervous tension, a small square panel ground open at the base of the wall, just big enough to crawl through.

We fed the scaffolding plank through first, and then shuffled through the opening in single file, pausing to close the hidden doorway up again behind us. This meant shoving one of the Aten discs back through the gash in the wall to the other side. Adam darted back through the hole and scooped it up so we could keep them both with us after the hole closed over. Leaving both Aten discs by the entrance, we lifted the plank and levered it forward across the pit shaft, which dropped away a few paces along the corridor. We'd made a good selection. The plank protruded by a good arm's length on both sides of the deadly drop. It was body-width wide and several inches thick, certainly strong enough to take a body-weight since that was its purpose.

Even so, we body-surfed along it. I went first, followed by Walid, and then Adam. Once on the other side, we stood up, brushed ourselves off, checked our flashlights were ok, and moved forward. It was only a few paces more to the main chamber of the tomb. The first thing to hit me in this deeper part of the corridor was the noticeable change in air quality. It was hot, musty and bone-dry. It caught in my throat, a choking mixture of dust and dead air that made it difficult to inhale. I breathed slowly and shallowly through my nostrils, trying to acclimatise to the lack of oxygen and the stale smell. Of course, the dust was not just the product of the ages. We had Mustafa Mushhawrar to thank for the quantities of rock dust that had billowed into the tomb when he'd set off the rock fall that killed him. It just made the suffocating atmosphere worse.

And it was heart-breaking to see how it dulled the glitter and gleam of the golden objects displayed in the treasure chamber. But no amount of dust could detract from their magnificence. Even though I knew exactly what to expect, my breath still caught in my throat and I felt my chest tighten as our combined torchlight cut a swathe of light across the chamber. As I'd noted before, this was no haphazard jumble of artefacts. Every object seemed carefully and lovingly positioned to show it off to best effect. Even coated in dust, the display was jaw dropping. As well as a fully assembled chariot and exquisite golden throne there were flawlessly painted and inlaid caskets; translucent alabaster vases; intricately carved ivory chests; finely wrought chairs; carved wooden gaming boards; a golden inlaid couch with a row of sun-discs serving as the headboard; jewelled stools of different shapes and design; and solid gold statues with obsidian eyes gleaming dully in the torchlight.

'My God, I'd forgotten...' Adam breathed.

'It's fabulous,' Walid whispered.

'Breath-taking,' I murmured.

I don't think we could have spoken in everyday tones had the sunrise depended on it. As before, I felt as if we were trespassing into a deeply holy place. Whispering was the only way to preserve its sanctity.

The chamber was rectangular, carved from the living rock behind Hatshepsut's temple. Every inch of space contained a priceless relic from the Amarnan court. Unlike in Tutankhamun's tomb, nothing was left in pieces. Every item had been reassembled, including the golden chariot, the ritual couch, a huge solar boat longer than a canoe, and a scale model of the city of Akhet-Aten, wrought entirely in gold. It had all been here, buried in this secret tomb for close on thirty-three centuries. It was a mind-boggling passage of time. As always, my mind tried to grapple with it, and failed.

Despite my previous experiences here, I still succumbed to the bone-softening thrill of stepping across space and time into a piece of history still radiating with ancient life.

'Well, Walid, I don't envy you your choice,' Adam remarked in low tones, sweeping his flashlight across the crowded space in front of us. 'I hope you gave your selection some thought before you got here. Otherwise it promises to be a long night.'

'Something small,' Walid murmured quietly. 'Easily portable and something I can readily pretend to discover once we reach Amarna.' He looked to me for help. 'You've spent so much more time here than have I...'

I wasn't too sure I wanted to be reminded of the time Adam and I had spent here before, since we'd been trapped and in fear for our lives on both occasions. But it was true I was pretty intimately acquainted with the contents of the tomb. I'd searched through most of them hunting unsuccessfully for something to fashion as a rope.

'What have you decided on?' I queried, just to be sure. 'Two small items, one to act as a cover for the sale of the other?'

'And perhaps a third if it becomes necessary to meet the blackmailer's full demand for LE ten million. I figure I should take that from here too since there's no other way on earth I'm going to come by that sort of money.'

'Your challenge is going to be taking items from here worth *less* than ten million Egyptian pounds,' Adam said wryly. 'This stuff's staggering. Most of it's priceless.'

Walid was wringing his hands again, looking sick. 'But there must be something...'

'What about a pectoral?' I suggested, taking pity on him. 'Or perhaps a ring or two, or a bangle. Something like

171

that should do for the down-payment item. And then maybe one of the smaller statues should it prove necessary to pay the full ransom. I'm sure one of your private collectors would be only too happy to pay the full asking price for a solid gold statue of Nefertiti, even if it does stand only as tall as your finger.'

'Yes, yes,' Walid nodded, looking happier. 'These are good suggestions.'

I showed him where Nefertiti's jewellery casket was lying with some of its contents spilling across the floor. He dropped to his knees and bent over the ancient relics almost reverently, his head dipped forward as if in prayer. I could see his hand was shaking badly as he reached out to touch the precious items.

Adam and I watched him for a moment and I knew we shared his horrible stomach churning feeling of sacrilege when Walid selected a small item, wrapped it carefully inside his handkerchief and slipped it into his pocket.

Adam drew me aside. 'I can't bear this,' he muttered. 'It was never meant to come to this.'

I knew exactly what he meant and read the sick sense of guilt in his eyes. He was thinking back to the night we first discovered this place. 'We were supposed just to take a sneak peak, leave Howard Carter's papyrus here, then lock up and leave,' I agreed. 'And then none of this would have happened.'

'Damn that bastard Hussein Said,' Adam said bitterly. 'I should have let him fall into the pit shaft when I had the chance.'

'Amen to that,' I agreed. 'And then that turncoat Mustafa Mushhawrar would never have known this place existed.'

'We could have done it, you know, Merry,' Adam said vehemently. 'We could have closed it up behind us and kept it as our secret. But now I'm starting to wish we'd never decoded that damn papyrus.'

'Don't say that!' I cried in distress. 'That's like me saying I wish I'd never broken that picture frame and found the hieroglyphics that started all this! And I could never regret that, Adam! I just couldn't. Because without all that I may never have met you! And since meeting you I've had the time of my life! You've made me the happiest woman alive!'

He pulled me against him in a crushing embrace. I could feel the anger washing through him. 'But to take just a single item from here and sell it to get a damn blackmailer off our backs,' he muttered against my hair in disgust. 'It's just plain wrong Merry. It makes me sick to my stomach.'

'But what choice do we have?' I whispered in defeated tones.

Adam set me away from him, but his eyes blazed into mine. 'I'm going to find that blackmailer and I'm going to wring the bastard's neck!' he vowed.

173

Behind us, Walid stood up and coughed to get our attention. 'The fault is entirely mine,' he said. 'I should never have insisted we write those damn letters.'

This was irrefutable so neither Adam nor I attempted to argue.

'Have you got what you need?' Adam asked.

Walid nodded to confirm he'd made his selection. He lifted a small golden statue from a box where it was nestled among some linen and placed it carefully into the inside breast pocket of his jacket. 'I... I feel as if I should make an apology, offer some words of atonement,' he murmured, looking uncertainly across the shadowed space towards the burial chamber.

Almost as if drawn there by some unseen magnetic force, we picked our way across the treasure chamber, taking care not to bump into anything, and squeezed through the small gap in the wall into the burial chamber. The wreckage caused by Mustafa's explosion of rock was far worse in here. A good portion of the cliffside had crashed into the small space. Boulders and stones littered the floor. The rock-dust wasn't just a coating; it was almost ankle-deep in places. I chose not to investigate what little was left of the anthropoid coffin of the princess Neferure, since I knew a combination of falling rock and my own efforts had destroyed it beyond recognition.

But that wasn't what we'd come to see. Two huge polished granite sarcophagi were jammed alongside each other in the confined space.

Walid bowed his head and murmured a few words in Arabic.

I whispered an apology of my own. By the look of him, Adam was still biting back anger, standing staring at he larger of the two with a pinched expression on his face. So, when he spoke, his comment was unexpected.

'Well, if Akhenaten's mummy is wrapped up safe and sound inside this great big stone box, it will certainly knock poor old Nabil off his perch.'

I think Walid and I both registered surprise in the same heartbeat, but I got there first. '*If?*' I stared up at the heavy stone lid set squarely on top of the sarcophagus. 'Did you say *if* Akhenaten is inside?'

'Surely there cannot be any doubt?' Walid questioned. But, looking at him, his expression was suddenly doubtful.

'We know Tutankhamun and Ay brought their 'precious jewels' for reburial from Akhet-Aten,' I said confusedly. 'And we know 'precious jewels' was the codename they used to refer to Akhenaten and Nefertiti. So Akhenaten *has* to be inside. It makes no sense otherwise.'

Adam was also staring up at the granite lid wedged firmly atop the sarcophagus. 'I'm not sure I meant to say "*if*",' he murmured, looking a bit quizzical. But now the thought's there… Well…' He shrugged. 'We'd need a damn strong pulley system to lift that lid and check. There's no point in us even attempting it.'

'Don't tell me you're starting to believe Nabil may be onto something with this whole Moses and Akhenaten theory?' I demanded, amazed.

'Seriously? No.' He tilted his head to one side. 'I'll admit I find some of his supposed *"evidence"* intriguing.' He made speech marks with his fingers around the word. 'But I'm not ready to suspend disbelief and run with a hypothesis I think will turn out to be a load of old hogwash.'

Walid was contemplating the great stone coffins in silence. 'Assuming Akhenaten and Nefertiti are indeed buried here; this is the biggest discovery of all time. I will need to give very careful thought to how we should proceed with regard to pulleys and levers when the time comes.' He added something in Arabic, bowing his head once more, and patted his bulging pocket.

'Ok, time to get out of here,' Adam said.

We swigged some water to slake the dryness in our throats and squeezed back into the treasure chamber, carefully making our way back to the corridor. Casting a last long look around us in the torchlight, as if imprinting the scene on our collective memories, we turned to leave.

Reaching the pit shaft, I stood back to allow Walid to shunt himself across the plank in front of me since he was the one carrying the priceless objects.

He held out his hand to help me as I shuffled my way across. Then Adam pulled himself over. Safely across, we reached back to haul the scaffolding plank back with us.

Upright again, I reached for Adam's hand and smiled up at him, hoping to end the night's thievery on a positive note. 'Well, it certainly makes a nice change to be leaving here under our own steam, without needing to be rescued from being incarcerated in the place.'

He squeezed my hand back. 'True, that,' he smiled. 'Even so, I have some fond memories of my times trapped in here with you, Merry.'

He reached down and picked up one of the Aten discs, pressing it firmly into the gash alongside the entrance. I counted heartbeats waiting for the ancient mechanism to groan into action, wondering if I'd somehow tempted fate and we'd suddenly discover the penny-in-the-slot device had stopped working from this side. My sigh of relief was loud and heartfelt when I heard the familiar rasping sound of the ancient stone shifting.

We fed the scaffolding plank through the space that opened up in the wall first. Then Walid crouched down and crawled through. I picked up the second Aten disc and was about to follow him through, when I heard a sound that made my blood freeze.

Adam yanked me back from the entrance. He'd heard it too. It was the sickening thud of Walid being whacked on the head with something. I heard his cry and the sound of him dropping to the ground on the other side of the wall.

We didn't have time to react. Almost before we'd registered what had happened, a voice from the chapel said, 'Please come out slowly and join your friend. That way you will not be hurt. I know there are two of you, so please do not try to be clever.'

Adam glanced back along the corridor. But without the scaffolding plank there was no way back into the tomb. Even if there were, there was no means of escape once there. The tunnel Mustafa Mushhawrar had dug through to the burial chamber was now a pile of fallen rock since he'd brought down half the mountainside. There was no way back, so we had no choice but to go forward.

'I'll go first,' Adam whispered. 'Just be ready to run if I give you the word.'

I watched him crouch down and disappear through the gap. Then, with a last look back into the darkness of the tomb, I followed him.

Chapter 9

My first sight in the torchlight was of Walid's slumped form, and of two sets of feet. Adam's were the ones laced into dusty walking boots. The others were shod in a pair of smart lace-up shoes in crocodile skin.

I almost shrank back thinking wildly this must be the ghost of Mustafa Mushhawrar come to do mischief. But a second glance told me they weren't polished enough to belong to Mustafa. Common sense also reasserted itself to remind me ghosts were unlikely to wear shoes.

Adam reached forward with a strong hand to help me up from my knees. Walid was groaning and trying to sit up. I breathed a sigh of relief and bent to assist him.

'Leave him!' barked Crocodile Shoes.

I straightened and sent him a narrowed glance, seeing him properly in the torchlight for the first time. His face was vaguely familiar but it took me a moment to place him. Mustafa's replacement from the Ministry office stared back at me. I daresay I shouldn't have been surprised. Frankly, there was a big part of me that wasn't. Nor was I particularly taken aback to see the baseball bat he wielded in one hand nor the knife he was pointing at us in the other.

'You!' I said accusingly.

'You don't even remember my name, do you?' he sneered.

He was quite correct, of course. I'd been so busy seeing him simply as Mustafa's replacement while Walid collected the key from him; I hadn't actually taken the trouble to really *see* him at all. Now I took a close look. He was of medium height, quite young, probably late twenties at a guess, with the dark skin of a Nubian, dressed for work in trousers and a crisp white shirt. He was still wearing his name badge pinned to the breast pocket of his shirt. I narrowed my gaze on it.

'I am Gamal Abdel-Maqsoud,' he introduced himself, catching my look. 'And you have tricked me. You made a copy of the key, I suppose.'

'Mustafa's replacement,' I murmured for Adam's benefit, since he hadn't come into the Ministry office with Walid and me. I didn't bother to respond to the bit about the key, since it was phrased as a statement not a question, and besides, it was staringly obvious that's what we'd done.

'Ah, yes; Mustafa,' Gamal Abdel-Maqsoud nodded. 'He behaved strangely for many months before his tragic death in the rockfall behind the temple. I was his apprentice, and I wondered why he was so tired on duty every day, yawning at his desk and trying to stay awake. This was out of character for Mustafa. He was usually so diligent and correct. I often wondered what was causing him so many sleepless nights. I imagine the answer might have something to do with whatever lies behind this hole in the wall. Am I right?'

I opened my mouth to speak but Adam got there first. 'You seem to be working it all out nicely, so why don't you tell us?' he invited smoothly.

'I see you are not in a mood to be friendly,' Gamal Abdel-Maqsoud said with a frown. 'Which reminds me...' He raised the baseball bat as if to wield a glancing sideways blow across Adam's temple.

'What the hell do you think you're doing?' I cried out.

'It strikes me I need to incapacitate your friend,' he said pleasantly.

'Hit him with that and I'll kill you!' I threatened.

He sneered at me again, running his eyes up and down me in an insolent manner. 'You and whose army?'

'I'm warning you!' I bit out, aware of Adam tense and watchful beside me.

Gamal Abdel-Maqsoud smiled suddenly. 'Alright have it your way. You may help me to tie him up. To tie both of them up,' he amended. 'I suppose you have some rope in that rucksack?'

It flashed through my mind to deny it. But he stepped towards Adam with the bat raised and the knife outstretched so I thought better of it.

He stood with the knife blade against Adam's throat while I slipped off my rucksack and fumbled with the fasteners.

Gamal's eyes gleamed darkly as I drew out a length of narrow rope.

'Ok, I will observe while you tie your friend's ankles together. You have more rope in the other rucksacks?'

He watched me closely while I emptied Adam's and Walid's rucksacks of the lengths of rope they'd also brought with them.

'That should be enough to immobilise both of your friends while you act as my tour guide and introduce me to what is on the other side of the wall.'

He kept the knife trained on Adam, with the baseball bat raised and ready to strike while I tied Adam's legs together at the ankle, then secured his hands behind his back. I could feel the leashed-in tension in Adam's body as I pulled the cord tightly around his wrists. I squeezed his hand before I let go. It was a small gesture but it felt important that I should make it.

Adam's silence was unsettling, even to me. His gaze remained fixed on Gamal's face throughout.

'I can't tie up Walid,' I protested. 'He's injured.'

Walid was conscious but I could see the blow he'd sustained to the back of his head had left him dizzy and dazed. He'd managed to push himself into a sitting position propped against the wall but seemed to be having some trouble focusing his eyes. As I watched, he groaned and rubbed the back of his head.

'Just his feet then,' Gamal said. 'You may leave his hands free.'

I set to work with the rope while Gamal Abdel-Maqsoud waited in the same threatening pose as before. When I'd finished he checked the knots and nodded his satisfaction. 'Thank you, and now we may continue our conversation. You can start by telling me what lies beyond this passageway.'

But I was in no more mood to be friendly than Adam, certainly not now. 'I thought you wanted to see for yourself,' I said, wondering how difficult it would be to push him into the pit shaft once we were both inside the corridor.

'It is a tomb.' He said flatly. 'But belonging to whom, I wonder?'

I wasn't inclined to enlighten him. Alongside me, Adam stood silent and still as a statue in his ropes.

Gamal Abdel-Maqsoud suddenly lost his temper. 'You will sit!' he barked, bringing the baseball bat down in a low swing that caught Adam behind the knees. Adam buckled and fell.

'You bastard!' I yelled, raising my palm as if to strike Gamal Abdel-Maqsoud across the face. He immediately turned on me with both the baseball bat and knife upraised.

'Merry, don't,' Adam grunted from the floor by my feet.

'I just wish you to be pleasant,' Gamal said with a swift return to good humour.

'I don't see how I can be pleasant to someone who's attacked both my friends,' I challenged. As if on cue, Walid let out a low groan. 'He needs water.' I reached back inside my rucksack for the plastic bottle. Gamal made no attempt to stop me as I unscrewed the cap, bent down and helped Walid to raise it to his lips.

'I am not usually a man given to violence,' Gamal Abdel-Maqsoud said conversationally. The two fallen men at my feet offered a rather stark contradiction to this assertion. 'But what am I expected to do when you trick me and come here behind my back? Stand back and applaud?'

I was impressed by his linguistic ability if not his way of conducting himself. It was evidently a requirement of a position in Luxor's Ministry for the Preservation of Ancient Monuments to be able to speak good English. Mustafa's had been equally flawless. It seemed Gamal Abdel-Maqsoud was Mustafa's understudy in more ways than one. I decided to hold my tongue in the hope it might encourage him to keep on practising his foreign language skills. The tactic worked. He kept talking.

'I felt sure this day would come,' Gamal said. 'My friend Abdul and I discussed Mustafa's strange behaviour many times after his death. After Abdul returned from the – how do you say – ? – *wild goose chase* – ? – Mustafa sent him on, we felt sure he must be hiding something.'

I felt the alert stillness seize hold of Adam on the floor at my feet. Adam and I are deeply in tune with each other and I immediately grasped what he was thinking.

'Wild goose chase?' I prompted.

'Is this not the correct expression?' he frowned. 'Mustafa sent Abdul in pursuit of a woman who had bought a necklace from his cousin Jamal's jewellery shop in the Souk. His instructions were to get it back from her, by force if necessary. Is this not an odd request to make of one's apprentice?'

'Mustafa had two apprentices?' I questioned. 'Yourself and Abdul …?' I let it hang, hoping he might give me a last name. My blood was suddenly fizzing with the possibility that Gamal Abdel-Maqsoud might be about to reveal the identity of Walid's blackmailer.

But our antagonist took my question at face value. 'Yes, the Ministry has a good instructional programme for those with an interest in preserving our ancient monuments. Mustafa was responsible for training both Abdul and myself.'

'And the necklace?' I asked.

Gamal Abdel-Maqsoud narrowed his eyes on my face. I think it suddenly struck him he might be saying too much. 'He was unsuccessful in retrieving it,' he said shortly.

Sensing he was about to clam up, I decided on one last attempt to get the whole story from him in the hope we could unmask the blackmailer. 'But that didn't matter, since after Mustafa's death, he got hold of Mustafa's bank box instead?'

I caught the look that flashed across Gamal's face before he could stop it. 'Too many questions,' he barked. 'I did not follow you here tonight for a friendly chat. I came to see what it was Mustafa was so het up about in the weeks before his death.'

'How did you know to come here tonight?' I pressed, not giving up.

'Before he left Luxor Abdul told me to watch for any strange activity at the Hathor Chapel. When your friend here came and asked for the key with so much unnecessary explanation, I felt sure it must be significant. So I decided to stay behind tonight and keep watch. I saw you all arrive and creep to the temple after dark.'

'So you followed us.'

'But when I approached the Hathor Chapel and let myself in you were not here,' he said. 'All was darkness and silence. It occurred to be there must be a hidden doorway. So I knew I must wait.'

'And then you heard the rock start to move and saw this passageway open up in the wall.'

'It gave me a fright, I admit,' he confessed.

'So, what happens now?' I asked.

'Now you are going to show me what is on the other side of this hole,' he said decisively.

'No,' Walid tried to get to his feet but immediately tumbled sideways again as the rope around his ankles tightened.

It was the distraction Adam had been waiting for. With a great heave, he launched himself bodily against Gamal Abdel-Maqsoud's legs. The sudden explosive movement knocked our opponent off his feet. He flung out his arms wildly trying to regain his balance. I darted forward and gave him a violent shove, yanking the baseball bat out of his hand as he fell. The knife clattered out of his other hand and Adam rolled himself on top of it.

Gamal Abdel-Maqsoud recovered himself quickly. He sprang back up off the floor and launched himself at Adam. The ropes were a serious impediment to Adam's ability to defend himself. Gamal brought down a glancing blow on Adam's face with his fist just before I was able to swing back the baseball bat. My strike landed cleanly on the back of our assailant's head, connecting in much the same place he'd hit Walid. It sent him sprawling across the stone floor, out cold. Walid levered himself forward, picked up the knife from beside Adam and held it poised above Gamal Abdel-Maqsoud's inert frame.

'Well done!' he approved, sounding shaky. 'Adam, are you ok?'

Adam sat up, rubbing at his left cheek with the tips of his fingers. 'He packs a mean punch, I'll give him that,' he muttered. 'Better check you haven't killed him, Merry, despite your earlier threats.'

I crouched over our attacker's still form. 'He's breathing,' I confirmed in relief. Even as I said so, Gamal Abdel-Maqsoud grunted and started to move.

'Better get these ropes off me and onto him then,' Adam suggested. 'Walid? How are you feeling?'

'Well enough to keep this knife poised at the ready,' our friend asserted. 'I am in no mood to be forgiving.'

Gamal Abdel-Maqsoud shifted, opened his eyes, saw the knife pointed at his throat and subsided again.

I made quick work of untying Adam and together we bound our victim so his wrists were locked together behind his back and his ankles similarly knotted together.

'That's better,' I said with grim satisfaction. Now, what are we going to do with him? We can hardly leave him here. His shouts will be heard in the morning.'

'We could gag him?' Walid suggested. He started to unbutton his shirt.

'We don't need to make a gag out of your shirt,' Adam said. 'I have a better idea.' His eyes darted towards the dark hole in the wall and I immediately divined his intentions.

'Adam, I'm not sure…' I started.

But Adam was already addressing our fallen assailant. 'Ok, Mr Gamal Abdel-Maqsoud, you wanted to know what lies on the other side of the wall. How would you like to find out now?'

Gamal stared up at us with wild eyes, 'You wouldn't,' he dared.

'Try me,' Adam warned. 'I'm willing to accept you were drawn here by curiosity tonight, and I daresay you're a nice chap when you're not wielding a baseball bat. But I don't take kindly to being threatened with either a bat or a knife, and certainly not both. Besides which, you seem to know the answers to a good many questions I would very much like to ask.'

Gamal started to struggle and attempted to sit up. But the ropes were leashed too tight.

'Ok, give the knife to me,' Adam said, reaching out to take it from Walid. 'Merry, keep the baseball bat at the ready. If he tries to run, whack him with it. I'm going to untie his feet.'

He fitted the action to the words, and then helped Gamal to stand up. 'Sore head?' he murmured when our attacker swayed with dizziness. 'I'm sorry about that. Merry's stronger than she thinks she is. Ok, after you…'

He stood aside to allow Gamal Abdel Maqsoud to approach the square hole in the base of the wall. Our assailant hesitated and looked at me.

I shrugged back at him, 'You did say you wanted to take a look,' I reminded him. 'Adam's nice like that.'

'I'll be right behind you,' Adam promised. He crouched down and shone the beam of his flashlight into the darkness on the other side of the entranceway. 'Just crawl through and wait for me on the other side.'

This was no easy task considering Gamal had his hands tied behind his back. He had to crouch and shuffle his way through the hole with his head bent forward.

Adam followed him, still with the knife, and I brought up the rear without letting go of the baseball bat.

'I'm going to sit here a moment and rest,' Walid called after us. 'Do you need the plank?'

'No, but could you shove our rucksacks through?' Adam called back.

He collected all three as Walid fed them through the hole, and then straightened.

With the three of us standing just inside the passageway, Adam shone his flashlight forward so the beam penetrated deep into the dark corridor. 'You do the same with yours, Merry, could you please?' he prompted. I noticed he kept the knife carefully trained on our guest.

With the beam of both flashlights lighting the gloom it was just possible to discern the dull gleam of gold in the treasure chamber, which opened out at the far end of the corridor. I heard Gamal Abdel-Maqsoud catch his breath.

'Sadly for you, my friend, this is as far as you go,' Adam said. 'Now, I am going to tie your ankles together again, but not too tightly. You'll be able to slip out of the knot again once we're gone. I just don't want you following us out.'

'But you can't leave me here!' Gamal cried wildly.

'Who is this Abdul from the Ministry who was instructed by Mustafa Mushhawrar to recover the necklace?' Adam asked. 'And where is he now?'

'I have nothing further to say on this subject,' Gamal said flatly.

'But Abdul is the one attempting to blackmail Walid, am I right?' Adam pressed.

'I have no idea what you are talking about,' Gamal replied.

'Your colleague, Mustafa's other apprentice, the one who stole the bank box from Mustafa's mother...' Adam said helpfully.

'I don't know what you mean,' Gamal said, refusing to look at Adam or at me. He stared instead into the darkness of the middle distance. Adam and I had both lowered our flashlights.

'You have a very simple choice to make,' Adam said nicely. 'Either you tell me what I want to know or I will lock you up in here until you find your tongue.'

'Show me what is at the other end of this corridor and I will consider it,' Gamal parried.

'I'll tell you what I'll show you instead,' Adam offered. He pulled Gamal forward a few paces and then stopped. I followed and, together, Adam and I shone the twin beams of our flashlights into the depths of the pit shaft. The deadly spikes reared up from the bottom, twenty odd feet below us.

'Tell me what I want to know or I will leave you here,' Adam warned again.

'You wouldn't dare,' Gamal breathed. 'My absence will be noted from the Ministry in the morning.'

'Ah yes,' Adam said smoothly. 'But they won't know where to look for you. Nobody will hear your shouts once the passageway is sealed.'

'Abdul will know!' Gamal shouted with bravado. 'He will find me!'

'Ah, so your friend Abdul *does* know about this place.'

Gamal maintained a mutinous silence, staring blankly into the depths of the pit shaft.

'But he will have no way of rescuing you,' I pointed out, deciding to join in. 'He'd need the Aten discs for that. And we have them. There is no way to open up the secret doorway without them.'

'So, I'll repeat it one more time,' Adam said alongside me. 'Tell me what I want to know or I will leave you here.'

'I have nothing more to say,' Gamal muttered.

Adam lost patience. 'Ok, you've made your choice. Just remember, you were offered one.'

Gamal Abdel-Maqsoud glared at him, then hawked and spat.

'That decides it,' Adam said grimly. 'Ok, Merry; tie his feet.'

'But...' I started.

'Please, Merry; just do as I say.'

It's very rare for Adam to use that tone. When he does, it brooks no argument. I set to work again with the rope. I was becoming increasingly proficient at tying knots thanks to the practise I was getting tonight.

'Not too tight,' Adam advised. 'It's not as if he can go anywhere when we've gone.'

Once our new friend was bound hand and foot again, Adam looked into his face in the torchlight. 'Ok, this is your last chance Gamal. Fail to speak out now and we lock up and leave.'

Gamal spat directly in his face.

'Charming,' Adam muttered, wiping his face on the arm of his shirt. He winced as he rubbed against his bruised cheek. 'Ok, have it your way.'

He pulled Gamal back towards the entranceway and then pushed him down onto the floor. 'Keep the baseball bat trained on him would you please, Merry?'

While I did so, wondering if I'd have the guts to use it on a restrained man should he take it into his head to try the same move on me that Adam had used so successfully on him earlier, Adam rooted around in the rucksacks. He drew out our three bottles of water, all still semi-full, and a

Tupperware lunchbox containing sandwiches, biscuits and fruit. I'd come prepared. Given the outcome on both my previous visits to the tomb, it had seemed advisable to come well provisioned.

'Ok, loosen the knot on his wrists,' Adam said. 'Not too much. Just enough to keep him out of harms way while we get out of here. It would seem a bit cruel to leave him food and water and no means of reaching them once we're gone.'

As I fiddled with the knot, Adam waved the knife in Gamal's face. 'Ok, now I want you to have a good, long, hard think while you're here. I'm leaving you both flashlights and some food and water, as you can see. You are not in any immediate danger of expiring. But you'll be completely on your own. Unless, that is, you choose to keep company with ghosts. It's possible there are one or two who might decide to make their presence felt while you're here. Don't believe in ancient curses, do you? Hopefully not, since this place is bound to be protected by one. Ok, Merry; after you…'

I cast our new acquaintance a last look, then crouched and crawled back through the hole at the base of the wall. Adam joined me a moment later. There was no sound of movement behind us. Gamal Abdul-Maqsoud evidently thought Adam was bluffing. But I knew him better. It's not often that anger takes hold of Adam. But when it does, its grip is vicelike.

'Right Merry, you know what to do...' Adam said quietly. Then he ducked and dived back through the hole again.

I bit my lip while I fitted the Aten disk into the gash in the wall and pressed down with all my strength. There was the usual long pause, just long enough for Adam to fling himself back through the hole with the disc clutched under his arm. He'd retrieved it where it had fallen on the other side of the wall. He was pushing himself to his feet when the familiar rasping sound accompanied the movement of the stone shifting back into place. Gamal Abdel-Maqsoud was now trapped on the other side with no means of freeing himself.

It flashed through my mind to feel a bit sorry for Gamal Abdel-Maqsoud. It was possible he'd simply come to investigate his suspicions. He was, after all, responsible for the protection of Hatshepsut's ancient monument. If so, he'd got a whole lot more than he bargained for. But the trouble was, I couldn't overlook the baseball bat or the knife; nor his willingness to employ them. Perhaps if he'd just used them to threaten us while he established exactly what we were up to, and then reported us to his superiors, he could have established and maintained the upper hand. And landed us in a whole heap of trouble to boot. But he'd proved more personally avaricious than that. And he'd whacked Walid over the head without a second's hesitation. No. I decided my momentary stab of conscience was misplaced. He'd come intent on violence and to wrest whatever prize might be on offer for himself. I consoled myself that he'd got what was coming to him.

'Right,' Adam said, dusting himself off. 'Time to go home. You ok Walid?'

* * *

The day was spent making the final preparations for our journey north down the Nile to Amarna. Khaled made all the final checks to assure himself the *Queen Ahmes* was fully functional and ready to make the trip. It would be her first proper voyage since her restoration. Adam and I had sailed her up and down the river around Luxor a few times, but never ventured far.

Walid retired to his room to sleep. He sported a nasty bump on the back of his head but thankfully no more serious damage.

Adam was developing a rather ugly bruise on his left cheek but was otherwise unscathed. As for me, I'd emerged from the night's activities with nothing more physical than bags under my eyes to show for our exertions.

'Surely you're not planning on leaving that poor man entombed behind Hatshepsut's temple while we go to Amarna?' I asked rather desperately. I'd known Adam angry, but never cruel.

'It would damn well serve him right if I did,' he said severely. I noted the *if* and breathed a sigh of relief. 'But, no; lovely Merry, I'm just going to let him sweat it out for a bit. Maybe then he'll be more inclined to tell us what he knows. If there's a way we can unmask the blackmailer before Walid is forced to sell a single one of the items he took from the tomb to a private collector, we have to pursue it; by fair means or foul.'

He was right of course. The ends justified the means. But I couldn't help but feel queasy every time I thought of Gamal Abdel-Maqsoud trapped inside the entrance corridor, mere paces away from the deadly pit shaft and with just our flashlights and meagre provisions to sustain him. Having been entombed there myself not once but twice, it certainly needed no flight of imagination on my part to picture him there in the stifling, dead-aired gloom of the sepulchre. I wondered at his ability to commune with ghosts, even without knowing whose company it was he was keeping. Shuddering, I tried to pull my mind onto something else. After a number of attempts I was able to finalise my shopping list for the trip to the supermarket I had planned for this afternoon.

In the meantime, Adam made a telephone call to Ahmed in Cairo. 'We think the blackmailer goes by the name of Abdul,' he said. 'I don't have a surname. But he was an apprentice to Mustafa Mushhawrar at the Ministry for the Preservation of Ancient Monuments in Luxor before our dear departed friend buried himself alive, so I'm hoping he shouldn't be too difficult to track down.'

He cut the mobile connection, and then turned to me. 'Ahmed is having his new teeth fixed in place tomorrow. He's as excited as a little kid on Christmas Eve.'

I grinned, glad to have something more prosaic to talk about. 'I can't wait to see him with his new smile. It was megawatt to begin with, so I daresay we'll need sunglasses in his company once Selim's finished with him.'

The day dragged. Nabil tried to engage me in another discussion about Akhenaten's secret life as Moses. But I was really in no mood to hear more of his supposed evidence. I asked after his Aunt Layla instead and was rewarded with an evasive response that she was quite well and continuing to enjoy the hospitality of The Winter Palace hotel, where he and the professor had enjoyed a fine meal last night. I suppressed a smile. Nabil Zaal was verbosity personified on his pet subjects but clammed up like a, well, like a clam when the territory became personal.

Adam gave Ted a brief appraisal of the night's activities. 'Ah well, my boy; you've acted as you saw fit,' was the professor's verdict. 'Let's hope twenty-four hours shut up in the tomb will serve to loosen the young fellow's tongue. Walid showed me the items he selected for removal. If there is any way to avoid their sale to pay this blackmail ransom, it must be pursued at all costs.'

Finally darkness swept in to claim the day. Adam and I were setting out alone to confront Gamal Abdel-Maqsoud tonight. Walid's head was still aching and I felt an early night was needed to set him on his feet again.

To be honest, this was how I preferred it. Adam and I had started out on our adventures in Egypt as a twosome for all that we didn't know each other well at the start. Our number had swelled as our various friends and hangers-on became involved in our escapades. But the two of us alone was how I liked it best. We were soulmates. We'd stand or fall together. The only possible exception I'd make to this general rule was for Ahmed. But since he was up in Cairo, eagerly anticipating his final sleep before getting his teeth fixed, I spared him only a momentary thought.

Adam and I travelled light for our second nocturnal trip to Hatshepsut's temple. The baseball bat and a single Aten disc seemed the only things we really needed besides water. Neither Adam nor I are comfortable around knives. They do tend to leave the most unsightly scars. Adam still sports one across his upper right arm where he was struck by the very first of our knife-wielding opponents. It's fair to say there have been a few. We travelled on Adam's scooter, him up front and me riding on the back with my arms circling his waist. Leaving the scooter parked behind a convenient knot of palm trees as before, we made our way across the parking lot.

The basin of desert in front of the temple was shadowed silver and grey in the starlight. It was an eerie colourless place at night. The stars looked close at hand, as if we might reach up and pluck them out of the sky. As ever, it was hot.

Stealthy as stray cats, we crept across the temple forecourt and up the lower ramp to the first elevation.

All was still and silent inside the Hathor Chapel once we'd let ourselves in with the replica key. The carvings leapt to life across the walls the instant Adam switched on the spare flashlight we'd brought with us. I succumbed to the usual chills for a moment, and then pulled myself together.

'Ok, Merry; let's see if a few hours of solitary confinement have made the bastard more inclined to talk.'

Adam slotted the Aten disc into the wall and gave it a mighty shove. Seconds beat by as usual before the mechanism groaned to life. The hidden door shifted open.

I'd expected to see the glow of the flashlights we'd left behind illuminating the hole. So I was surprised by the stygian blackness on the other side of the opening.

Adam flashed his beam through the hole. 'Gamal? You can come out now.'

His words were met with a profound silence.

'Gamal?'

We looked at each other in confusion. Adam kneeled down and started to crawl through the opening, keeping the baseball bat at the ready and with the flashlight swinging in arcs before him.

I saw him straighten on the other side. 'Well, I'll be damned,' he said, sounding a bit sepulchral as his voice drifted back through the opening in the rock.

It was enough to have me dropping onto all fours so I could follow him.

He helped me up as I reached the other side. Adam swung the flashlight in consternation. It was impossible. But it seemed to be true. Gamal Abdel-Maqsoud had gone. The corridor was empty.

Chapter 10

'What the hell...?' Adam exclaimed, straightening and flashing the beam of his torch in wild arcs. 'It's impossible! He can't have just vanished into thin air! There's no other way out!'

I'm sure the expression on my own face was every bit as shocked and unbelieving. Adam bent to pick up the Aten disc where it had fallen through the gash in the wall onto the floor inside the corridor. In the narrow beam of light a movement caught my eye. 'Adam! Watch out!'

There was a slim ledge set into the wall above the square hole in the base of the wall. It was a sort of lintel, jutting proud of the stone. I'd never noticed it before, although it was set at about head height. Somehow Gamal Abdel-Maqsoud had climbed up there. And now he launched himself off it, diving at Adam in much the same way a lion might lunge at prey.

My warning came too late. Adam wasn't quick enough to leap aside. Gamal landed on top of him, sending them both sprawling.

The baseball bat spun out of Adam's grasp and the Aten disc rolled back towards the entrance hole.

I leapt forward to grab the bat but Gamal was too quick for me. He'd recovered himself quickly and snatched it away before I could reach it.

Adam dived at Gamal's legs knocking him off his feet again. A violent struggle for the baseball bat ensued. Grunting and swearing, Adam and Gamal wrestled each other for control. As they writhed and rolled I rescued the flashlight, which Gamal had knocked from Adam's hand when he crashed him to the floor. It was at risk of tumbling into the pit shaft. A fight was bad enough, but a fight in the dark was not to be contemplated. The beam darted madly as I leapt back and forth trying to get within striking range of Gamal's head. The flashlight would serve me equally well as a weapon. But with arms and legs thrashing in all directions, it was impossible to get a clear aim.

The two men were pretty evenly matched. Gamal was young and fit. But Adam kept his strength up working on the *Queen Ahmes*. One moment Gamal seemed to have the upper hand, but the next, Adam was fending him off and pressing him back.

Neither was able to land a clean punch. Gamal was clinging onto the baseball bat for dear life, trying to pull at Adam's hair and fight him off with the other hand, kicking and scratching and trying to bite. Adam had one hand under Gamal's chin, forcing back his head so Gamal couldn't head butt him. As they struggled and flailed, they edged closer and closer to the pit shaft.

I contemplated jumping between them and it to act as a sort of lifeguard. But one misplaced kick could send me hurtling down onto the spikes so I thought better of it. 'Adam! Don't let him push you any further! The pit shaft…!'

Adam heeded my desperate warning. With a loud grunt, he pulled back and managed to bring his fist in a nice uppercut to Gamal's jaw.

The Egyptian reeled backwards. But Adam's blow wasn't clean enough to knock him out. In the split second of space it gave him, Gamal swung back the baseball bat and brought it in a vicious strike against the side of Adam's head.

Adam let out a cry and fell.

I screamed and hurled the flashlight with all my strength at Gamal's face. I had the satisfaction of hearing the loud crack as it hit him squarely on the nose and saw the immediate gush of blood before the flashlight dropped to the stone floor and smashed. Everything plunged into darkness.

I heard a scrabbling sound I took to be one of the men trying to get to his feet. As the only other noise to accompany it was a groan, it was impossible to say which one of them it was. I dropped to all fours and knelt head down with my arms folded on top for protection. If it should prove to be Gamal, I didn't doubt he'd attempt to shove me into the pit shaft. So a position curled up on the floor seemed my best bet. It kept my weight low and meant I couldn't easily be pushed.

Adam had fallen behind Gamal, closer to the entranceway. So I could only hope Gamal wouldn't fancy the prospect of dragging Adam towards the shaft just in case he should happen to misjudge it in the dark and send them both hurtling to their deaths.

I proved correct both in my assumption that it was Gamal getting to his feet, and also in my judgement that he'd simply step over Adam slumped on the floor to make good his escape. This became apparent when his rather disembodied voice penetrated the protective cover of my arms over my head.

'I have the golden disc.' I lowered my arms so I could hear him better. 'And I know how to use it. Now it is my turn to leave you here to contemplate your fate. Do not expect that I shall come to release you. The next time I pay a visit here it will be in the company of either Abdul or the Authorities. Which of these it proves to be will depend very much on the actions of your friends. Either way, you will be dead. In this dry atmosphere you may well desiccate rather than rot. I will be most interested to see which it turns out to be.'

It was impossible to see him. But I could make out the sound of him crawling through the hole into the Hathor Chapel beyond. A moment later I saw the glow of light beyond the square opening. He'd evidently taken one of the flashlights we'd been stupid enough to leave him last night. Sparing only a quick, frightened glance at Adam's inert form sprawled on the stone floor, I leapt towards the hole even as I recognised the sound of the Aten disc being wedged into the gash in the wall.

I landed on my stomach in the gap, reaching wildly for Gamal's feet. But he saw me coming. He brought down the baseball bat in a sharp strike at my grabbing hands.

Struck across the wrist, I cried out in pain and instinctively pulled back out of range of another blow. Just as the Aten disc dropped onto the floor beside me. I knew I had just seconds until the ancient mechanism growled to life and the stone shifted closed. But Gamal, sadly, wasn't stupid. He'd obviously been paying attention to Adam's actions last night. Even as I snatched up the Aten disc, knowing we could use it to set us free, Gamal flung himself back through the opening and wrested it from my grasp. I let out an involuntary scream, part pain at my damaged wrist, part frustration at Gamal's quick thinking. As Gamal ducked back through the gap, I grabbed at his legs, trying to pull him back. But I was neither quick enough nor strong enough. He kicked back at me and I fell back as his foot connected painfully with my shoulder. There was a familiar rasping sound and the hidden door ground closed, trapping Adam and me in the dark in the entrance corridor to our tomb.

I sat slumped on the floor for a moment, giving in to the crushing sense of defeat. My wrist burned with pain and my shoulder was sore where he'd kicked me. It was no compensation to feel the patch of wetness I was sitting in and know it was blood from the violent nosebleed I'd inflicted on him. Then the need to check on Adam took over and I crawled forward, wincing as I groped blindly with my hands and put pressure on my wrist, 'Adam?'

His groan helped me locate him in the darkness.

'Adam, are you ok?'

He groaned again, and pushed himself slowly up into a sitting position. I could sense he was pressing his fingertips against his temple, testing for broken skin and blood. I held my breath, and then let it out in a big rush of relief when he spoke. 'You know, Merry, once was unlucky, twice might be considered careless. But to be trapped in here three times is starting to feel like a jinx.'

'Or maybe a curse,' I muttered. 'I think the bastard broke my wrist.' But my heart was lighter knowing Adam was unharmed and still in possession of his faculties. A blow like the one Gamal had landed on him could cause brain damage.

'Something tells me tonight didn't go exactly according to plan,' Adam murmured wryly.

'I didn't even know that shelf was there above the doorway,' I admitted. 'We should never have left him the flashlights, or his watch. It obviously enabled him to predict when we'd come back, knowing what time the temple floodlights are switched off.' I pushed myself to my feet and stumbled backwards to where the hidden doorway was positioned in the wall, feeling above it for the narrow shelf Gamal had used as a launch pad. I retrieved the Tupperware lunchbox, unsurprisingly empty and three empty plastic bottles. 'He's downed the lot!' I said in dismay.

'The lack of food doesn't particularly bother me,' Adam said. 'That was a nice meal you cooked for us tonight, Merry. But the lack of water might soon start to cause us some concern. It's unpleasantly hot and bone dry in here.'

'Not to mention dark,' I added. I'd retrieved the spare flashlight from the shelf. But a single flick of the switch was enough to confirm the batteries were dead. Blackness engulfed us. The darkness and the dry heat were almost physical, pressing in on all sides.

I heard the sound of Adam getting to his feet. 'Hmm, a bit dizzy,' he admitted, 'But no permanent damage done, so far as I can tell. Now, we need to concentrate on staying away from the pit shaft. But, first things first, let's see about your wrist, Merry.'

I held my arms out so he could find me in the dark. 'Ouch!' I cried as he inadvertently made contact with my wrist and a stabbing pain shot up my arm.

He was close enough that I was aware he was pulling his shirt over his head. A moment later a ripping sound told me he'd torn it in two. 'Not the first time we've had to tear up a shirt to use for bandages, eh?' I could hear the smile in his voice. 'Alongside getting trapped, it's turning into a bad habit.' He made another loud rent in the fabric. 'Ok, hold out your arm,'

I obliged and bit my lower lip as he gently felt my wrist with his fingertips. 'My brave girl,' he murmured as he wound a long strip of cotton around it, then another and pulled tight so he could tie a knot to hold it in place. 'Trying to save the day, as always.'

'Failing, as always,' I muttered, suppressing a gasp of pain as he secured my substitute bandage.

Letting go of my wrist, he pulled me closer. A moment later I felt his lips touch mine. It was a soft, sweet kiss. Inexplicably, tears sprang into my eyes. 'The last thing on this earth you are, my lovely Merry, is a failure – quite the reverse, in fact. You know, there's something almost cosy about being stuck in here with you again. It has a kind of warm familiarity about it, a bit like coming home. Put it this way, there's nobody else on earth I'd rather be trapped with inside a dead-aired tomb with no imminent prospect of release and no water.'

I reached up and touched my lips to his again. 'I feel exactly the same way.'

'Which reminds me,' he said. 'There's something I've been meaning to ask you…'

He took both my hands in his and held them up to his face, kissing my fingers.

'...Meredith Pink... Merry... will you marry me?'

More than anything I wished I could see his face. His voice was deep and full of emotion. His warm hands grasped mine and I swear I could feel the energy radiating from his touch.

As I caught my breath I realised actually I didn't need to be able to see his face. Everything important was transmitted through his hands and his voice. I could feel the emotion flowing through each. My heart started to sing. It didn't matter that this proposal was in the pitch-black darkness of an ancient tomb where fresh air hadn't circulated for something like thirty-three centuries. Adam loved me and he wanted to marry me.

'Yes!' I cried happily. 'Oh, yes please!'

He caught me against him and kissed me, deeply and thoroughly. 'Just for the record,' he said against my lips, still holding me pressed against his bare chest, 'I don't mean someday, somewhere, if or when we get out of here. I mean right here, right now.'

'What?' I felt a strange euphoria take hold of me, and giggled. Maybe his dizziness was transmitting itself onto me along with his emotion. He was the one who'd taken a blow to the head from a baseball bat. But suddenly I was the one reeling.

'Why not?' he challenged. 'Who says you need a church and a vicar or a fancy venue and a registrar plus loads of guests and a cake to have a wedding?'

'But...'

'But nothing.' He kissed my fingertips again. 'I've been wanting to ask you ever since that email from Dan landed in your Inbox and you looked so hurt. Hang that; I think I've wanted to ask you since the day we met. Why should we allow Dan and Jessica to steal a march on us?'

'Don't you think Merry Tennyson sounds a bit funny?' I asked, feeling giddy.

'Keep Pink if it makes you happy,' he offered, and I could hear he was grinning. 'I don't care what you call yourself, so long as we're together. I think I've loved you from the moment I first clapped eyes on you, walking across the forecourt of this very temple looking all day-dreamy and preoccupied.'

'Even though back then you thought I might be an antiquities thief or a con artist?' I teased.

'That just made you more intriguing,' he smiled. Strange, to be able to hear a smile, but it was right there in his voice. 'And I've spent every moment since falling more and more deeply in love with you. I adore everything about you, lovely Merry. To be able to call you my wife would make me the happiest man on the planet.'

I didn't know quite how to respond to this. I'm not as good with words as Adam is. I threw my arms around him instead, found his mouth and kissed him with all the passion bubbling up in me. Funny, how the throbbing of my damaged wrist melted away. Sure, I was crying. But it was tears of joy, not pain. It struck me how lucky I was to have found a man who knew how to express his feelings. A decade with Dan had left me wondering if maybe men didn't actually have any, let alone know how to put them into words if they did.

Adam set me gently away from him. 'Ok, I'm going to do my best to get this right but feel free to correct me if you think I miss a bit.' He took my hands back in his. I'm sure his eyes were looking adoringly into mine, so I gazed back at where I imagined his eyes to be, letting all the love I was feeling shine out. After a brief pause while he collected his thoughts, he cleared his throat, and then began, 'Dearly beloved, we are gathered here in the sight of... well... maybe not just our God. Let's just say we are gathered here in the sight of possibly the entire ancient Egyptian pantheon, plus hopefully our own God since we believe him to be all seeing, all knowing. Anyway, the point is, we are gathered here to join this man and this woman in holy matrimony.' He broke off and kissed me again before admitting, 'I don't remember the next bit, Merry.'

'Something about the solemn state of marriage, I think,' I frowned, 'Which is not to be entered into lightly or thoughtlessly.'

'Do you feel light and thoughtless Merry?'

'Light-headed, certainly,' I grinned. 'A bit drunk actually.'

'Good! Me too. But hopefully not thoughtless.'

'Thought*ful*,' I smiled, emphasising the last syllable.

'That's alright then,' he smiled. 'We can continue.'

'I think the next bit might have something to do with being given away or with witnesses.'

'Ah! As in who gives this woman…?'

'Yes, something like that.'

He paused again, and then asked quietly and with a soft seriousness, 'Are you willing to give yourself to me Merry?'

I spared a fleeting thought for my father, seeing him in my mind's eye bent over his stamp collection back in England. Whilst this ceremony might be unorthodox, I knew both my parents approved of Adam and would welcome him into the family with open arms. 'I am,' I whispered.

'Now, as to witnesses,' Adam murmured. 'I think there might be one or two ghosts we could call upon. How do you fancy having Akhenaten and Nefertiti as our best man and matron of honour?'

'I'd be delighted,' I smiled. 'And perhaps the princess Neferure as a bridesmaid.'

'Of course. So, all the major roles are filled. We may proceed.' He clasped my hands gently, careful of my injured wrist. 'So, now, let's cut to the important part. Do you, Meredith Jane Pink take me Adam James Tennyson to be your lawful wedded husband? Do you promise to love and cherish me and, forsaking all others keep yourself only unto me as long as we both shall live?'

'I think you forgot the *richer or poorer* and *in sickness and in health* bits,' I murmured. 'But since it's possible we may not get to live all that much longer, I'm willing to overlook it. Oh, and I most certainly do, by the way!'

He claimed my mouth with his for another kiss. This time it was me who pulled back. I rested my hands against the warm skin of his chest, almost as if I could absorb him through my touch.

'My turn,' I murmured. 'Do you, Adam James Tennyson take me Meredith Jane Pink to be your lawful wedded wife? Will you love and cherish me, for richer or poorer, in sickness and in health and, forsaking all others keep yourself only unto me as long as we both shall live?'

'You've mixed that up delightfully, Merry!' he accused. 'I'm not sure if I'm supposed to say *I do* or *I will*. Take it as read the answer is a resounding *Yes!* to both! So please can we just cut to the part where I get to kiss the bride?'

'But you haven't finished the ceremony yet!' I chided.

'Oh? Oh, yes. Right. Sorry. Ok, so it gives me great pleasure to pronounce you man and wife! Please Merry, may I now kiss the bride?'

I took this to be rhetorical since his mouth had already descended on mine. I swiped at the tears running freely down my cheeks.

'Leave them,' he ordered. 'I like your salty wet kisses Merry.'

I held his face in my hand and peppered it with my salty wet kisses.

He pulled away abruptly. 'Dammit!'

'What?'

'We forgot the whole bit about *with this ring I thee wed*, not to mention my favourite part about *with my body I thee honour*. Is that right? I'm not so sure about the whole *honour* bit. I'd just like to make love to you as much as possible, if that's alright with you?'

'I've no complaints,' I whispered.

'If we could just get into the treasure chamber, I'd choose you the nicest ring from Nefertiti's collection… To give it to you somehow wouldn't feel like stealing. Something tells me Akhenaten and Nefertiti would understand.'

'It's ok. I don't need to have a ring on my finger to feel married to you. No ceremony in front of a vicar or a registrar and a crowd of guests, with flowers, dresses, music, rings, or any of the other paraphernalia that goes with weddings could ever feel more meaningful to me than the one we've just shared.'

'Even so, if we ever get out of here, I'd be more than happy to put on a show for everyone else's benefit. Especially if it means we get to say the bits we might have forgotten.'

'It won't make it any more real to me,' I said staunchly.

'So, whether we expire in the next couple of days from dehydration or somehow make it out of here and die at a ripe old age having lived a full and adventurous life, it really makes no odds,' he said. 'I can die happy, knowing we've said everything that needs saying.'

I wished I could see his face. But the darkness was loaded with intimacy. I had a feeling it might not have been quite such a tender or significant experience in the light.

'I love you Adam,' I said, realising it was the one thing I hadn't put into words.

'And I love you Meredith Pink Tennyson; heart, body and soul.'

I have a feeling we might have made love right there on the hard stone floor if the familiar rasping sound of rock shifting against rock hadn't cut through the closeness holding us intimate and spellbound.

A flashlight beam dazzled our eyes. I winced away from it; blinking at the spots it sent spinning before my eyes.

'Merry? Adam? Are you in there?' The professor's voice spoke from the darkness behind the light. I couldn't look at it, not even squinting. 'Ah, yes – there you both are! I'd have been here earlier. But I caught a blood-soaked young man trying to steal your scooter near the parking lot. The poor young devil's had the most awful nosebleed. I imagine from his jabbering one of you young people might be responsible for his broken nose. Is that correct?'

'Ted! Thank the Lord!' Adam proclaimed. 'And don't worry about your timing. It's pretty damned perfect!'

'Where is the blood-soaked young man now?' I asked rather more prosaically, feeling not even slightly repentant for the broken nose.

'I'm afraid I found it necessary to clunk him over the head with my walking cane while his back was turned trying to jump onto the scooter. You see; he was kicking up the most awful fuss about accompanying me back to the *Queen Ahmes*. I was pretty sure he must be the young man you'd described from the Ministry office, Gamal Abdel-Maqsoud. It struck me he must somehow have given you the slip, and simultaneously managed to reverse your positions with regard to being locked inside the tomb. And since he might be our only lead when it comes to unmasking Walid's blackmailer, I knew I couldn't let him go free. When the Aten disc rolled out from under his arm when I hit him, I had my proof of his identity. It also seemed to confirm what had happened, since

I'd been able to get no sense from the young man at all. Luckily, I didn't need his disc to rescue you since I'd brought the other one along with me. But I confiscated it from him all the same.'

'And where is he now?' Adam repeated my question since, despite his lengthy explanation, Ted had failed to answer it.

'I'm afraid I found it necessary to leave him tied to a tree,' the professor admitted. 'I couldn't risk him recovering his senses and following me here, or raising the alarm. Luckily I had a good strong length of rope in my rucksack, since we agreed never to visit the tomb again without one.'

'Ted, you are a miracle worker!' Adam exclaimed. 'But what brought you out here to the tomb tonight? I didn't think you'd register our absence until morning, and I was rather worried Merry and I might be dying of thirst by then.'

'Since this was our last night in Luxor before departing for Amarna, it occurred to me this was my only opportunity to visit the tomb. Walid showed me the items he selected for possible sale. It reminded me just how staggering the tomb contents are. I thought I might be able to meet up with you here and treat myself to another little look-see; especially since we may be forced to go public with the tomb if the whole blackmail scenario blows up in our faces.' He paused. 'But I daresay as things have turned out it's more important we should untie young matey boy from his tree and get him back to the *Queen Ahmes* for a proper interrogation.'

Adam and I had been crawling through the opening in the wall while the professor was speaking. As Adam reached back to help me to my feet, Ted caught sight first of Adam's naked torso and then of my wrist, bound tightly in Adam's shirt. He let out an exclamation,

'Oh my goodness, Merry, you've been injured. We must get you back to the dahabeeyah with all possible speed and get that properly strapped up.'

'It can wait,' I said gamely. 'Honestly, it barely hurts at all. I don't want to stop you visiting the tomb.'

'No no, I won't hear of it. Come. We must collect up Mr Abdel-Maqsoud on the way. If we can persuade him to reveal the identity of the blackmailer, there's every chance I can still come here for a private viewing before Walid decides to announce its discovery to the world.'

Since Adam agreed this was the best plan, I said no more. But I was strangely reluctant to lock up and leave. I sent a last longing look into the darkness of the passageway beyond the hidden doorway. I couldn't help but wonder how long it would take for the magical moments Adam and I had just spent in there to take on the dreamlike hue of unreality. I didn't want what we'd shared to slip away. I wanted to hang on to it and bring it with me.

Reading my thoughts as usual or perhaps because he felt the same way I did, Adam piped up. 'Ted, we have some important news to share with you. And we'd like you to be the very first to know and to offer us your congratulations.'

'Ah, how lovely!' Ted exclaimed before Adam could say more. 'You've asked Meredith to marry you. Congratulations on your engagement, my dears. I couldn't be more delighted. Now I have two weddings to look forward to!'

Chapter 11

Gamal Abdel-Maqsoud was a sorry sight indeed bound tightly to the narrow trunk of a palm tree with dried blood from his violent nosebleed splattered all down the front of what had once been his pristine white shirt.

He'd regained consciousness but clearly had an almighty headache.

'If his difficulty in focusing is anything to go by, I think you've given him concussion,' Adam ventured.

Whether or not this was the case, he offered us very little resistance as we untied him.

Ted had borrowed my scooter to make his trip from the dahabeeyah to Hatshepsut's temple. We decided Adam would take Gamal back with him, while Ted rode with me. We took the precaution of securing Gamal to Adam's scooter with Ted's length of rope, just in case he should take it into his head to try any kamikaze moves along the way.

Thankfully he was too spaced out to try anything brave, reckless or suicidal. We reached the *Queen Ahmes* without mishap.

'Now what?' I asked.

'Now I think we lock him in one of the staff cabins below deck and make sure the window is secured,' Adam said.

'Should we call a doctor?'

'We'll see how he is in the morning. I'd prefer to avoid that if at all possible. But I think we need to allow him some recovery time before we attempt to interview him.'

'Should we search him?'

'Search him?'

'Just to check he doesn't have a mobile phone on him. It didn't matter back inside the tomb since we know there's no signal from there. But here it's a different matter.'

Adam performed a quick body search. 'Nothing,' he confirmed. 'He's clean.'

'Speaking of which…'

'Yes, we should take his shirt away to wash and get the poor chap a fresh one. It strikes me he got a little more than he bargained for when he decided to stake out the Hathor Chapel.'

There was a sink already installed in the tiny staff cabins situated on the lower deck at the back end of the dahabeeyah. I busied myself bringing a flannel, soap, fresh towels and a clean T-shirt borrowed from Adam's wardrobe, while Adam divested our guest of his soiled shirt. Gamal was limp and unresponsive during this procedure. I was rather worried by the way his eyes kept rolling back in his head. Ted must have whacked him pretty damn hard with his walking cane.

'We'll leave him to sleep,' Adam decided. 'And we'll see how things are looking in the morning.'

Dawn was fingering its way across the horizon by the time Adam and I fell into bed. He pulled me into his arms even before our heads could hit the pillow. 'Hey Mrs,' he said. 'I hope you're not too tired to consummate our marriage.'

Suffice it to say, it was rather a long time before we got off to sleep.

By lunchtime of the following day when Adam and I finally surfaced having treated ourselves to a little 'honeymoon' in our cabin, it was to find Gamal Abdel-Maqsoud very much recovered but in the mood to be truculent.

'You cannot detain me against my will,' he asserted.

Adam was disinclined to be sympathetic. 'Oh yes we can; and we absolutely will. Until you tell us what we want to know, you will remain here as our guest, by force if necessary.'

'I will be missed at the Ministry office.'

'I've thought of that,' Adam said calmly. 'I suggest I stand here and wait while you put in a call to your boss. I'm sure he'll understand your need for some time off in view of the head injury you sustained falling off your scooter.'

'You can't make me…'

'What I *can* do is make your stay with us very uncomfortable if you don't comply with my requests. My – er – Merry here is a very good cook. I assume you'd like to be fed while you're with us?' Adam pointedly held out his phone towards our guest. Sulkily, Gamal took it.

'Just pass me the baseball bat, would you please, Merry? I don't want to take any chances.' Then he turned back to Gamal. 'Don't think I'll baulk at using it if you try to be clever.'

Gamal made the call.

'Well done,' Adam approved. 'You've earned yourself a sandwich. Now if you'd like dinner later I suggest you tell us what we want to know. The questions are very simple and they both relate to this Abdul you so carelessly mentioned. Number one, who is he? By which I mean what is his full name? And number two, where is he? You told us he'd left Luxor. We presume him to be in Cairo. But Cairo is a big city. We'd like to narrow it down a bit.'

'Keep me here as long as you wish,' Gamal sneered, 'but this information I will never give to you.'

'Then you'll go hungry,' Adam said cheerfully.

Gamal shrugged. 'I can play a waiting game. You will have no choice but to give Abdul what he demands. If you do not you know what the consequences will be. And then the tables will be turned once more. Is that not your English expression?'

Adam cocked an eyebrow at him. 'If it's a waiting game you want, a waiting game you shall have.' Then he held the cabin door open for me so I could precede him out. 'Scrap the order for a sandwich, Merry. Let's leave him here to think about his options while we have lunch with the others.' And he closed and locked the door behind us.

Before we set sail I paid a visit to the medical centre in Luxor to have my wrist looked at. I was much relieved when the medic examined it and decided it was badly bruised rather than broken. Properly strapped, it felt much better. He advised me against putting too much pressure on it but otherwise declared I could go about my normal day-to-day business. I grinned and very nearly told him there was very little normal about my day-to-day business. But, sharing a smile with Adam, I chose to hug this knowledge to myself instead. In actual fact, I think he was more concerned about the absolute shiner of a black eye Adam was now sporting than he was about my damaged wrist. A punch in the head was one thing, but to have sustained a direct hit from a violently wielded baseball bat was quite another. Adam submitted to lights being shone into his eyes and all manner of balancing exercises with good grace.

Much relieved when we were both pronounced fit enough to leave, we returned to the *Queen Ahmes* and prepared for the off. In terms of the changed status between us, Adam and I decided, as far as everyone else was concerned, to run with the story that he'd asked me to marry him while we were shut up in the tomb. Let's face it; it was the truth – just not the whole truth. Keeping our private wedding ceremony as our secret made it more special somehow.

'We don't need to invite people in on it to make it real,' Adam asserted. 'We were both there and that's what matters. We can act as each other's witnesses. I'm perfectly happy to do it all again for the sake of form. But make no mistake, Merry; we're married. And that's final.'

So we accepted the rhapsody of congratulations and promised to make haste with the wedding plans. In truth, I was quite upbeat at the prospect of flowers and rings and confetti and, more importantly, my Dad there to give me away while my Mum shed a discreet tear. I'm a girl after all, and I've read possibly more than my share of romantic fiction. But Adam was right. We'd done the important bit. The rest was just fluff, convention and for the benefit of everyone else. Besides, I *felt* different. I'd made promises, call them vows if you like, and every one of them had been heartfelt and true.

I stood with my good hand tucked inside Adam's watching Khaled unfurl the sails, feeling quite ridiculously happy and complete. The prospect of Dan and Jessica's wedding was something I found I could now contemplate with total equanimity. I hope I'm not given to one-upmanship. But

I admit it was quite a gratifying feeling to think I'd got there first.

Once Khaled had the dahabeeyah on course for Amarna and the wind was billowing in the sails, Adam and I joined the others up on the sundeck. We knew we could leave the business of sailing in Khaled's capable hands. The Nile current was in our favour since we were travelling downriver. The breeze was behind us and Khaled was a skilled skipper. He knew to avoid the sandbars and keep the *Queen Ahmes* on course along the deepest channel of the mighty river.

The *Queen Ahmes* with both sails unfurled is quite a sight. I wished I could somehow transport myself to the riverbank so I could take some video footage on my camcorder of her gracefully transporting us down the Nile, almost as if she were back in her heyday of Victorian cruising.

Arriving on deck we found Nabil had buttonholed Ted and Walid and was lecturing again. I rolled my eyes at Adam, poured myself some chilled homemade lemonade from the jug I'd brought up earlier and settled myself in one of the cushioned steamers in the shade to listen.

'Just take the Ten Commandments as an example,' Nabil was saying. 'As we know from the Bible, they were given by the Lord God to the Israelites on Mount Sinai. Yet they are clearly in the Egyptian tradition and would appear to have common roots with the Egyptian *Book of the Dead*.'

Walid and Ted both greeted this assertion with silence. Whether they were humouring him, rapt with wonder or bored out of their minds was impossible to tell. Whatever, Nabil needed no encouragement to continue. Perhaps he came from the school of thought that silence was golden. Anyway, he took a leisurely sip of his lemonade and went on,

'As you are both extremely well placed to know, the ancient Egyptians believed that after their death they faced a trial in the underworld before Osiris and his forty-two judges in the Hall of Judgement. Spell 125 of the *Book of the Dead* contains a sort of 'negative confession' that the dead person has to recite on this occasion. It contains such assurances as: *I have done no falsehood / I have not robbed / I have not stolen / I have not killed men / I have not told lies.*'

He paused and looked around at his small, assembled audience with the familiar glint in his eyes. It seemed to me it didn't matter one jot to Nabil whether his audience was small or large. That it was an audience was enough. A single listener would do if they were attentive. I don't think it even mattered overmuch to Nabil whether his audience agreed with him or not. I'd seen him handle dissenters. In actual fact I think he rather relished the opportunity of counter argument to add a sense of theatre to his speeches.

Sadly for Nabil, his audience today was unresponsive. So he spoke quite happily into the void. 'It's clear to me the Ten Commandments are a kind of positive reframing of this

Egyptian negative confession. So we find: *Thou shalt not kill / Thou shalt not steal / Thou shalt not bear false witness against thy neighbour,* and so on.'

I sipped my lemonade, interested in spite of myself. Nabil's was a different way of looking at the ancient Egyptian theology. I found myself agreeing with Adam's verdict that Nabil's hypotheses were intriguing. Even if some of them were wide of the mark, he was able to draw enough links between ancient Egyptian religion and many of the founding principles of some of the major religions of the world today that I couldn't dismiss him out of hand.

Nabil refilled his glass. 'It therefore seems likely to me that Akhenaten, who did not believe in Osiris or his underworld, turned the moral code according to which the ancient Egyptians believed their dead would be judged into an imperative standard of behaviour for his followers.'

Adam smiled and reached across for my hand. 'I've looked at some of this Moses/Akhenaten stuff online,' he said. 'It seems to have quite a following. Have you told them about Akhenaten's *Hymn to the Aten* yet Nabil? Apparently it's a virtual mirror image of *Psalm 104*.'

'Ah yes,' Nabil beamed at him, 'Thank you, Adam, for reminding me. Yes, many believe the later Hebrew writer who set it down in the Biblical writings must have known the earlier Egyptian hymn. You are correct of course. Many of the passages are almost identical. Both are a song of praise to the creator. So I will go one step further and say that the Hebrew writer may have believed he was setting down a psalm handed down from Moses. He may or may not have known it was a carbon copy of Akhenaten's hymn, and so had its roots in Egyptian theology.'

I zoned out while Nabil started quoting from both the psalm and the hymn to demonstrate their similarity. I was a bit surprised at Adam for encouraging him. Especially considering how recently we'd been keeping company with whatever was left of Akhenaten's earthly remains. Or had we? The trouble was, Adam had used the word *if* on our visit with Walid to the tomb. For such a small word, it punched well above its weight. Now that the seed of doubt had been sown about whether or not the heretic pharaoh was actually interred inside his huge stone sarcophagus, I couldn't help but wonder if he had such a rock solid alibi after all from Nabil's claims of his Biblical alias. It gave me a headache to think about it. So I decided not to. I looked at the passing scenery instead.

This part of the Nile was especially beautiful. We'd left Luxor behind us and swiftly approached the town of Qena, where the beautiful Denderah temple is situated. I'd been horrified on my one visit there to find myself looking at a replica of the famous Denderah Zodiac carved into the ceiling of one of the chapels. The original had been hacked from the temple by the early explorers and was now to be found in the Louvre in Paris.

Adam and I had often engaged in debate about whether Egypt's plundered treasures ought by rights to be returned from the major museums of the world. I tended towards the view that they should. How much more magnificent might the temples and tombs of Egypt be with their statuary and artefacts returned to them and displayed in their original locations?

Adam generally took the opposing view that it was better to bring Egypt to the people of the world if it wasn't possible, either through political expediency or financial constraint, for the people of the world to visit Egypt.

'Egypt is the first and finest civilisation in the world,' he'd said to me on more than one occasion. 'As such, Egypt is the nation that holds the key to the beginnings of the entire human enterprise. We all have a stake in that. So it should be accessible to people wherever they happen to be. If that means they touch Egypt through the British Museum or the Metropolitan, or the Louvre, who cares? The important thing is they touch Egypt.'

'But surely it's theft,' I'd argued, 'To have taken so many priceless artefacts and scattered them throughout the world, sometimes with no provenance whatsoever. There are items on display in the British Museum, for heaven's sake, that have no labels on them at all, because the curators have simply no idea where they originated from.'

We'd gone round and round it and never reached a definitive view. Perhaps it was because we were both right.

I think I fell asleep. When I woke up, it was to find the conversation had shifted to the News.

'Three people have been killed in Alexandria during clashes between pro- and anti-Morsi protesters,' Adam said, reading from the screen of his iPad. 'It says here one of them was a 21-year-old American student. He was reportedly stabbed to death as he observed the demonstrations. My God, things are turning ugly. It will be hard for the international community to stand idly by if foreign nationals start being killed.'

'The crowds will descend on Tahrir Square this weekend to demand Morsi's resignation,' Walid said. 'I fear more blood will be spilled on our streets.'

It was the worst possible news and didn't bode well for a return any time soon to a robust tourist trade in Egypt. I decided to enjoy this opportunity to cruise the Nile since it may well turn out to be my last for a long time. This part of the Nile north of Luxor had been a no-go zone for many years due to the threat of terrorism targeted at tourists in and around the modern Egyptian province of Minya. This had been a stronghold of Al-Gamaa Al-Islamiya, the same terror group who'd so nearly had one of their former associates appointed Governor of Luxor. Before their campaign of attacks it had been possible to cruise the length of the country from Cairo to

Aswan. The restrictions had been relaxed recently, possibly because an Islamist president was in power, hence our ability to make this journey now. But I feared they would be imposed again if a compromise could not be found between President Morsi and his opponents in the next few days.

We moored overnight near to Abydos, where the famous temple of Seti I is situated. Then it was a full day's sailing to reach Amarna. We arrived after sunset, so moored on the banks of the Nile and spent the evening planning our time here, with reference to the big maps Walid had brought with him and various websites on the Internet. I'd taken pity on Gamal Abdel-Maqsoud and taken him dry bread and water periodically throughout our journey, plus some painkillers. His broken nose had stopped bleeding but it was clear it was healing to be somewhat mis-shapen. I tried to feel sorry about this. Tried; and failed. My shoulder was still bruised where he'd kicked me. And it would be a few days before my wrist strappings could come off. I was quite content to keep him on meagre and unappetising rations. But I had no desire to have him die of starvation or dehydration during his voyage with us. So bread and water it was. For the rest of us I cooked one of my tasty tagines for our evening meal. We'd managed to keep it a secret from Nabil Zaal that we had another 'guest' on board, so dinner could proceed without any awkward questions being asked. We ate up on deck under the stars, reading about the ancient city on whose shores we were now moored and letting our excitement mount.

Excavation and preservation of the site of Akhenaten's ancient city to the sun had been on-going for most of the last century and beyond, since the so-called Father of modern Egyptology, Flinders Petrie started work there during the latter part of the nineteenth century. The site was now under the jurisdiction of an international team known as the Amarna Project, who worked there with the cooperation of the Egyptian government and the Ministry of State for Antiquities.

Thanks to the efforts of this team of experts the ancient city was taking shape once more, rising from a sand blown basin of desert where it had lain buried and in ruins for millennia. There were numerous birds-eye images on the Internet showing the layout of the city from above, with the huge rectangular perimeter shapes of the temples and palaces excavated from the sand that had blown in over the centuries to cover them.

Amarna occupies a large bay of almost flat desert hemmed in for much of its perimeter by a semi-circle of cliffs that rise to a high desert plateau. Both the north and south headlands approach close to the Nile, giving the site a feel of being situated within a broad arc of open space between the river and the curve of the cliffs. The distance between both headlands is about ten kilometres long, with the broadest extent, between river and cliffs, being nearly five kilometres across.

It was a nice D-shaped parcel of virgin land, and I could understand why the heretic pharaoh had chosen it as the site for his new city. That the sun rose between a cleft in the backdrop of cliffs was a bonus that must have seemed prophetic to the rebellious king.

Next morning, Adam and I stayed behind on board the *Queen Ahmes* with Khaled, while Nabil, Ted and Walid went to introduce themselves to the field director and his team and show their credentials and the official Egyptologists permit they'd been given.

They returned, excited and eager to make a start.

'It's the tombs I'm most interested to see,' Nabil asserted. 'I feel sure I will find something in the wall carvings that has been missed by other scholars.

Ted's smile was tolerant. 'Yes the tombs will be a good place to start. They tell much of the story of this fascinating place.'

Walid looked somewhat uncomfortable. Since excavators and archaeologists had been crawling all over the Amarnan tombs for decades, they weren't the most promising location for his staged 'discovery' of the artefacts he'd brought with him from the tomb. But we had to start somewhere. And I think we were all itching to see for ourselves the tomb of Akhenaten over which so much controversy raged. Forget the whole question about whether or not Akhenaten was also Moses. Egyptologists were divided into two camps: those who believed he had been interred in his tomb, and those who believed he had not.

The Amarnan tombs are carved into the dried valleys and torrent beds – called wadis – that cut through the cliffs behind the city. Perhaps Akhenaten, having abandoned Thebes and its ancient burial ground, chose this location thinking it most closely resembled The Valley of the Kings, for all that it was on the east bank not the west.

The field director from the Amarna Project had been kind enough to put a jeep at our disposal so we could easily make the journey from the Nile, across the site of the ancient city to the cliffs beyond. It was a beaten up old vehicle with an overpowering smell of diesel, and very poorly sprung suspension. Every one of the innumerable years it had spent out in the heat and sand of middle-Egypt showed in the scratched and corroding bodywork and the worn interiors. But it was transport, so we were grateful. The five of us crammed inside, with Adam at the wheel and the professor alongside him in the front in deference to his seniority in both years and Egyptological status. We set off, armed with plenty of bottled water, sunhats and a packed lunch. A hot southerly wind was blowing, whipping up the sand as we drove across the desert basin towards the cliffs.

The Royal Tomb, as Akhenaten's intended burial place is known, lies in a narrow side valley leading off from the Royal Wadi at a distance of nearly four miles from its mouth. We were able to drive most of the way, but then had to get out and walk.

'It is this cleft in the rocks through which the sun rises every morning,' Nabil Zaal said excitedly. 'Many scholars believe it resembles the ancient Egyptian hieroglyph for *horizon*, perhaps explaining why the rebel pharaoh called his new city Akhet-Aten, or Horizon of the Sun.'

I felt my anticipation mount as we approached the entranceway. 'What's that?' I asked, looking at the modern construction covering the tomb entrance.

'It's a flood barrier,' Ted explained. 'It's there to protect the tomb from the occasional heavy rains that send water sweeping down the wadi.'

'Sadly this protection has come a little late,' Walid said. 'As you will see, the tomb is in a poor state of preservation.'

'Hardly surprising considering the campaign of destruction waged against Akhenaten's memory back in ancient times,' Adam remarked.

Falling silent, we filed through the entranceway and started to descend the steep steps of the first corridor.

I found it hard to breathe for much of our tour around the tomb. It had none of the colour or grandeur of some of its

Theban counterparts, although in its dimensions it could rival many of them. But it had an atmosphere I found quite chilling.

Recently added to Nile cruise itineraries, the tomb was equipped with electricity and ramps. Yet these modern contraptions to facilitate tourism or comply with health and safety regulations did nothing to counteract the overwhelming sense of desolation and abandonment that echoed through the rock hewn chambers.

'It was intended for Akhenaten, his second daughter the princess Meketaten, and probably for his mother Queen Tiye,' Ted said as we moved through the tomb.

'There is also an unfinished annexe probably meant for Nefertiti,' Walid added. 'As with Akhenaten himself, debate rages about whether his queen was ever actually interred here.'

'The rock is of poor quality, so much of the decoration was wholly or partly cut in a thin layer of gypsum plaster spread on the walls,' Walid said. 'As you can see, much of this has been lost, due both to dampness invading the tomb and possibly the destruction waged by Akhenaten's enemies. Most of the surviving decoration is in these chambers here, cut for the princess Meketaten.'

We moved into these chambers as Walid spoke. Despite the ambient lighting, Nabil Zaal had brought along a flashlight and was running the beam in long sweeps along the wall.

'I've read about Princess Meketaten,' I said. 'She was the second daughter of Akhenaten and Nefertiti and died young. Some people believe she died in childbirth, is that right?'

'It's all a bit confused,' Ted said. 'Nobody has been able to provide a definitive interpretation of these images. But, yes, that's certainly one suggestion, although she's likely only to have been in her mid-teens at the time of her death. Another is that a plague swept through Akhet-Aten, possibly brought into Egypt by foreign dignitaries who came to pay tribute at a festival hosted by Akhenaten. Some believe it was the beginning of the end for Akhenaten, a sign the pantheon of gods were displeased and taking their retribution.'

As he spoke we were gazing up at the remains of the wall carvings, still discernable despite the erosion of time and the damaged sections.

'These scenes of grief for their lost child are unique in ancient Egyptian art,' Walid said. 'The naturalistic style is probably at its most moving. One can almost hear the wailing of the mourners.'

I stared at the faded wall reliefs and swallowed hard to unblock the painful constriction in my throat. His words brought the wailing of Mrs Mushhawrar to mind, which was not comfortable at all. The death of a child was intolerable at any age. Gazing around me, it was impossible not to contrast the hollow, echoing tragedy of this place with the glorious tomb carved into the cliff behind Hatshepsut's temple. Even coated in rock dust, the splendour of our tomb shone from every artefact. The colours of the paintings on the plastered walls of the burial chamber had retained so much vibrancy they might almost have been painted yesterday. Yet here everything was empty and achingly sad, the plaster flaking away from the walls with none of its original colour remaining. If Akhenaten was indeed buried in our tomb having been moved there by Tutankhamun shortly after his death, I could only be glad for him. It may not have been what he intended or even wanted; to rest forever behind a temple dedicated to the god he'd turned against, Amun. But to my eyes it had to be better than the stark isolation of this place. Our tomb was a celebration of the life Akhenaten and Nefertiti shared. Here it was just about death.

I shivered. 'Nabil, have you seen enough?'

He continued to wave his torch in wide arcs in front of the wall. 'No... I mean, yes...' He sounded agitated. 'I mean... it's just... well, I thought there would be more in the way of inscriptions...something that may have been overlooked or misinterpreted... But...'

'But archaeologists and excavators have been crawling all over this place like ants for more than a century,' Adam said wryly. 'The wall reliefs, or what's left of them, have been copied, photographed and printed in more books than you can shake a stick at. Everybody who's anybody in the field of

Egyptology has had a bash at interpreting them. It was always going to be a long shot, Nabil... But I'm sorry you're disappointed.'

Nabil shrugged, brightening. 'It is of no matter. This is just the start. We can make a slow study of all the tombs. I will find something. I am sure of it.'

I could only admire his optimism and his ability to bounce back.

He made a last flourish with his torch, 'I am confident of one thing. Akhenaten was never buried in this tomb. I may not be able to prove it here and now. But prove it I shall!'

Since none of us seemed able to think of a suitable response, we took this as our cue to leave. I don't mind admitting it was with some relief I stepped back into the aggressive glare of the sun.

'Shall we head back now towards the excavation site of the old city?' Walid asked with a return to his earlier edgy impatience.

'There are a couple of other tombs I would very much like to explore first,' Nabil appealed. 'If I may crave your indulgence...?'

'Just two?' Ted asked with an ironic lift to one eyebrow. He immediately reached up to push his glasses back up onto the bridge of his nose since they'd slipped forward.

'Yes, those of Panehesy and Meryre,' Nabil said. 'They are key in helping me prove Akhenaten's alias as Moses.'

We all stared at him. I could feel myself growing fidgety. Not one of us encouraged him. He went on nevertheless,

'These two men were Akhenaten's two highest priestly officials at the Akhet-Aten temple,' he explained. 'Meryre was the High Priest of the Aten and Panehesy was the Chief Servitor of the Aten. Now, listen to this...' his earnest gaze swept across each of us in turn. 'The two highest priestly officials under Moses were Merari and Pinehas. The Egyptian equivalent of Merari is Meryre and of Pinehas is Panehesy! I believe Meryre and Panehesy left Egypt with Akhenaten to lead the Hebrew people out of Egypt in what has become known as the Israelite Exodus. I think we will find clear evidence that they were never interred in their tombs.'

We looked to Ted in his capacity of something akin to an Egyptological elder statesman among us. To my surprise, he looked quite eager. I sent him a quizzical glance, which he noticed. He smiled at me.

'I am thinking of the Copper Scroll,' he admitted.

'My goodness! I'd almost forgotten that!' I exclaimed.

'There is a column in the Copper Scroll which appears to give the location of certain of the buried treasure as relating to ancient storehouses in Akhet-Aten,' he said. 'It reads something along the lines of *"Go north from the house of the stored produce and you will find a tomb. The tomb which has a tunnel opening towards the north has the key buried in the mouth of the tunnel".*

'The key?' Adam questioned.

Ted fixed his gaze on him. 'Some believe it is the key to unlocking the Copper Scroll itself.'

'As in a code breaker?' I asked.

Ted smiled, 'Yes, something like that. Now, what is interesting is we know from the excavation work here in Amarna where the ancient storehouses were located. Bearing exactly due north, as instructed, one does indeed arrive at a line of tombs, running along the edge of the plateau. The tomb of Meryre is located there, and has a tunnel opening running north. I would like to see this tomb for myself.'

We retraced our steps to the jeep, all buzzing with a renewed excitement. It was severed abruptly when we reached the beaten up old vehicle to find a note taped to the windscreen. It read *"Go Home. Leave our Pharaohs alone. They are Egyptian NEVER Jewish!!!"*

'Oh, good grief, they've followed us here,' I exclaimed.

Nabil ripped the note off the windscreen and stared at it thoughtfully. 'I have made no secret of my movements,' he said. ' I publish a daily blog, you know.' Then he smiled. 'This means there are those who believe I may be right. And since this truth is unpalatable to them, they seek to divert me from finding the evidence to prove it.'

'Maybe we should turn back,' I said uncertainly. 'These people might be dangerous. The smoke bomb and stone throwing may have been just a warning.'

'Nothing and nobody will divert me from accomplishing my mission,' Nabil said boldly, if a bit too zealously for my liking. He was not to be budged. So we squeezed back inside the jeep, gulped down some water and set off for the northern tombs.

Our experience there was a virtual re-run of the one inside the Royal Tomb. The northern tombs were poorly preserved and it was almost impossible to discern what little remained of the wall reliefs. Even Ted looked disappointed when he returned from making a thorough check of the corridor that may have been the tunnel alluded to in the Copper Scroll.

'Ah well, maybe it would be better if we cultivate a friendship with the field team working here,' he suggested. 'We are not equipped to do any proper excavation work of our own. And I am reluctant to step on their toes.'

'But I must "stage" the discovery of my Amarnan artefacts,' Walid reminded us, whispering so Nabil couldn't hear and nervously twisting his hands together. It was becoming a bad habit of his. 'I need to give the appearance of excavation work to make my finds believable.'

Adam took pity on him. 'Let's head back to where the main archaeological work is going on in the remains of the city and see if we can find a promising location,' he suggested.

We piled back inside the jeep and, leaving the bay of cliffs behind us, drove back across the desert road towards the ruins that had once been the temples, palaces and suburbs of the ancient city.

'It's close to here that the world-famous bust of Nefertiti was found by the German expedition in 1912,' Ted said as we entered Akhet-Aten proper. 'The remains of the sculptor's workshop were uncovered and the statue was discovered inside.'

'It makes you wonder what else might be lying buried under the sand waiting to be unearthed,' I said, then nudged the curator and murmured softly in his ear, 'It bodes well for your "discoveries", Walid.'

The words had barely left my mouth when I heard a popping sound. It was almost like a Christmas cracker being pulled or a party popper being let off. I jumped out of my skin. 'What was that?'

Catching a glance of the upper portion of Adam's face in the rear view mirror, I saw his sudden look of panic. He started pumping one of the foot pedals.

'Hold tight!' he called out urgently. 'I've lost the brakes!'

Chapter 12

Wedged as I was between Nabil and Walid on the back seat, there was little I could do but thrust my hands out to brace myself against the back of Adam's driver's seat. Thankfully Ted, sitting in the front passenger seat, was strapped in. Even so, it was a nerve-shredding experience as Adam frantically shifted down through the gears, trying to slow us down for the inevitable impact. He seemed to be having trouble with the steering too. We veered sharply right, and then left as he fought to bring the jeep under control.

Portions of suburban Akhet-Aten jutted from the sand all around us in low-rise stone walls. If we hit any one of them it could rip through the underside of the jeep. Peeking out with my eyes screwed up, I could see Adam aiming for a sand bank directly ahead. 'Hold tight!' he shouted again.

I gripped the backrest in front of me and pressed down hard with my feet to try to secure my position. Even so I jolted wildly forward at the moment of impact. My backside lifted off the seat. I was powerless to prevent myself flying forwards and smacking headfirst into the windscreen. Nabil Zaal saved me in the nick of time, grabbing me forcibly from behind. I thudded back into my seat and let out a loud grunt.

It was a while before I was brave enough to open my eyes. When I did I rather wished I hadn't. 'Adam!' I cried, seeing him slumped forward over the steering wheel. I'd heard of accidents where the impact of the driver slamming into the steering wheel crushed their ribcage and punctured their heart. 'Adam!' I cried again, feeling the grip of hysteria take hold of me. If Adam's heart was punctured he wasn't the only one who'd bleed to death. I'd loved him before our impromptu and private marriage ceremony. But ever since, I'd felt as if my heart had taken up residence inside his chest cavity and was walking around inside of him. Any damage to Adam's heart would kill me too.

'Adam!'

His groan was the sweetest sound I'd ever heard. He slumped backwards in his seat and took a couple of deep breaths.

'Oh, thank God,' I breathed. 'Adam, are you ok?'

'My fault for not strapping myself in,' he grunted. 'Ah well, Merry; I seem to remember you quite liked me with a bruised chest. It can be just like old times.'

I didn't know whether to hug him or hit him. Since neither was especially achievable from the back seat of the jeep, I belatedly turned my attention to my companions, starting with Nabil Zaal on my right.

'Nabil, I think you saved my life. Thank you.'

'It was just an instinctive reaction,' he said, making light of it and rubbing his shins where they'd slammed into the ridge across the bottom of Adam's seat.

Walid, on my left, had adopted the full brace position for impact, with his head between his knees and his arms upraised over his head. As a small, wiry man, this was easier for him. 'No harm done,' he assured me.

Ted, in the front passenger seat was obviously shaken. 'Thank God for seat belts,' he said tremulously. 'Oh dear, I seem to have lost my glasses.'

We found them in the foot-well in front of him once we'd all climbed out of the jeep. Testing for broken bones we found none.

'That could have been a whole lot worse,' I exclaimed in relief. 'What the hell happened?'

Adam was inspecting the jeep. 'That popping sound we heard,' he frowned, 'I think someone inserted a small charging device behind the brake pedal. It acted like a firecracker going off. I think it split the master cylinder, which meant the piston stopped working and all the brake fluid drained out. It's a pretty sure fire way to ensure the brakes fail.'

'This is all my fault,' Nabil said, looking quite devastated. 'My claims have clearly made me some enemies. And it seems these people will stop at nothing to… well… to stop me. But I am sorry, my friends, your lives have been put at risk to serve my own ends. Merry, you tried to warn us...'

'But I didn't think they'd actually go so far as to try to kill us all by sabotaging our vehicle.' It was true, and it made me wonder just how deeply rooted were the hostilities Nabil and his latest theories were stirring up.

'It's clearly unacceptable in some quarters for Akhenaten and Moses to potentially share an identity,' Adam said.

'And I fear this may be just the tip of the iceberg,' Nabil added. 'I can see Christians having just as much trouble accepting an Egyptian pharaoh as the forefather of their religion, as any of these secular groups.'

Walid had wandered a little way away from the crashed jeep while we were talking. 'Look!' he shouted. 'What's this?'

His excitement had us all running. He'd found a stone step revealed by the sand our jeep had sprayed in all directions in its emergency stop. We all fell to our knees and started frantically scraping back the sand with our bare hands.

One stone step led to another, and then another.

'Oh my god, now I know exactly what Howard Carter felt like when that young water-carrier unearthed the first step leading down to Tutankhamun's tomb,' I breathed.

'I don't think we've uncovered a tomb,' Adam commented.

'It looks like a cellar to me,' Ted said with his more trained eye. 'We're in the suburban part of the ancient city. This may well have been the home of one of Akhenaten's nobles.'

'Yes, yes,' said Walid, who also knew what he was talking about. 'I think we are in a private dwelling.'

Adam forgot his bruising and I forgot my swollen and strapped wrist. The only thing we cared about was to discover where the descending stone steps might lead us.

We were lucky that this section of ancient Akhet-Aten was some distance from the main excavation sites. Nobody disturbed us while we worked energetically to uncover the stairway. We were fortunate to be dealing with sand rather than the more solid infill that often needed to be chipped away from the entrance passages to tombs in the Valley of the Kings.

We cleared eight downward steps. And then found a doorway, like a trap door set into the ground that led to a subterranean room. Breaking through, I think we all succumbed to the thrill, or maybe chill, of stepping backwards across perhaps thirty-three centuries to a place left as a freeze-frame of history after the last person locked up and left, back in the days when the city was still occupied. I know I did. Succumb to the thrills and chills, that is.

'Good Lord,' Ted breathed. 'What have we here?'

'I think it's a wine cellar,' Walid posited, looking in all directions at once. 'Look at these jars…'

'And what's this…?' Nabil still had his flashlight hooked to his belt. He'd released it and was penetrating the gloom with the narrow beam of torchlight. 'Is it some kind of box?' He shone his torch-beam on the square object about the size of a shoe box set against the wall in one corner.

We all crowded around. Gingerly, Nabil lifted it and set it on a shelf jutting from the wall. He ran his flashlight over the surface, blowing away centuries' worth of dust at the same time. 'Can you read the inscriptions, Professor?'

Ted squinted over the box, holding his glasses in place on the bridge of his nose with one forefinger. He was a master in philology, the study of ancient languages. 'I'll need to check my reference books to be sure,' he started. 'But to the naked eye, it seems to say something along the lines of… "*I, the servitor of Aten, will follow my Lord on every step of his journey to lead our people out of Egypt. I leave these honours here that my family may make use of them in my absence…*" That's the best I can do' Ted finished.

"*Servitor of the Aten*"?' Nabil repeated on a rising note of excitement. 'This is Panehesy's house?'

'That or one of his close relatives,' Ted agreed, peering back at the inscription set into the lid of the box. 'Yes, his name is here at the top. I think it reads "*Panehesy*". But I'm sure his house has already been excavated. This must belong to a member of his family.'

But Nabil wasn't listening to these conjectures. 'Did you say, *"every step of his journey to lead our people out of Egypt"*?' he pressed.

'That's what it looks like,' Ted agreed.

Nabil looked as if he'd been electrocuted. I'd swear his hair was standing on end. 'You realise what this means...?'

Adam rubbed his bruised chest and then applied his fingertips in a gentle circular motion to his temple and receding black eye. 'This is the clearest proof to date that Akhenaten may have led his people out of Egypt in what's been handed down to us as The Exodus,' he said.

Nabil stared back at him, transfixed with wonder. But I was concerned with more prosaic matters. 'What's inside the box?' I pressed.

Adam looked uncomfortable. 'I'm not sure we should open it up, Merry. We're here on a visitor's permit. We should probably hand it over to the local team.'

Ted saw how hard I was trying to mask my disappointment, and stepped in. 'I think we have the necessary Egyptological credentials between us, especially Walid, Nabil and myself, not to be unduly concerned about protocol. I see no harm in taking a look providing we hand it straight over to the local team of experts straight afterwards.'

We gave Walid the privilege of breaking the seal. He caught his breath and was silent for a long moment, staring into this relic that had survived from antiquity. 'It looks like a golden collar,' he whispered.

I think we were all familiar with this term. Notwithstanding how badly damaged they were, the Amarnan tombs abounded with images of Akhenaten and Nefertiti bestowing honours on their faithful subjects from the Window of Appearances in the Royal Palace. These took the form of neck-braces of pure gold. They were evidently highly prized by their recipients. Whilst the tombs of the nobles we'd visited today were in a poor state of preservation, they all bore scenes of these ceremonies, during which the collars of gold were bestowed upon the loyal subjects of Akhet-Aten. One might almost describe the scenes as mass-produced, so popular did they seem to be. To be fair, the artisans at Akhet-Aten didn't have the back catalogue of traditional religious scenes to draw upon when decorating the tombs. They had to look for inspiration to the everyday scenes being enacted around them in the city. The royal family clearly played an important, if not over-riding, role here. So it was perhaps only to be expected that images of Akhenaten and Nefertiti were to be found plastered all over the walls of the tombs of the people who lived in the virgin city alongside them.

The collar was heavy. Unsurprising perhaps, since it was made of solid gold. Carefully we passed it between us, exclaiming over the workmanship and weight.

But one of our small party had no interest whatsoever in the priceless collar. 'This box proves it,' Nabil breathed. His awed expression hadn't changed. 'Akhenaten led his people out of Egypt, and Panehesy went with him. Panehesy obviously left the gold collar for his family in case they should fall on hard times after he'd gone. It was something they could sell. How wonderful, that they never did! Please... I must take photographs; lots of photographs.' He meant of the box, not the golden collar.

While Nabil busied himself with his camera, the rest of us traded glances. 'We need to find a way to lift the lid on that stone sarcophagus,' Adam murmured in my ear. 'It's the only way we'll know for sure if Nabil is barking up the wrong tree or not.'

We were still exclaiming over our find when a shout from above alerted us we were no longer alone. 'Hey! Are you ok down there...? What have you found...? We saw your jeep embedded in the sand dune at the side of the road... We're coming down...'

I flashed a meaningful glance at Walid. Catching my drift, he thrust one hand into his pocket and drew out a small wrapped object. It was one of Nefertiti's rings, taken from our tomb and wrapped in Walid's handkerchief. He frantically loosened the protective cotton wrapping and flung the ring hurriedly, and with no care at all, among the clay wine jars resting in rows against the wall.

Just in time! Two young people joined us in the wine cellar. They introduced themselves as Steve and Sally from the Amarna Project excavation team.

'My God! What have you found here?' Steve demanded excitedly, once cursory introductions were over.

'It was an accident,' I babbled. Seeing Walid toss the ring among the wine jars had made me ridiculously nervous. I felt as if guilt was writ large across my features. 'We managed to crash the jeep your field director loaned us.' I wasn't sure I was ready to own up to Nabil's anti-Semitic stalkers just yet. 'As we swerved, I think we dislodged the sand covering the foundations of this building. We found a step... which led us here.'

'We think it may have something to do with one of Akhenaten's nobles; a chap called Panehesy.' Adam volunteered.

'Yes, yes,' Steve agreed, his eyes shining with Egyptological fervour. 'This is right alongside what we've so far excavated of Panehesy's house. I think you've simply approached it from the back and broken through into a chamber we hadn't found yet. How thrilling!'

'It looks like a wine cellar,' Sally's excitement matched her colleague's. 'This could be incredibly significant in helping us more accurately date the years of Akhenaten's reign. 'We need to get Barry over here!' Barry was the field director, the man in charge of the Amarna Project.

Within half an hour the small subterranean room was crammed with archaeologists, excavators and Egyptologists, all clamouring for a bit of the action.

We told our story again and again, always omitting the part about the jeep being deliberately sabotaged. I'm not quite sure why we drew a line at telling the whole truth. Perhaps it had something to do with not wanting to reveal too much about Nabil's theories before we'd had a chance to test out how strong an alibi our rebel pharaoh might actually have. Or maybe it was because we didn't want to admit to bringing trouble along with us on our visit here.

We stood back, politely and deferentially, while the experts made their study of the place. Naturally the team took away the golden collar and the box it had been stored within to be properly catalogued and preserved. I was glad Nabil had made good use of the little time he'd had with his camera.

Each of the wine jars was meticulously registered using a hand-held technological device, bigger than a mobile phone but smaller than a tablet. Steve and Sally referred to them as PDAs. Since I'm not especially technology-savvy, I had no idea what this acronym might stand for.

'Hey! What's this?!' Sally called after a while spent bent over among the wine jars. 'I think we have another bezel ring! Flinders Petrie found hundreds of them. This one, unusually, seems to be pure gold!' She was silent for a long moment. 'Oh my goodness, it's inscribed for Nefertiti!'

While we hung back lest our expressions should betray us, everyone else crowded around her for a closer look.

Our hosts proclaimed that Nefertiti must have given Panehesy a ring bearing her cartouche as a token of appreciation in much the same way Akhenaten had bestowed the golden collar upon his loyal subject, the Chief Servitor of the Aten. If that was their expert opinion, who were we to disabuse them?

It was a long time before we returned to the *Queen Ahmes*.

I flopped down on one of the sofas in the air-conditioned lounge-bar. 'Mission accomplished!' I congratulated Walid. 'Nobody suspected for a moment that Nefertiti's ring hadn't been there among the wine jars of Panehesy's cellar since antiquity.'

'The Press will be here in no time,' Adam said encouragingly. 'Walid, it's your big opportunity to lay the groundwork to meet the ransom demand assuming we're not able to get to your blackmailer first.'

But when the TV crew and journalists arrived on the scene a couple of hours later, it was Nabil Zaal they wanted to talk to. The interviews took place in the headquarters building of the Amarna Project, where it was cool, and to give it the kudos of a proper archaeological discovery. An interview on board the *Queen Ahmes* wouldn't have set quite the right academic tone. I considered this a shame since it might have been good for business.

The journalist thrust a Dictaphone under Nabil's nose, and the camera was trained on him. 'Mr Zaal, your recent lecture at the Egyptian Antiquities Museum in Cairo kicked up quite a storm. Your claims have been met with anger and hostility in some quarters. There are those who say you are setting out to prove that certain ancient Egyptian pharaohs were in fact Jewish.'

We'd cautioned Nabil against saying too much, not knowing how dangerous the anti-Jewish group might be, or precisely where they were now. But, for Nabil, the opportunity to speak on prime time TV was simply too good to pass up.

He made a gesture of conciliation with both hands outspread, and smiled. 'My friends, let us be accurate,' he said gently. 'The Jewish religion did not exist at the time of the 18th Dynasty of Pharaonic rule. Like Christianity and Islam, Judaism emerged later. And, as we all know, the Nation of Israel was established only relatively recently. So, to say I am claiming the Amarnan Pharaohs, by which I mean,

Akhenaten, Tutankhamun, Smenkhkare and Ay, were Jewish is to misunderstand me. I would like to emphasise that I mean no disrespect to any of the great faiths of the world. And I certainly have no wish to stir up political unrest. Sadly, there is enough of that in Egypt at the moment as it is. I am an historian and an Egyptologist, in that order. I seek only the truth.'

'But at what cost, Mr Zaal? There are those who would clearly do you harm rather than see you prove your claims. The smoke bomb at the museum was thankfully harmless. But the brakes on your vehicle today were tampered with.'

Adam and I exchanged uncomfortable glances. We were sitting at the back of the room so we could observe proceedings without actually taking part. It seemed investigative journalism was exactly that; intrusive might be another word for it. Our care in keeping the cause of our crash under wraps from the local field team had been for nothing. To be fair, a cursory glance at the jeep's master cylinder was enough to expose the large crack running through it. Things like that didn't happen simply by accident.

'I would like to reassure these people that I mean no harm,' Nabil said equably. 'Further, I would like to ask them to consider their position from a different perspective. Ancient Egypt is credited as the first and finest civilisation in the world. If that civilisation can lay claim to a pharaoh who's beliefs and thinking went on to spawn the major monotheistic religions of the world, surely that is something to be proud of. The fact this pharaoh may have had Hebrew blood in his veins does not make him any less Egyptian. He was equally descended from the mightiest Pharaonic house of them all, the Thutmosides, who made Egypt the first great empire on earth. I think this is something for all Egyptians, whatever their faith or political persuasion, to celebrate, not seek to refute.'

I had to admire him. Nabil Zaal was a man who knew how to think on his feet, and how to play to an audience. If it had been appropriate I might even have applauded. But since this interview was being filmed, discretion remained the better part of valour.

The journalist appeared unmoved by the author's rhetoric. 'There has evidently been a significant find here in Amarna today,' he went on. 'Can we ask if it sheds more light on your identification of historical Akhenaten as Biblical Moses?'

Nabil Zaal met my eyes. We'd coached him to be circumspect. After all, we didn't want him to look a complete fool as and when we were able to announce our tomb and lift the lid off Akhenaten's sarcophagus. In the meantime, I'll admit the wording on the box we'd found containing the golden collar was incredibly suggestive. All the while that tiny seed of doubt remained, sown by Adam's thoughtless use of the word *if*, nothing could be certain.

'Let's just say I am cautiously optimistic,' Nabil said guilelessly.

The interview moved on. Exclamations were made over the gold collar and the field experts from the Amarna Project were able to wax lyrical about the artwork that abounded in the city showing Akhenaten and Nefertiti bestowing these lavish tokens of appreciation upon their loyal subjects.

Finally, Walid was given his opportunity to comment on the gold bezel ring bearing Nefertiti's cartouche. He'd evidently rehearsed what he wanted to say and spoke about finding it among the wine jars with the calm authority I'd observed on previous occasions. 'The quality of the workmanship is superlative,' he finished. 'It gives me much hope that there remains more to be found as the Amarna team here excavate ancient Akhet-Aten out from the sand that has buried it for millennia. Who knows what other treasures from the Amarnan period await discovery, and how they might further illuminate this most fascinating period of Egyptian history? In the meantime, the museum in Cairo will be delighted to have this latest addition to its collection.'

I daresay he had his fingers crossed behind his back the whole time he was speaking.

'And may I ask *your* opinion, Dr Massri, on the possibility that Pharaoh Akhenaten might have led the Biblical Exodus out of Egypt as Moses?'

For the first time, Walid looked flustered. 'I find it an intriguing hypothesis,' he stuttered, 'but one that it will be very difficult to prove.'

'Perhaps if Akhenaten's mummy were to be positively identified...?'

Walid darted a hunted look across the room at Adam and me. His expression put me in mind of a fox who'd unexpectedly found himself clamped in the jaws of a hound and didn't know how to shake free.

Ted, also seated up front as befitted his rank as a long-standing Egyptologist with impeccable credentials, came smoothly to his rescue. 'There are many historians and archaeologists who believe the skeleton found in tomb KV55 in the Valley of the Kings is Akhenaten. DNA testing has proved these remains to be Tutankhamun's father. But if this skeleton is Tutankhamun's father he cannot also be the father of the female mummy known to be Ankhesenamun, since this DNA is close but does not match. Yet we know from the historical record quite unequivocally that Akhenaten was Ankhesenamun's father. Debate still rages, and the prime candidate for the KV55 mummy surely must be Smenkhkare.'

This was either too much information, or possibly too complicated for the journalists to follow.

Ted smiled at them. 'I'm saying I believe Akhenaten's mummy has never been discovered,' he qualified.

'Does that mean, Professor Kincaid, that *you* believe Mr Zaal's claims that Akhenaten was Moses? Perhaps the reason his mummy has not been found is because he was alive when he left Egypt, hence there is no mummy to discover.'

Now it was Ted's turn to meet my gaze momentarily. He covered the look we exchanged under the guise of pushing his glasses back into position on his nose. 'I mean only that Akhenaten's final resting place may yet be out there awaiting discovery,' he said, choosing his words with care.

Adam leaned over and whispered in my ear, 'It will be discovered sooner than anyone may think, if Walid is unsuccessful in silencing that damn blackmailer.'

Adam's comment brought the urgency of our situation sharply back into focus. Time to further explore the remains of the heretic's ancient city was a luxury we didn't have. We needed to get Walid back to Cairo so he could make contact with any private collectors he'd selected for an off-the-record approach. We were still praying it might yet prove unnecessary. So our first priority once we were back on board the *Queen Ahmes* and the journalists had dispersed was to call Ahmed in Cairo. Adam put him on speakerphone so we could both hear him.

Ahmed started speaking almost before we'd finished saying hello. 'My friends, you should know... de man who let off de smoke bomb at de museum was released yesterday wid only a police caution.' He rattled off the words with all the subtlety of a machine gun firing bullets. 'De scarab, it has been recovered and is back on display at de museum. I think Nabil Zaal will be pleased to learn this, yes? And Walid also; he will be glad to have it back at its proper home.'

'The return of the scarab is great news,' Adam agreed.

'But you must be careful,' Ahmed warned urgently. 'Nabil has posted news on his website to say he is in Amarna to make his researches. It is not a long journey from Cairo to Amarna by train. Dese people, dey may follow him dere. You might be in danger!'

'You're right to warn us, Ahmed,' Adam said. 'But I'm sorry to say it comes a little late.' In a few sentences he described the note on the windscreen and the sabotaged brakes.

'You could have been killed!'

'We had a lucky escape.'

I murmured, 'Lucky in more ways than one. Tell him to watch the evening news tonight to see for himself what we unearthed thanks to our little *accident*.'

Ahmed made all the suitable noises, but then took control of the conversation once more. 'And now I have told you de bad news about de released robber of de scarab, I can now tell to you my good news...'

'Ahmed! Your teeth! I'm sorry, mate. It should have been my first question. Are you pleased with your new smile?'

'No, no – I mean, yes, yes. Yes, my friend. Selim has done a very fine job. He is my brother for life and I am a new man! But it is not my toothses to which I refer.'

Ahmed had never mastered pronunciation of the word *teeth*. I let him off since in every other way his English was so vastly improved.

'Oh, when you said *good news* I thought...'

'No! It is even better dan dat.'

Adam and I exchanged a hopeful glance.

'I have carried out my investigations and I have discovered who is dis Abdul who was de second apprentice to Mustafa Mushhawrar.'

'You have?' we both cried out in unison. 'That's really why we're calling,' Adam admitted. 'What have you found out?'

I visualised Ahmed pulling himself up to his full impressive height with self-importance. He gave us the essential information he'd been able to discover about Abdul's identity and current whereabouts.

'His name is Abdul Shehata. I have not been able to arrest him yet as I do not have de evidences to make it stick. But I have my surveillances trained on him!'

We both smiled. 'Ok, we'll be heading back to Cairo tomorrow. We should arrive just in time to see for ourselves the demonstrations against President Morsi as they kick off. Hopefully we can get to this Abdul Shehata before Walid approaches anyone about selling the artefacts.'

I grinned, starting to feel quite optimistic. Things were beginning to fall into place. I reached over and kissed Adam's cheek, then said 'Oh, and we have some news for you, Ahmed!'

'What news is dis?'

Adam took my hand and smiled into my eyes. 'It seems there are some words I need to say in public to make things between Merry and me official.'

'My friends! You are getting married!?'

Adam squeezed my hand, 'To be sure to be sure,' he murmured.

Our captive houseguest Gamal Abdel-Maqsoud was starting to look a little thinner. I daresay his subsistence diet of bread and water might have something to do with it. The swelling from his broken nose was going down but it was quite clear it was healing crookedly. It was his own fault. He should never have hit Adam with the baseball bat.

He looked up with a sullen expression from the bed when Adam unlocked his cabin door and we stepped inside. He might be hungry but he couldn't complain about the temperature. We'd had air conditioning installed at great expense throughout the *Queen Ahmes*. It was pleasantly cool despite the ferocious temperatures outside.

'We've tracked down your friend Abdul Shehata,' Adam announced without preamble.

Gamal's expression was suddenly guarded. This was all the confirmation we needed that Ahmed had identified the correct person. Adam carried on anyway,

'After Mustafa's untimely death, Abdul was transferred to Saqqara to finish his apprenticeship for the Ministry for the Preservation of Ancient Monuments. You were the lucky one promoted to fill Mustafa's shoes. Abdul was the junior apprentice. Perhaps that's why Mustafa sent Abdul, not you, on the wild goose chase to try to recover the stolen necklace. And maybe that's why Abdul was so suspicious about Mustafa's behaviour in the time leading up to his death. It was a stroke of genius to hit on the idea of stealing the strong box from Mrs Mushhawrar when she went to collect it from the bank. Abdul must have thought all his Christmasses had come early when he found the letter inside.'

I coughed meaningfully and Adam caught my drift.

'Ahem, no, you don't celebrate Christmas, do you? Ah well, you know what I mean…'

'I know nothing about a letter.' The sullen expression was back.

'Really? Now that is most interesting. So, tell me Gamal, exactly how much do you know? There might be a hot meal in it for you. We know exactly who Abdul is, and also where to find him. I can assure you, we'll get to him long before you can, so you might as well look after your own interests.'

'I know nothing about a letter.' Then his expression changed. He looked from Adam's face to mine, and back again and seemed to come to a decision. 'Abdul talked with me often about Mustafa's strange behaviour and his troubles trying to get back from the scary lady the necklace Mustafa's cousin Jamal had sold her. But he didn't tell me anything about a letter. When he was transferred to Saqqara near Cairo, he simply told me to keep a watch on the Hathor Chapel and to let him know of any unusual activity there. You are the ones who told me of the letter, and his attempts to blackmail you.'

It was possible this was true, I thought, trying to think back. We'd probably given away far more than we'd intended, assuming he knew far more than perhaps he did.

'And did you?'

'Did I what?'

'Did you let him know when Walid Massri from the Egyptian Museum turned up asking to carry out an impromptu inspection?' Adam pressed.

'I wish I had,' Gamal said dully. 'Then perhaps I could have avoided all this.' He gestured at the cabin to indicate his resentment at his captivity. 'But I decided to see what I could find out for myself first since he was being so secretive.'

Adam stared at Gamal for a long moment as if weighing him up. Then he turned to me. 'You know what, Merry? I'm inclined to believe him. I think you may bring him some dinner on a tray tonight. Now, Gamal, I have some good news for you. We're going to Cairo and you're coming with us. We need to have a few words with your friend. And then we need to decide what we are going to do with you.'

Chapter 13

The five of us – Ted, Walid, Nabil, plus Adam and myself travelled to Cairo by train early the next morning. Speed was of the essence. Silencing Abdul Shehata was our top priority. Ideally we needed to get to him before the mass rallies against President Morsi kicked off on Sunday. These had the potential to make much of Cairo a no-go zone, so we needed to act quickly.

We'd thought we might have some difficulty persuading Nabil Zaal to leave Amarna so soon. But he seemed quite happy to make the trip. His discovery of the box in Panehesy's wine cellar with its intriguing inscription, plus the publicity he'd achieved for his cause in his unexpected television interview seemed enough for him right now. He'd evidently concluded he was unlikely to find anything other scholars had missed in the tombs of ancient Akhet-Aten and declared himself content to rely on the Internet and the museum archives for further research into the new book he planned to write.

Ted, of course, knew of the reason for our urgent need to return to Cairo and so raised no objections about our swift departure. 'I shall continue to study what is known about the

Copper Scroll, and hope we will be able to return for a more leisurely visit in due course,' he said equably.

Thankfully, we received no further threats or communication of any sort from the anti-Jewish group so keen to stop Nabil proving any link between Akhenaten and Moses. We could only hope they'd high-tailed it back from whence they'd come and, having forcibly made their point, might now leave us alone.

We left Khaled to sail the *Queen Ahmes* to Cairo and meet us there. We gave him strict instructions to keep Gamal Abdel-Maqsoud locked in his cabin. We'd relented on Gamal's food rations now we no longer needed him to help us unmask Walid's blackmailer. Having a police officer among our closest friends definitely had its advantages. Gamal was now permitted to share in meals, delivered to him on a tray. Not that he seemed even remotely grateful. Ah well, at least it was a salve for my conscience.

Walid's mobile phone rang while we were still speeding northwards. It was Shukura. We could all hear her quite plainly since she tends to speak excitably and at the top of her voice. There was certainly no need for Walid to put her on speakerphone, although we took the precaution of prevailing on Nabil to fetch us drinks from the dining car before we allowed her gush of words to pour forth.

'My dear, you have received another communication from that despicable blackmailer. I managed to intercept it since I asked for all of your post to be delivered to me in your absence.' Shukura spoke in her high-octane Home Counties English. The accent was courtesy of her Oxford education. The high-octane delivery was a speciality all of her own. 'He demands that you leave the agreed deposit in an envelope behind the sarcophagus of Akhenaten in the forecourt of the museum on Sunday at 3pm.'

Adam and I exchanged a glance. This was the reconstructed sarcophagus, re-assembled from the multitude of bits found smashed in the Royal Tomb at Amarna. I suspected he'd picked it deliberately; to let us know he knew of the other sarcophagus resting with its lid firmly in place in a secret tomb carved into the bedrock behind Hatshepsut's temple on the west bank in Luxor.

'But he gives me no time...' Walid wailed.

'Your journey to Luxor and Amarna has used up a number of valuable days,' Shukura agreed without further comment. This was unusual for her. But then she hadn't been told of our purpose in leaving Cairo. Her abbreviated comment managed to convey disapproval at being left out as well as a question mark that invited us to fill in the blank spaces. She's clever like that.

Ted stepped smoothly into the breach. He'd had a brief dalliance with Shukura many years ago, and knew her well. 'Sunday is when the demonstrations will be at their height in

Tahrir Square,' he said. 'It marks the one-year anniversary of Morsi's election.'

'He told me he would use the anti-Morsi rallies as a cover in his last communication,' Walid reminded us. 'What can I do? There is no way I can raise the down-payment with so little time.'

I put my thinking cap on. 'I suggest you take a photograph of the other ring you took from the tomb and put in in an envelope alongside a newspaper cutting of the interview you and Nabil gave in Amarna yesterday. Perhaps take a photograph of the Nefertiti statue too. Add a short statement to tell him you're now putting out feelers for sale to raise his blackmail demands, but tell him he needs to hold to the original deadline of one month. We need to play for time.'

Everyone agreed this was a reasonable holding strategy as we could be pretty sure no one else would be close to the sarcophagus on Sunday to accidentally stumble across Walid's communication and blow the whistle on us.

'But we need to nab the bastard first,' Adam said.

Ahmed's call came swiftly on the heels of Shukura's and told us the same thing. Abdul Shehata had hand-delivered a note to the museum early this morning and then returned for duty at Saqqara.

'Ok, time to turn the tables,' I smiled as we pulled into the Ramses station in Cairo. 'Wasn't that the expression Gamal Abdel-Maqsoud used?'

A taxi ride was all we needed to transport us from downtown Cairo to Saqqara. We dropped Walid, Nabil and Ted at the museum en route and stared agog at the crowds already massing around Tahrir Square. The atmosphere was more party than protest, but that didn't seem to be the point. 'My goodness, I've never seen so many people in one place,' Ted said, looking alarmed. 'Last time the people took to the streets like this it signalled the end of the Mubarak regime. Things aren't looking good for President Morsi.'

It took ages for our taxi driver to weave his way through the jam-packed streets of downtown Cairo and reach the outskirts. Finally we left the suburban sprawl behind us and drove across the agricultural land towards the ancient burial ground of Saqqara. As well as pre-dating the Valley of the Kings as the Pharaonic necropolis of Memphis, Saqqara is famed for the earliest of all the pyramids, the stepped pyramid of Djoser, conceived and built by the legendary architect Imhotep.

The palm tree-lined open desert was a relief after the dirty, traffic-clogged and people-choked streets of Cairo. I watched the stepped pyramid grow closer as we approached and tried to put my thoughts in order.

'Surely we're not going to approach Abdul Shehata here and now?' I frowned. 'I'm not sure a confrontation while he's on duty is a great idea.'

Adam agreed. 'Ahmed's already here, keeping him under observation. Let's join him and just get a feel for who it is we're dealing with,' he suggested.

Joining Ahmed in his hired and nondescript car, we first remarked on our police buddy's new teeth.

'Ahmed! You look amazing!' I pronounced. It was true. His megawatt smile was transformed into one of radiant perfection. Ahmed had always been a good-looking man. Now, he was stunning, head-turning, show-stopping – you choose the expression. The combination of flashing dark eyes, a seal-like cap of black hair and even white teeth, set in a walnut brown skin was quite a sight to behold, despite his size. I found myself wondering if I weren't so madly in love with Adam…

I severed the thought abruptly. Ahmed would make some woman, some day, a fine partner or husband. But that woman was most definitely not myself. Still, I think it can never hurt to appreciate the physical attributes of the opposite sex when such an opportunity presents itself. I smiled at Ahmed and paid him the compliments he both expected and deserved.

Ahmed accepted these as his due, grinning and trying, unsuccessfully, to look modest. Then he became serious. 'Abdul Shehata delivered de note to de museum early dis morning,' he told us 'He walked as bold as brass up to de guards at de entrance and handed over de note addressed to

Walid.' He shielded his eyes with his hand, looked towards the stepped pyramid and let out an exclamation. 'Ah, yes, I can see him now. Dat individual; it is he.'

He pulled a pair of binoculars from the glove compartment and handed them to Adam, pointing towards the administration buildings close to the ticket office at the entrance to the ancient burial ground. Left to fend for myself, I squinted against the bright sunshine and followed the direction Ahmed was indicating.

'But he's little more than a boy!' Adam exclaimed.

Narrowing my glance on the slim, youthful frame of our blackmailer I saw what Adam meant. He was a slip of a thing, surely barely into his twenties. I raked my memory for the only time I'd caught sight of him during his stalker days trying to rob Eleanor of the necklace she'd bought from Jamal Mushhawrar. I'd caught a glimpse of him legging it from the shrine where the mummified crocodiles were displayed at the Kom Ombo temple. Eleanor claimed he'd ravaged her. But in truth he'd merely been trying to ascertain if she was wearing the sought after necklace when he accosted her and pulled the collar of her blouse apart. My impression back then had been one of youthful opportunism, too. Perhaps it was his stock in trade – an immature confidence that if he kept trying, the odds would eventually turn in his favour. He'd certainly met more than his match in the redoubtable Eleanor. I could only hope we'd prove more than a match for him too.

Watching Abdul Shehata from our position obscured behind other vehicles at the back of the car park, it became obvious he was about to leave. He called out a comment to a colleague who followed him out of the administration building, and then raised his hand in a farewell salute, striding towards us.

'What do we do?' I asked. 'Do we follow him? Or should we attempt to intercept him now?'

His colleague locked up the building, and started more slowly to follow Abdul down the path.

'I don't think we can risk a confrontation now,' Adam said, lowering the binoculars. 'We're too far from anywhere and I don't think we want a witness. Besides, he's unlikely to have Mustafa's letter with him while he's at work. It looks as if they're shutting up shop for the day here. Probably sensible in view of what's about to kick off in Cairo. And it's patently obvious there are no visitors here today. I suggest we trail him and see where he goes.'

'He lives in de Heliopolis district, not far from de presidential palace,' Ahmed informed us. 'It may be worth us visiting him dere later. We can have de element of de surprise, yes?'

Abdul Shehata jumped on a moped, fired it up and sped out of the car park in a cloud of dust. Moving at a rather more sedate pace, we followed him in the hire car, with

Ahmed at the wheel, Adam in the front passenger seat and me in the back.

As expected, the young opportunist headed into Cairo and turned towards Heliopolis. We hung back at a safe distance so he didn't suspect us of following him.

'I don't see how we can possibly hope to trail him through these traffic jams when he's on a moped and we're in a car,' I said in frustration, losing sight of him as he threaded between two lines of stationary cars and then zipped down a side street.

'It is of no matter,' Ahmed reassured me. 'I know de place where de young rascal lives. I followed him dere yesterday.'

It took us nearly an hour to get there. Crowds surged in the streets creating gridlock.

'Where the hell are all these people going?' I burst out, gaping at the tens of thousands of people swarming through the city. 'Tahrir Square is on the other side of town.'

'They've come to demonstrate outside the presidential palace,' Adam guessed. 'Didn't you say it was in this suburb, Ahmed?'

'My friends, I fear we must leave de car and walk de rest of de way,' Ahmed said by way of reply. 'It is not far.'

We had little choice but to abandon the car by the roadside. It was impossible to find a space to park it properly. Most people were using their cars to support their rally cry, virtually standing on the horns. The noise was incessant and unbearable.

I clung to Adam's hand and we followed closely behind Ahmed as our big friend cut a swathe through the massing throngs. He was dressed in a crisp white galabeya rather than his police uniform. Even so, his physical stature and purposeful air issued a warning against getting in his way. I was grateful. There was a very real danger of being crushed. Crowds pressed around us on all sides, with much shouting, chanting and banner waving. Although generally good-natured in tone, it was really quite intimidating. I had no doubt I'd be trampled underfoot if I fell. It was a heaving mass of pushing and pulling humanity. Adam kept a fast hold on me and we moved as quickly as we could with our heads down, eyes focused on Ahmed's broad back in front of us.

Finally Ahmed stopped. 'Dis apartment block here,' he pointed across the packed street and raised his voice so we could hear him. 'Dis is de place.'

It was a nondescript concrete building rising to about ten floors with tiny balconies overlooking the street, very similar to all the others in the vicinity. I kept a tight hold on Adam's hand and tried for a better look. It was nigh on impossible to stand still. The surging crowd carried us further along the street. It was a bit like riding a wave.

Ahmed spied a small side alleyway where refuse bins were stored. He pulled us into it with him, a momentary release from the crushing melee swarming towards the presidential palace with their banners at the ready.

'Phew!' Adam exclaimed, wiping perspiration from his top lip with the back of his shirtsleeve. 'I was starting to feel a bit claustrophobic hemmed in on all sides like that. It's a struggle to breathe, don't you think?'

'I hate crowds,' I agreed. 'I remember Dan almost broke things off with me one year when he bought me tickets to see Robbie Williams at Wembley. I felt so panicky with the audience leaping and jumping all around me we had to leave early. I didn't think he'd ever forgive me. The tickets cost a fortune. And Dan doesn't even much like Robbie Williams!'

Adam looked at me disapprovingly. 'To compare Egypt's national crisis to a Robbie Williams pop concert! Merry! I'm surprised at you! Where's your sense of proportion?'

I knew he was ribbing me, helping ease the stress of finding ourselves enmeshed in the street demonstrations. Even so, I felt chided, and rightly so. My comment had been fatuous. But in reality this was exactly the same feeling I'd experienced at the concert. This breathless, frightening sense of being caught up in something frenzied and a bit out of control.

'What's the plan?' I asked, deciding it might be a good idea to change the subject and refocus on the task at hand. Looking back out onto the street was a bit like looking at a river that had burst its banks. Only it was a flood of people rather than water surging past. 'Do we knock on his door and attempt to reason with him? Somehow I don't see him handing over the letter without a fight.'

'I wasn't expecting him to be such a kid...' Adam started and trailed off. One look at his face was enough to tell me he relished the thought of perpetrating violence against the young ruffian about as much as he'd like to throw himself under the feet of the passing masses.

Ahmed gave a sudden shout. 'Look! Dere he is!'

Adam and I were just quick enough to spy the youthful Abdul Shehata leap down the steps in front of his apartment block and join the throng pressing forwards towards the presidential palace.

'He's going to join the demonstrations!' I cried unnecessarily. The wooden placard Abdul held clasped between both hands made what he was doing abundantly clear.

The three of us stared at each other in consternation.

'Now what?' I demanded of neither Adam nor Ahmed in particular.

Adam came to a quick decision. 'Ahmed, follow him!' he ordered. 'Merry, you and I are going to do a quick sweep of his flat while the coast is clear. Ahmed, which number is it?'

Ahmed gave us the essential information and thrust himself back into the crowd. It immediately swallowed him up.

I could just about see his head, since he was so much taller than those massing around him.

Adam grabbed my hand. 'Deep breath, Merry,' he advised. And then we, too, plunged back into the noisy, jostling torrent of humanity.

It was no easy task to fight our way against the oncoming swarm of people. I didn't care to count the number of times I was bumped, kicked or shoved by those whose path we were blocking. I wouldn't go so far as to say any of this was intentional. We were simply a pair of salmon swimming against the tide. But finally we pushed our way to the other side; breaking free of the stream of people as we reached the steps we'd just seen Abdul Shehata descend with his placard.

Luckily for us, Abdul's flat was on the ground floor. Perhaps more fortunate still, it was at the back of the building, overlooking a scrubby yard and out of sight of onlookers. Our third stroke of good luck was finding the window partially open, secured with an old-fashioned lever Adam was easily able to break.

He gave me a leg up so I could crawl through the window space and tumble inside. He climbed in behind me a moment later.

Straightening, we surveyed young Abdul Shehata's living quarters. To call this a flat or apartment was massively to over-inflate its proportions. It was actually little more than a bedsit, and a rather squalid one at that. There was a single mattress on the floor topped with a grubby pillow and a sleeping bag. A small fridge hummed noisily in one corner. The only items of furniture were a wardrobe and small chest of drawers. There was a sink, which looked as if it doubled both as a kitchen and bathroom facility, a toaster, kettle, and a stack of plates. Tables, chairs and any kind of soft seating were notable by their absence. The poster of Michael Jackson taped amid the peeling paintwork on the wall struck a rather incongruous note.

Nodding at it Adam commented, 'I prefer his taste in music to yours, Merry; for all that I doubt he was even out of nappies when MJ was topping the charts. Robbie Williams indeed!'

I gazed about me feeling more than a little depressed. This was no way to live, even for a kid of little more than student age. 'I can understand why he wants the money,' I said. 'And despite his almost laughable lack of success in getting the necklace back from Eleanor, he must have some talent. Judging by Mustafa Mushhawrar and Gamal Abdel-Maqsoud, they don't employ idiots at the Ministry for the Preservation of Ancient Monuments.

'Hmm, somewhere along the line he evidently learned something about snake charming,' Adam remarked, remembering the final showdown with his sister-in-law.

'And his detective-work piecing together the reasons for Mustafa's strange behaviour was pretty impressive,' I added.

'As you said, it was a stroke of genius for him to hit upon the idea of stealing the strongbox from Mrs Mushhawrar.'

'Was it a stroke of genius for him to hit on the idea of blackmailing Walid, too?' he asked, narrowing his eyes on my face.

'No, of course not; but I can't help but think it shows an enterprising spirit.'

'Careful, Merry; you'll have me either admiring him or feeling sorry for him, and I'd rather not feel anything about him at all if it's all the same to you.' But I saw his eyes dart towards the wall poster. Catching sight of the youngster attempting to blackmail Walid, and now seeing the pathetic place he lived, humanised him somehow.

'Shame about the cut-and-paste ransom demands,' I said. 'Perhaps they were our clue to his youth and naïveté. I always thought them a crude and rather unoriginal way of communicating.'

'But effective,' Adam muttered. 'Now, Merry; to work... If you were a twenty-something kid, where would you hide your collateral to keep it safe?'

'You mean Mustafa's letter?'

'Of course, Mustafa's letter! What else?'

'Just checking. Well, under the bed, I guess...'

We turned the mattress upside down, unsurprised if a bit repulsed when a few cockroaches scuttled out from underneath it; then turned the pillow out of its dirty pillowcase and inspected the seams. We put the sleeping bag through a similar inspection.

'Inside the fridge?' I suggested instead.

'Nope,' Adam confirmed, wincing at the smell and slamming the door closed again. 'Some rancid cheese; and milk that's going the same way. I assume he lives on Kentucky Fried Chicken.' The empty carton in the bin did seem rather to uphold this view, so we moved on with our search.

'Behind the poster?' I suggested.

'Nothing.' Adam re-taped Michael Jackson to the wall.

We hunted through the wardrobe and chest of drawers, checking for secret panels or an envelope taped to the undersides of the pull-out drawers. There was nothing in the pockets of any of the items of clothing we rooted through; not that this took us long. Abdul Shehata clearly hadn't the means to pursue fashion. Apart from the clothes he was standing up in, he possessed just a couple of pairs of jeans, a few shirts, a modest collection of T-shirts and some boxer shorts. I wondered to what extent this might change should he prove successful in securing his ransom money from Walid, whether in full or in part. Ten million Egyptian pounds could buy a heck of a lot of pairs of designer jeans and the fancy tops to match.

Frustrated, Adam and I stood in the middle of the room and took stock. 'There's a shared bathroom down the corridor,' Adam said, having checked. 'He won't risk leaving it there.'

'So where…?' I asked, scanning the meagre contents of the room once more.

'He must have it with him,' Adam concluded.

'But wouldn't you expect him to have taken copies?'

'Maybe he has a lockable pedestal at work,' Adam conjectured. 'P'raps we should have broken in there instead.'

Alerted by a sudden noise outside the door, Adam grabbed me and we froze. I barely had time to think that surely Ahmed would have warned us if either he'd lost sight of our quarry in the crowd or, worse, if he suspected Abdul Shehata was coming home. He had Adam's mobile phone number, and mine; and we had both phones with us.

There was no time for us to escape back through the window. With an almighty kick from the other side, the front door flew open, swinging off its hinges after it smacked into the wall.

Ahmed stood there covered in blood. In his arms he was carrying a slight and inert form. Blood-soaked wasn't adequate to describe the horrific state of this individual. Even so, it took less than a moment to identify Abdul Shehata.

'He is badly hurt,' Ahmed declared unnecessarily, striding into the room.

'Ahmed, what the hell happened?' Adam demanded, recovering himself more quickly than me.

'We failed to read de words printed on de placard he carried,' our police pal said sadly. 'Young Abdul Shehata here, he is a pro-Morsi supporter.'

'You mean, he stepped out there into that rioting mob all baying for Morsi's blood and sought to defend the president's democratic right to rule?' I cried.

'He found himself in de minority,' Ahmed confirmed. 'Outside de presidential palace de protests dey turned ugly. Some people burned an effigy of Mohamed Morsi and clashes broke out between de supporters and de opponents of de president. At first it was just fighting. And den dey started using knives. De army did not want to intervene for fear dey would be accused of taking de sides. And dat is when de gunfire it started. I tried to get to Abdul to pull him away. But someone dey threw a grenade at de supporters of Morsi trying to block de entrance to de palace. It blew up right in front of dis young man's face.'

I could see that.

While he'd been talking, Ahmed knelt down and laid his badly injured charge on the pitiful mattress at our feet.

'You should have taken him straight to hospital,' Adam said.

'Dere was no point,' Ahmed said, looking grim. 'Look at him. He is not going to make it.'

Frankly, I'd rather have looked just about anywhere else. But it was impossible to look away.

'Damn Mustafa Mushhawrar to Hell,' I said bitterly, feeling sick. 'This young man didn't deserve the fate that bastard set him out on.'

Of all the possible outcomes to the blackmail scenario, this was the last I could possibly have envisaged. Standing here, it was the last I wanted. When I thought how casually we'd talked about silencing him, I felt quite ill with disgust. Despite the number of dead bodies we'd amassed during our adventures in Egypt, I'd never witnessed death at close hand before. It was hideous, and humbling.

'We should have let him have the damn money,' Adam muttered bitterly.

'Or let him blow the whistle on our tomb,' I added.

Somehow, against the loss of this young life, neither the money nor the tomb seemed worth it.

Young Abdul Shehata survived barely half a minute outside of Ahmed's arms. I thought back to the young stowaway who'd stalked Eleanor so unsuccessfully from the *SS Misr* and felt my eyes pool with tears.

Adam turned away, bringing his emotions under control. 'Well, he's not going to blow the whistle on our tomb now,' he said tightly. 'Best get on the phone to Walid and have him put a stop to any feelers he's been putting out.'

Ahmed was the one who took it upon himself to conduct the body search that confirmed Abdul Shehata was not carrying Mustafa's letter about his person.

'We'd better take him to the morgue or the hospital, or somewhere,' I said a bit desperately. 'We can't leave him here.'

Ahmed was the one who took on this task too. It's easy sometimes to see Ahmed as a bit of a buffoon. But when the chips are down he's a man I'd want in my corner any day of the week.

Adam and I went back to stay with Shukura and Selim that night. I think we wanted to be among friends. We shared their daughter's room, since Ahmed was on a camp bed in their boys' bedroom.

Laying alongside each other in the darkness, we held hands and shared the sorrow. Silence was best. There were no words to do justice to what had happened today.

'Damn Egypt and its fledgling democracy,' Adam muttered.

Since I knew he didn't really mean this, but also knew exactly what he meant, I squeezed his hand, and said nothing.

Next day, we managed to fight our way through the crowds converging on Tahrir Square, to join Walid at the museum.

His relief was palpable. But even Walid could only regret the loss of life that had led to his release. 'That poor young man,' was all he said.

It was probably one of the strangest days of my life. From the window of Walid's office we watched hundreds of thousands of people converge on Tahrir Square. The feeling of the whole world watching Egypt's unfolding political drama was overwhelming.

Just before 3pm Ahmed joined us. He'd been out to Saqqara to give Abdul Shehata's colleagues the tragic news of his death, and also to check through the young man's personal belongings.

'I finded de box he robbed from Mother Mushhawrar,' he declared, holding it aloft.

I let out a huge puff of relief. But Ahmed had only paused for breath.

'But de letter of Mustafa Mushhawrar, it has disappeared into de thin air,' he finished. 'It is not inside de box!'

We crowded around to see for ourselves. Of course, Ahmed was right. There was some cash, a passport and a few small items of jewellery. One appeared to be an engagement ring.

'Abdul didn't even spend the cash,' I said in a choked voice. Somehow this really got to me. 'He was happy to blackmail Walid for millions but wouldn't spend the few hundred Egyptian pounds he stole from a crippled old lady.'

Adam took my hand and squeezed it. 'Ah well, at least Mrs Mushhawrar can now have back her son's few bits and pieces.'

'But where is the letter?' Walid asked desperately. 'Why wasn't it in the box?'

Since none of us could offer an explanation, nobody answered.

We fell silent as the clock struck three. In a different reality Walid would, even now, be outside, placing the envelope beside Akhenaten's reconstructed sarcophagus for Abdul Shehata to retrieve later.

I wished we could perhaps have lived out this alternative scenario to preserve the young man's life. But I had no idea how we might have silenced him if we had. So perhaps events had taken their pre-ordained course and natural justice had been served.

I'm not one usually given to philosophical musings. This was possibly just as well since, on this occasion, they were cut short. It was Adam's mobile phone that rang, not mine, but it cut into my thoughts just the same.

Adam listened intently, and then stared at me in horror. 'It's Khaled. Gamal Abdel-Maqsoud ambushed and attacked him, and then threw him off the *Queen Ahmes*. My God, we need to get to the docks! There's no knowing what he might do!'

Chapter 14

It took us forever to get to the river. The demonstrations against President Morsi were in full swing, not just in Tahrir Square but in locations right across the city. Horns honked, loudspeakers blared and people were letting off fireworks even though it wasn't yet dark. The noise was deafening.

Finally we made it. Khaled leapt up from some stone steps where he'd been sitting with his head in his hands. Blood oozed from a gash above his right eye, although he'd done his best to clean the wound. And he was drip-drying having been quite recently soaking wet. 'I am so sorry, my friends,' he started.

'Khaled, what happened?' I cried in distress.

'I took Gamal his lunch on a tray,' he explained, dripping onto the decking boards that lined the marina as he spoke. 'But he was waiting behind the door of his cabin. As I went through, he smashed the door back in my face. Hot soup spilled all over me.' This much was evident from the bright stains all down the front of him, which his dunking in the Nile had failed to wash away. 'Scalded, I let out a yell, dropped the tray and tried to grab him. But he was too quick for me. By the time I recovered my wits, he'd made it to the kitchen and armed himself with one of the butchers knives.'

Khaled looks like an Egyptian, albeit with blue eyes. But he speaks like a Scot, courtesy of mixed-race parentage.

'Are you alright?' I asked in concern.

'I daresay I'll live,' he said with an ironic lift to his eyebrow. A fresh trickle of blood spilled from the wound above it. He wiped his eye with the antiseptic wipe I handed him. 'But that young man needs whipping,' he added. 'He pointed the knife at me and when I tried to wrestle it away from him, he jabbed it at me, as you can see.'

'Khaled, you could have lost an eye,' I exclaimed in horror.

'The gush of blood blinded me for a moment. He used the opportunity to manhandle me outside and fling me overboard. I tell you; when I get hold of that young man I won't be held responsible for my actions!'

Ahmed growled like an angry bear. But it was Adam who asked the essential question. 'Is he still onboard the *Queen Ahmes*?'

Khaled gestured along the river. 'He has at least an hour's lead on us.'

Spanned with bridges and bordered with high-rise buildings on both banks, the Nile in Cairo was more like the Thames in London than the mighty river cutting through either desert or lush vegetation on both sides that I was more used to.

'We have to follow him!' I cried.

Ahmed was already on the move, off to hire a boat.

'Does he have the sails unfurled?' Adam asked urgently.

'No, he'll need to use the motor. I'd rolled in the sails once we reached Cairo since we'd have the wind against us for the journey back to Luxor, and it's against the flow of the current.'

'Oh my God, he'll run her aground or crash her into a bridge, or collide with another vessel and capsize her!' I wailed. 'Does he even *know* how to sail a dahabeeyah?'

'He'll be alright if he stays towards the centre of the river,' Khaled said. 'The traffic out on the Nile today is mostly further downtown to join in the political demonstrations. And he won't need to steer between any sandbanks until he's much further upriver. It's fitted with cruise control. Don't worry, it takes a lot to capsize a dahabeeyah.'

But how could I not worry? Our new nemesis, this Gamal Abdel-Maqsoud, had control of our most prized possession, the *Queen Ahmes*. He'd turned the tables on us once more. We had to stop him.

Whether Ahmed used his sheer physical stature, his new beaming megawatt smile, his police badge or his wallet to secure us a boat I didn't ask. Perhaps it was a combination of the lot. I was just delighted to see the keys dangling from his outstretched hand when he returned an agonising few minutes later. With every moment that passed the gap widened between Gamal aboard the *Queen Ahmes* and us in the Cairo marina hopping impatiently from one foot to the other.

It was a motorised cabin cruiser rather than the speedboat I'd have preferred. Even so, it was a good deal faster than the dahabeeyah.

'We'll catch her in no time!' Khaled approved. He took the wheel as we jumped on board.

Dusk was descending as we pulled away from the mooring platform and set off in pursuit of the *Queen Ahmes*. Fireworks exploded overhead as we steered along the Nile. The people of Cairo remained out in force, ensuring the attention of the world was focused on their demands to remove the president. As for us, we just wanted our boat back.

I sat on the bulkhead at the front of the cruiser with my legs crossed and my arms folded, nervously kicking one foot up and down and scanning the river ahead of me for a first glimpse of the dahabeeyah. Adam was alongside me in a similarly fraught pose. Ahmed was pacing the deck, bemoaning the fact he'd had his gun confiscated when he was suspended from his police duties in Luxor. 'De man needs shooting,' he mumbled. 'First to imprison you in de tomb, and now to steal de dahabeeyah. He is a menace and should be locked up!'

It was almost dark when my straining eyes picked out a familiar shape up ahead. We were out in the suburbs now, sailing past Giza. The pyramids were way off in the distance. The main city of Cairo was far behind us, with fireworks still lighting the skyline in flashes of brilliance. 'There!' I shouted, jumping up. 'There she is!'

The relief at seeing the dahabeeyah the right way up and all in one piece was overwhelming. I had to sit back down again in case my legs gave way beneath me.

Khaled steered the boat as close alongside the *Queen Ahmes* as we dared. 'Hey! Gamal Abdel-Maqsoud!' Adam shouted, cupping his hands around his mouth. 'Come out so we can talk to you!'

The cabin cruiser was fitted with floodlights, which Khaled now switched on. They did their job well, literally flooding the dahabeeyah with light. If he hadn't heard, there was no way Gamal could pretend not to have noticed. We could see him in the engine room at the waterline at the back of the boat. He looked like a startled rabbit in headlights, which was all well and good.

'Come out!' Adam shouted again. 'Just hit the autocruise button! It's on your right!'

Shading his eyes against the glare of the lights trained on him, Gamal left the engine room and climbed the spiral staircase at the back, which led up onto the deck. Ahmed took this as his cue to join Khaled at the controls of the cabin cruiser, out of sight.

'You can do nothing!' Gamal shouted across to us. 'I have your boat and I am not giving her up!'

Adam grunted at me, 'Ahmed's right; his gun would have proved pretty handy right now. We could have just shot the bastard.' Then he cupped his mouth in his hands and raised his voice again. 'Ok Gamal, you win! We're willing to enter into negotiations. Let us have our dahabeeyah back and we'll tell you about the tomb!'

'No deal!' Gamal yelled back. 'You will trick me! At every turn, you trick me!'

Even as Gamal shouted this accusation at us, Ahmed was lowering himself silently into the Nile from the back of the boat. Since Gamal had never met Ahmed and knew nothing about him seeing as our police pal had been in Cairo for the duration of our previous battles, it seemed a good idea to use Ahmed as the element of surprise while we kept Gamal distracted up on deck.

'No tricks!' Adam called back. 'Just a fair exchange. Our boat for a share in the most spectacular tomb ever discovered.'

'Tell me about the tomb now,' Gamal shouted. 'I want to know about those round discs you used to gain entry.'

'Why don't you let us on board so we can talk about it properly?' Adam traded.

'You will not set foot on this boat until you have told me what I want to know! Whose tomb is it?'

Off to the side, I caught sight of Ahmed slowly doggy paddling his way towards the dahabeeyah. Until very recently, Ahmed had not been able to swim. He'd been so embarrassed by this inadequacy on a recent occasion when Adam had been forced to rescue him from drowning, he'd made it a priority to rectify the situation. He'd been taking lessons for weeks. It was fair to say he wasn't a natural. But his splashing wasn't bad enough to attract Gamal's attention, since our opponent wasn't expecting to see anyone in the dark waters of the Nile.

'I will not tell you anything more about the tomb until we're safely back on board,' Adam parried loudly.

'So, we have a stalemate,' Gamal called back. 'Isn't that what you say in English? So what, I wonder, will it take to break it? Ah, I have an idea!'

'I don't like the sound of that,' I muttered to Adam. 'Sounds like a threat to me.'

Sure enough, Gamal spun away from the handrail and seemed to be searching for something. He was back a moment later, holding a long object aloft.

'It looks like a rolled-up newspaper,' I frowned. I kept a wide range of magazines, newspapers and journals in a basket on the sundeck. 'Adam! My God! What does he think he's doing?'

Gamal produced a cigarette lighter from his pocket. As we watched in horror he flicked it alight and held the small flame to the top of the newspaper. It immediately caught light and blazed brightly as he held it up.

'Aha! Who has the upper hand now?' he shouted. 'Tell me whose tomb it is or I will set your beautiful dahabeeyah alight!'

'Don't you dare!' Adam bellowed.

'So, tell me about the tomb,' Gamal repeated, waving the burning newspaper towards the cushioned sunloungers up on deck. Just about everything on board the *Queen Ahmes* was made of wood, including the beams and rafters of the lovely old dahabeeyah herself.

I heard the horrified shout Khaled let out behind me. He'd painstakingly restored the dahabeeyah to her former Victorian splendour. I knew if Gamal carried out his threat he'd make an enemy for life.

'No!' I screamed as the tip of the fiery newspaper touched the fabric of one of the reclining steamers. It immediately blazed and caught light. Damn Egypt, and its bone-dry climate. The whole thing would go up like a tinderbox in moments if we couldn't put out the flames.

'Don't be a fool, man!' Adam yelled. 'You'll burn to death along with it!'

'Tell me about the tomb!' Gamal barked back, madly waving the burning embers of what little remained of the newspaper. Sparks flew in all directions, immediately bursting alight where they made contact with anything (and let's face it; that was just about everything) flammable.

I nearly fainted clean away at the sight of my beloved dahabeeyah in flames. The only thing that stopped me was the glorious sight of Ahmed hauling himself over the railings on the lower deck. But he still had the spiral staircase to negotiate in his soaked galabeya.

Adam didn't waste another second. Diving into the water he started to swim. The splash behind me told me Khaled had done the same.

I darted to the controls. But Khaled had taken care of things. We were dropped at anchor. The only problem this gave us was that the dahabeeyah, set on autocruise, was moving further and further away.

I contemplated leaping into the Nile too. But actually found myself quite powerless to tear away my terrified gaze from the blazing dahabeeyah. Ahmed had made it onto the upper deck. He was engaged in an out and out fight with our foe, trading punches back and forth as they both hopped around the blazing sunloungers. Ahmed was bigger and stronger. And I knew him to be remarkably light on his feet for such a heavy man. But Gamal had youth and fitness on his side. I watched in agony while they danced around each other, each looking for a chance to land a killer blow. And, in the meantime, the dahabeeyah was burning.

I let out a huge grunt of relief as I saw first Adam and then Khaled, following closely behind him, heave themselves out of the water onto the dahabeeyah's lower platform. Leaving Gamal to Ahmed, Adam darted up the spiral staircase and grabbed the hose secured against the handrail. We used it to wash down the decks every day. Khaled followed close behind with a bucket. Putting out the fire was all they cared about.

I sagged onto the cruiser's bench and watched, limp with relief, as Adam and Khaled doused the flames.

Gamal suddenly realised he risked being outnumbered three-to-one. Picking up one of my brass planters, he hurled it at Ahmed's head. I screamed and Ahmed ducked. But it was the distraction our adversary wanted. Spinning around, he shoved Adam bodily against Khaled sending them both sprawling. Then he climbed up on the railing, clamped his fingers around his broken nose and jumped feet-first into the Nile, landing with a loud splash.

I darted to the side of the boat, waiting to catch sight of him when he resurfaced. I wished I had a handy rock I could throw at his head when he did. Long moments ticked by and the waters smoothed over again where he'd landed in the river.

'Where'd he go?' Adam shouted across at me from the dahabeeyah.

'I don't know! I don't think he's come up yet!'

We continued to stare at the inky waters of the Nile, me from the cabin cruiser, Adam from the smoking dahabeeyah. Khaled had darted to the engine room and jammed on the brakes. The *Queen Ahmes* was resting now at anchor too.

Adam ran across the deck to the railing on the other side and scanned the water. I did the same, just in case Gamal had somehow managed to swim right underneath the cabin cruiser. There was enough light from the floodlights to illuminate a good stretch of river on both sides. I raked the riverbank and the expanse of water between it and me for any sign of movement. There was none.

'He's vanished!' I shouted.

'But that's impossible!' Adam yelled back. 'Unless he's drowned!'

'Please God!' I prayed fervently.

We waited and waited to see if Gamal would suddenly reappear. But the surface of the Nile remained smooth and unruffled all around us.

Khaled and Ahmed were taking stock of the damage caused by the fire.

'I can't stand this,' I muttered. Pausing only to slip off my shoes, I dived into the water.

I half expected to encounter a drifting body as I swam out through the cold water. But nothing hindered my progress. Soon I too was hauling myself onto the little platform at the back of the *Queen Ahmes*. It wasn't the first time I'd boarded her this way. Muttering a few imprecations against those who dared debar us from our own dahabeeyah, I joined the others up on deck, dripping with Nile river water as I went.

'It could be a lot worse, Merry.' Adam soothed as I burst into tears. 'The steamers and rugs can all be replaced.'

'I can sand down the floorboards and re-varnish them,' Khaled added.

'A bit of charred woodwork, well it just adds to de charm,' Ahmed said, looking anguished to see me in such distress.

'At least the damage is just up here on deck,' I nodded, sniffing and wiping my eyes with the back of my hand. 'Thank God it didn't take hold enough to set alight to the interiors.'

'We'll have it as right as rain in no time,' Khaled promised.

I couldn't bring myself to leave the dahabeeyah, and I think Adam felt the same. So Khaled swam back to the cabin cruiser. We swung both boats around and headed slowly back towards Cairo, keeping a sharp lookout for a swimmer or a drifting body en route, but saw nothing.

Cairo didn't sleep that night. The mass demonstrations continued well beyond first light. Next morning, we met up with Nabil, Ted and Walid in the lobby of The Four Seasons Hotel, where Nabil was staying.

'The American Embassy wishes to repatriate its citizens currently staying in Egypt,' he informed us. 'I am booked onto a flight home this afternoon.'

I looked at Adam in dismay. 'Please don't tell me the British Foreign Office is going to do the same and order us home.'

He powered up his iPad and flicked through a couple of screens. 'British citizens are advised against all but essential travel,' he read aloud. 'But there are no repatriation orders as yet.'

'Thank God!' I breathed.

'The American Consulate is responding to the death of that poor student during the protests in Alexandria last week,' Nabil explained.

Like most of the people sitting around in the lobby, our eyes kept darting to the big flat-screen television mounted against the wall. It was set to the BBC World Service News Channel, with a red bar of text scrolling continuously across the bottom of the screen. The sound was muted. But the pictures were all flashing images of the huge anti-Morsi rallies held in Cairo and across Egypt yesterday.

'The Aljazeera News Channel reported almost a million people took to the streets of Cairo yesterday,' Ted said. 'And something like four million across the country.'

Adam was scanning the News on his iPad. 'Earlier this morning anti-Morsi protesters ransacked the national headquarters of the Muslim Brotherhood in Mokattam, here in Cairo,' he said. 'It says here the protesters threw objects at windows and looted the building, making off with office equipment and documents. The health ministry has confirmed the deaths of eight people killed in the incident. My God, it's getting worse!'

Even as we sat there, a newsflash appeared on the screen above us. I read aloud, 'The military has delivered a nationwide television and radio statement giving both President Morsi's government and the opposition a 48-hour ultimatum to resolve the political crisis and meet the people's demands. Or else it says the armed forces will intervene to restore order.'

'Clashes between the pro- and anti-Morsi factions are growing increasingly violent,' Adam added, still looking at his iPad and shaking his head. 'So far more than thirty people across Cairo are reported to have lost their lives.'

The hideous image of Abdul Shehata's bloodied body flashed across my mind and I shuddered. 'Perhaps we should head back to Luxor sooner rather than later. The Foreign Office advice is aimed at tourists, not those of us living here. I don't see things settling down here over the next few days. And I have no desire to see more blood shed on the streets.'

'Then I will love you and leave you,' declared Nabil Zaal, getting up. 'I have already started work on my new book called *Akhenaten's Exodus*. Now I have the proof of Panehesy's box, I can pull together my theories around this central piece of evidence and tell the story of how Akhenaten led his people out of Egypt and transcended his original identity to become that towering figure of the Bible, and father of the Jewish faith, Moses. I have received no further threats from the group who tampered with our brakes in Amarna.' He smiled with a complacency I hoped was not misplaced. 'I daresay they saw my television interview and realised the faultiness of their thinking. As an Egyptian myself, I can only say I am proud to know one of our pharaohs was responsible for spawning the great monotheistic religions of the world.'

We exchanged glances after he'd bidden us farewell and gone back to his room to pack.

'There are more reasons than one to return to Luxor,' Adam said. 'It seems to me the first item on the agenda needs to be to get back inside our tomb and lift the lid on that damn sarcophagus.'

We decided Adam, Ahmed and Walid would travel ahead to Luxor by the overnight sleeper train, while Ted and I followed more slowly, sailing the *Queen Ahmes* up the Nile with Khaled once more at the helm. He would complete the repair work once we had her safely back in Luxor.

Walid reluctantly conceded that we needed to check inside Akhenaten's sarcophagus to see whether or not Nabil Zaal risked making a fool of himself in pursuing his quest to prove the historical pharaoh and the biblical giant were one and the same man.

'The inscription on top of the box we found in Panehesy's wine cellar in Amarna,' Walid queried. 'Remind me again what it said.'

Adam pulled his iPhone from his pocket and flipped to the photographs. But Ted had learned it by heart.

'"*I, the servitor of Aten, will follow my Lord on every step of his journey to lead our people out of Egypt. I leave these honours here that my family may make use of them in my absence…*"'

'Well, I can certainly see why it has got our friend Nabil Zaal all fired up,' Walid remarked. Then he frowned, patting at the wispy hair a sudden breeze from the revolving door lifted from his head. 'But proving Akhenaten's alias, or indeed his alibi, is not my reason for agreeing we must re-enter the tomb.'

We all stared at him, waiting while he gathered his thoughts.

'Firstly, it strikes me that poor young man, Abdul Shehata, who lost his life so violently outside the presidential palace on Saturday must have stored Mustafa Mushhawrar's copy of the letter somewhere. Since we have no idea where this somewhere might be, exposure of the tomb by person or persons unknown must remain a risk.'

It seemed strange in a way that we'd switched from referring to Abdul Shehata as a loathsome and feared blackmailer to calling him a poor young man. That's death for you.

'Secondly,' Walid went on, 'there is the young man who absconded with your dahabeeyah to consider. This Gamal Abdel-Maqsoud who has led us such a merry dance. With our fingers tightly crossed, we suppose him to have drowned in the Nile. But this may not be the case. He knows of the tomb. He had all the time in the world to stare at its contents, admittedly from a distance, while he was incarcerated inside the entrance corridor with two flashlights at his disposal.'

Adam squirmed uncomfortably alongside me. I was quite sure he regretted his decision to lock Gamal up inside the tomb that night. But really, what choice did he have?

Walid allowed a long pause to draw out while we absorbed what he was saying. 'I am not happy with the loose threads we have left hanging,' he said. 'Not happy at all.'

We all shifted under his critical gaze as it came to rest on each of us in turn. He'd felt the strain of the last couple of weeks more keenly than any of us. So it wasn't difficult to read the continued anxiety in his expression now, or blame him for his concerns.

'I fear we will have no choice soon but to announce to the world the discovery of our tomb,' he went on. 'I can only hope the political turmoil will have settled down a little by then. In the meantime, I would very much like to see for myself whether we do indeed have the secret reburial of Akhenaten and Nefertiti on our hands.'

So it was agreed. Adam, Walid and Ahmed would go on ahead and work under the cover of darkness every night to erect a pulley system inside the burial chamber to prise the lid off Akhenaten's sarcophagus. Ted and I would sail down the Nile with Khaled and join them in Luxor as soon as we could.

It was a strange thing to sail the Nile between Cairo and Luxor. It seemed the Foreign Office travel advice had been put into immediate effect, that of our own government and all the other European nations as well, so it seemed. Egypt was officially a no-go zone. The Nile cruise boats usually to be seen ploughing through the water, however emptily, with diesel fumes belching out the back, were conspicuous by their absence. We passed a few feluccas and water taxis, but very little else in the way of river craft. Ted and I kept our eyes on the News while we sailed southwards. On the evening following our departure, President Morsi delivered a late night speech rejecting the ultimatum issued by the military. He claimed he was the elected president who represented the will of the people and declared he would defend the legitimacy of his office with his life. He added, "There is no substitute for legitimacy", and vowed not to resign.

'How can he claim to represent the will of the people?' I demanded. 'Doesn't he watch the television? Is he stone deaf? The noise from the protests in Cairo on Sunday could probably be heard clear across the Mediterranean in Cyprus!'

The next day the Supreme Council of the Armed Forces issued a statement on its official Facebook page. Entitled "The Final Hours", it read: "We swear by God that we are ready to sacrifice our blood for Egypt and its people against any terrorist, extremist or fool".

'Amen to that,' I said, 'The military has finally nailed its colours to the mast.'

The next day the 48-hour ultimatum was due to run out. It started violently when unknown gunmen opened fire on a pro-Morsi rally in Cairo, killing sixteen people and wounding more than two hundred.

'This bloodshed needs to stop,' I said emotionally, as the image of Abdul Shehata's ruined body flashed before my eyes again. 'It's bringing Egypt to its knees.'

Ted and I spent the day tensely pacing the charred upper deck while the hours that would decide Egypt's future ticked by. The news came through just as the 16:35pm deadline approached that Morsi had offered to form a consensus government. But it was too little too late. The armed forces responded to say they were meeting with a number of religious, national, political and youth icons and would release a statement from the General Command as soon as they were done.

Ted and I had just finished dinner and were sharing a bottle of wine in the lounge-bar with the television muted when it flashed on screen that General Abdel Fattah el-Sisi, the head of the Egyptian Armed Forces and Defence Minister was about to give a live televised address. We immediately zapped up the volume.

The General said the army was standing apart from the political process but was discharging its responsibility to the Egyptian people who were calling for help. Then he delivered the news we had all been waiting for. Mohamed Morsi had been deposed and the draft constitution suspended. Morsi had been placed under house arrest at the Republican Guard headquarters in Cairo while several other government officials and Islamist figures supporting Morsi had been arrested. He named Chief Justice Adli Mansour as the interim president, and finished by declaring these actions the result of what he called "the Revolution of 30 June 2013".

'And now we wait to see,' Ted said slowly. 'Can democracy in Egypt survive the coup d'état that has removed its president?'

I looked at him and attempted a smile. 'Well, Nabil Zaal would have us believe monotheism survived the coup d'état that removed its pharaoh, so we can but hope.'

Chapter 15

Thankfully there was some good news on a more personal level as we journeyed southward. Adam called to let us know Ahmed's actions in scooping up the badly injured Abdul Shehata from outside the presidential palace and later depositing his body at the hospital morgue had not gone unnoticed. He'd earned a commendation from the military. This combined with the recovery and return of the bank box and its contents to Mrs Mushhawrar meant he'd had the complaint against him dropped. He was now happily free once more to report for duty as an officer of the tourism and antiquities police in Luxor.

'Thank heaven for that,' I said with feeling. 'With the investigation over and done with, and with a new smile to dazzle everyone with, I imagine Ahmed el-Rassul is one very happy man right now.

'You can't begin to imagine, Merry.' Adam laughed, and, saying how much he was longing to see me, rang off.

After four solid days of sailing, we approached the familiar bend in the Nile and the Theban Hills came into view. I stood at the handrail on the upper deck, drenched in hot sunshine, with my back to the burnt remains of the loungers and recliners, and allowed a powerful sense of homecoming to steal over me. I loved this noisy, dusty city, with its magnificent temple ruins, dainty minarets piercing the skyline, unfinished buildings with construction poles sticking up in the air, ramshackle suburbs full of wandering farmyard animals, and general air of faded glory. On the west bank, the strip of gauzy green cultivated land bordered with golden desert gave way to the tawny bronzed cliffs of the Theban Hills rising in the distance. I sucked in a deep contented breath and narrowed my eyes on the horizon. Our tomb was carved into those rugged cliffs. Soon we would know for sure if we'd discovered the greatest royal burial of all time, or whether Tutankhamun and his vizier Ay had perpetrated some fantastical hoax. 'He *has* to be there,' I breathed. 'The papyrus makes no sense otherwise.'

Adam, Ahmed and Walid were standing lined up on the riverbank waving in welcome as we approached the causeway we called home. I ran down the gangplank and into Adam's arms as soon as we docked. 'I *missed* you!'

'You too,' he grinned, spinning me around. 'But I'm pleased to report our time apart has not been wasted. We have the pulley system all rigged up and ready to go in the burial chamber, thanks to some equipment Ahmed's been able to squirrel out of the police stores.'

'Is that such a good idea?' I frowned. 'He's only just won back his job. Isn't it a bit soon to risk losing it again?'

Adam laughed. 'You know Ahmed. He's an adrenaline junkie. Sailing close to the wind makes him feel alive.'

'Hmm,' I grunted. 'Once a tomb robber, always a tomb robber; if you ask me. It's in his blood!'

I suspect Ahmed heard this little exchange, but pretended not to. He flashed his new smile instead. It really did make the most incredible difference to his appearance. 'Tonight's the night!' he exclaimed excitedly.

Khaled wasted no time now we were back and the *Queen Ahmes* was moored at her stone jetty. He immediately set to work on the repair of her upper deck. 'I'll have her looking as good as new in no time,' he declared. Thankfully we could afford his services since Nabil had paid us generously before departing for America. Khaled had argued that he'd work for free, but there was no way we could agree to that.

With time to kill before tonight's visit to the tomb, the rest of us sat in the air conditioned comfort of the lounge-bar and conducted a post mortem on Egypt's latest Revolution.

'I feel mostly relief that Morsi is gone,' Walid admitted. 'I certainly don't feel inclined towards the wild rejoicing that followed the fall of Mubarak. I think as a nation we are not so naïve this time. The events of the last couple of weeks have been proof to me that the path to democracy is long and laborious.'

'We must hope to get dere in de end,' Ahmed nodded solemnly.

'Sadly, I think there may be some little way to go yet before we're out of the woods,' Ted warned. 'There have already been reports of more violent clashes on the streets in Cairo, with claims the military is harshly suppressing protests in favour of Morsi that call for his reinstatement. I'm not sure I see things settling down any time soon.'

Adam looked grim. 'The situation's not helped by such mixed international reactions. Most Arab leaders have been generally supportive or else neutral. But Qatar and Tunisia have strongly denounced the military's actions. In the West, governments have either condemned or expressed concern over Morsi's removal.'

'Of course they have,' I said cynically. 'Or else how precarious would it make their own positions? If the people can rise up against a democratically elected president here and succeed in toppling him, it might just put the idea into people's heads elsewhere in the world that the same thing might be possible.'

'Heaven forbid!' Adam said with feeling. 'Democracy might have its failings, but I wouldn't much fancy the alternative.'

'America's reaction has been interesting,' Ted remarked. 'They can't seem to decide whether to call it a coup d'état or a revolution.'

'It's all in the label,' Adam said, sounding as jaded as I'd just done. 'Depending on which one they opt for, Egypt either benefits from continued US support financially, or loses it. There are lots of dollars at stake, so they'd better jump the right way.'

'Whatever happens, we need to see exactly whose body we have inside that tomb and then decide what to do about it,' Walid concluded.

We all tried to get some sleep before nightfall. This was easier for the men than it was for me, since they'd missed out on several nights' sleep already. I tossed and turned a bit, but couldn't settle.

'Merry, if you don't stop wriggling, I'm going to have to do something about it,' Adam growled threateningly.

I made a concerted effort to lie still. But I'm rather pleased to say Adam did something about it anyway. I'd been told marriage could take the gloss off certain interactions between a couple. I was quite delighted to have Adam prove to me that so far in our case this wasn't true.

As usual darkness came quickly. The frogs started croaking along the riverbank and bats came silently flapping through the treetops. We waited until we knew the floodlights were about to be switched off. Then it was time to go.

I didn't quite know how I felt as we made our way in Ahmed's car towards Hatshepsut's temple. A mixture of nervous anticipation and genuine trepidation probably described it best. I couldn't really explain the feeling that this might be the last time we'd have the tomb to ourselves. I crossed my fingers on my lap in the back of Ahmed's car at the thought. Considering our previous experiences, there was every chance someone would either follow or ambush us and we'd find ourselves locked in, entombed, and fighting for our survival. Considering the number of enemies we seemed to make, with no effort at all on our part, this remained a very real possibility. Perhaps this explained the huge quantities of rope, water and provisions we'd brought with us, not to mention both Aten discs.

And yet, I couldn't shake the instinctive feeling that I should savour every moment of this nocturnal visit – literally treasure these moments with the treasure.

Of course we remained as silent and stealthy as cats as we left Ahmed's car hidden off-road and made our way by starlight and the weak incandescence of a perfect crescent moon across the desert basin in front of Hatshepsut's darkened temple. It would be just our luck if the guards picked tonight of all nights to spot us, considering the number of times the men had made nocturnal trip here over recent nights. I marvelled at the nonchalance with which Adam unlocked the Hathor Chapel and stood back to let us all enter ahead of him. But then, this was a route he, Ahmed and Walid had travelled every night since last weekend, and usually weighed down by the various bits of the police equipment Ahmed had been able to filch. Either the guards were particularly unobservant, or we'd been incredibly lucky.

Whatever else I was feeling, it was still a moment of breathless fright when the flashlights were switched on and the ancient deities sprang to life across the walls. And no less a moment of breathless wonder when the Aten disc was pressed into the wall and, after counting heartbeats, the stone panel shifted sideways to reveal the blacked out passageway beyond.

As chivalry demanded (yes, it was still alive and kicking among my male companions), the men stood back for me to crawl through ahead of them with my flashlight lighting the way. Once through, I was quite tempted to turn it off. A huge part of me wanted to give in to an overwhelming sense of nostalgia, allow darkness to engulf me, and re-live every moment of the time Adam and I had spent in here alone so recently. As I'd feared, this memory had already taken on a soft-focus haze of unreality. Yet, now I was back again, I felt I could close my eyes and hear the words we'd spoken so emotionally to one another echo from the stone walls.

But I was quickly followed through the gap in the wall by the others so had to cut short these romantic recollections. Adam reached for my hand as he got up from his knees; pulled me towards him, and planted a kiss on my lips. 'I'll remember it always,' he murmured. That's the thing I love most about Adam: he always knows exactly the right thing to say.

I was interested to note the makeshift bridge the men had secured across the pit shaft, screwing each end in place so it was safe. 'Makes a nice change not to be dicing with death just to get across,' I approved, stepping carefully onto the lovely, wide, thick, secure plank of wood.

'Better all round when we had stuff to carry,' Adam explained.

A few more paces, and the treasure chamber opened out in front of us. 'Goodness me, what a wonder!' Ted exclaimed.

Of course, I thought, of all of us, he hadn't been here for the longest time.

'It takes a while to let it all sink back in, doesn't it?' I murmured.

'I thought I'd taken a mental snapshot,' Ted murmured. 'But now I realise just how faulty memory can be.'

Walid came up beside us. 'We played a game last night to see who could come up with the best word to describe it. We tried marvellous, staggering, and incredible. But we had to give up in the end. There wasn't a word we could think of that came close.'

'It's all very well, except for the dust,' I remarked sadly. 'It does rather take the shine off, don't you think?'

'I've been considering that,' Walid said. 'It seems to me we have no hope of putting this tomb back into the perfect condition it was in when you and Adam found it. So I think if we conclude we have no choice but to announce it to the world, we should leave it as it is. Who's to say the rockfall was not a natural phenomenon? I, myself, fail to find a more adequate explanation that will satisfy a curious public.'

He was right, of course. There was no way we could set about clearing the mess Mustafa had caused, not if we didn't want to risk discovery. We were already courting exposure as it was, being here on so many nights in a row. To leave it as it was certainly saved us an unenviable task. And I noted he'd used the word *we*. Perhaps Walid didn't want sole responsibility for the decision anymore.

Adam drew a deep breath. 'So, the time has come. Are we ready to lift the lid on this thing?' It was quite clear he meant literally as well as metaphorically.

It was more nervous dread than anticipation I could feel coursing through my veins now as we carefully picked our way across the treasure chamber. Squeezing through the gap in the wall into the burial chamber, I caught my breath. Ted did the same as he came through behind me. The pulley system the men had assembled seemed to encase the larger sarcophagus and had metal handles already clamped onto its stone lid.

The men had swept aside the dust, small rocks and loose chippings that had exploded into the cramped space. And they'd somehow hefted Nefertiti's sarcophagus to one side. This just about made room for the pulley system they'd rigged up.

'And so we approach the moment of truth,' Adam said. 'I rather feel we ought to have a camera rolling.'

'Our five sets of eyes are all the record I need,' Walid said severely. 'I have learnt my lesson well. There must be no evidence of what we are about to do that can accidentally fall into the wrong hands.'

'I'll second that,' Ted approved.

We exchanged apprehensive glances. I'm sure we were all thinking the same thing. The magnitude, the importance, the significance – call it what you will because words fail me – of what we were about to do was inescapable. Put it this way, it was a momentous occasion the gravity of which impressed itself on every one of us.

Ahmed took up position at one of the pulley ropes, while Adam and Walid jointly manned the other. 'Ok, on a count of three,' Adam directed. 'Merry and Ted, I want you to say the word.'

Almost paralysed with the awesome sense of responsibility that shifted heavily onto my shoulders, I reached for Ted's shaking hand. 'Ok, let's do this together… Are you ready ...? Right, here we go. One...Two..Three... *HEAVE!...HEAVE!...HEAVE...!*

Ted's voice was a faint echo of mine, but it didn't matter. The excitement was overwhelming. His clutching hand told me how exhilarated, terrified, downright panic stricken he was. We'd all seen the movies. I think every one of us expected the angels of death from *Raiders of the Lost Ark* to scream out of the ancient coffin, and hear Adam order us to keep our eyes closed and not look. At least, it was certainly what was going through my mind.

But there were no screaming angels, and there was no swelling movie score to add atmosphere to these moments. The grunting, puffing and heaving of three men was all we had to lend character to the scene being played out before our eyes.

To begin with, I thought the lid was stuck fast, perhaps welded in place by the same sticky resinous substance that lodged Tutankhamun in place inside his coffin. But finally, and with ever more desperate cries of '*HEAVE*' the solid stone started to shift. At first, it was just a shaky inch, which threatened to crash closed again. Concerted effort widened the gap and, with the ropes straining and the men sweating, I finally called for the ropes to be tied off. The gigantic stone sarcophagus rested with its heavy stone lid dangling precariously about a metre above it. Ahmed's police issue kit was doing its job; but only just.

Asking for a volunteer to peer inside was akin to asking one of us to place his (or her) head inside the jaws of death. We'd underestimated the weight of the solid granite lid. The pulley was creaking and groaning its protest at bearing such a load.

'I'll do it!' Adam offered; making sure the section of rope he shared with Walid was tightly secured.

'No! Adam, please! It's too dangerous!' But there was no one I was willing to volunteer in his place. So Adam it was.

I watched in an agony of dread as, using the pulley system as a kind of climbing frame, he levered himself up onto the outer rim of the sarcophagus, almost as if he was clambering onto a kayak with his legs clamped on either side. 'Ok, just hold those ropes steady,' he murmured, shifting himself forward until he had a clearer view. I passed him up a flashlight and we all held a collective breath.

There was a long pause. 'We don't appear to have the golden nest of coffins Tutankhamun was buried in,' Adam said at length. 'There's just one. It seems to be a wooden anthropoid coffin, covered in gold leaf. It looks very much like that one Theodore Davis found in KV55.'

'Any inscriptions?' Walid asked in a strangled tone of voice.

Adam was silent for a long moment, sweeping the flashlight in long arcs to illuminate the inside of the sarcophagus. Then he pulled his head back out from underneath the granite lid and stared at us one by one. 'It's him alright,' he said at length. 'It's Akhenaten. I don't know how we could ever have doubted it.' He ducked his head back inside again, focused the beam of the torch and started to read the inscriptions. His voice sounded sepulchral and a bit unreal, echoing out of the great stone sarcophagus. "*Neferkheperure-waenre, Akhenaten, Kanakht-Meryaten, Wer-nesut-em-Akhetaten, Wetjes-ren-en-Aten.*"

Ted frowned in concentration and translated, 'Beautiful are the Manifestations of Re, the one of Re; Living Spirit of the Aten; The strong bull, beloved of the Aten; Great in kingship in Akhet-Aten; Who upholds the name of the Aten.'

Walid sat down on the hard stone floor with a sudden bump. His knees had given way. 'By all that is holy,' he breathed. 'We have him. Oh my! I hardly know what to think.'

Ahmed was breathing heavily, and mopping his damp face with a tissue he'd pulled from his pocket.

'Whatever else he may have been or done, Akhenaten most definitely did not lead the Israelites out of Egypt in the Exodus,' I murmured, feeling a bit choked. 'He wasn't Moses.'

'Poor Nabil,' Ted remarked alongside me. 'He's going to be so disappointed.

'Hang on, there's something else in here,' Adam said from his position perched on the edge of the sarcophagus.

We all stared up at him, alerted by the excited note in his voice.

'There seems to be something wrapped in cloth. It's been wedged between the foot of the coffin and the inner casing of the sarcophagus.' He leaned forward, straining every muscle as he reached forward. 'It's no good; I can't get to it. I'm going to have to climb inside.'

'No, Adam! It's too dangerous! If the ropes break you'll be trapped inside with no air.' I darted a glance at the rope Ahmed had tied off. It was starting to fray.

But Adam was already moving. Ahmed dropped the tissue and immediately took up position, adding his strength to his side of the pulley to take some pressure off the rope. Walid climbed shakily to his feet and he, Ted and I shared the strain of the other one.

Watching Adam tip forward inside the sarcophagus did not rate as one of the most enjoyable sights of my life. But I suspect it's one I'll never forget. I had my heart in my mouth the whole time.

'I don't want to put any pressure on the coffin in case it breaks,' Adam grunted, trying to keep his weight on the stone. 'Ok, just a bit more.' He leaned further forward.

As he did, one of the strands of rope snapped. I yelped in fright, all of my nerve endings screaming. 'For God's sake, Adam! Come out of there!'

'Just a tiny bit more… Ok… Nearly there…Got it!'

He grabbed whatever it was he was reaching for and scrambled backwards. Just in time. The rope on Ahmed's side gave way. With an almighty crash, sending the rope spinning free of the pulley, the gigantic lid of the sarcophagus smashed back into place.

Adam fell backwards, landing heavily on the floor at my feet. He was hugging what looked like a pile of old cloth against his chest. Winded, it took him a moment to get his breath back. This was probably just as well since I needed the time to get my heart started again. I'd swear it had stopped beating.

As the dust settled all around us, we dropped to the floor around Adam.

'What is it?' Walid lifted the linen wrappings out of his arms and started gently to unfold them. 'My goodness, what have we here?'

'It looks like a set of clay tablets,' Ted said excitedly.

Ahmed shone the beam of his flashlight directly onto the ancient artefacts emerging from their protective wrappings.

'Good lord, they look just like the Amarna letters! Ted exclaimed. 'Except these are clearly written in hieratic script rather than Akkadian cuneiform.'

'Amarna letters?' I asked, while Adam pushed himself up and turned over onto his knees for a closer look.

'The Amarna letters were found by peasants digging in the ruins of Akhenaten's ancient city in Amarna in 1887. They record several years' worth of diplomatic correspondence with the states of Canaan and Amurru during and after Akhenaten's reign.'

'Is that what we have here?' I asked, peering closer. 'Diplomatic letters?'

'I don't think so, because these are written in Egyptian.'

Walid, very carefully, held up the first of the tablets so the beam from Ahmed's flashlight could more clearly illuminate the closely packed letters carved into the surface. 'Yes, definitely hieratic,' he murmured. 'It's an abridged form of hieroglyphics used by priests. Can you decipher anything of what it says, professor?'

Ted pushed his glasses up onto the bridge of his nose and frowned through them, squinting myopically at the tablets in the torchlight. Then he caught his breath and stared. 'Oh my good Lord...!'

'What?' we all asked simultaneously. 'What is it?'

'Unless I'm very much mistaken, this looks to me like a prototype of the Copper Scroll!'

Ahmed gaped at him. 'De treasure map?' he demanded. 'Dis is de treasure map you have been telling us about?'

Ted raised a shaky hand to his brow. 'Well, this is written in hieratic, whereas the Copper Scroll is in an ancient form of Hebrew. But, yes, I'd stake my reputation on it being the same basic text. I've been studying it quite closely.' He

328

ran a shaking hand over his brow. 'Scholars have been theorising some link between the Copper Scroll and Akhenaten. Heavens above! This would seem to prove it. But I don't understand... Why would it be buried here with the pharaoh?'

Walid was frowning at the first clay tablet. 'Look! Professor! Do you recognise this name? Does it say what I think it says?'

Carefully Ted took the tablet from him and held it to the light. Very slowly, he started to translate. 'The name reads *Meryre*,' he said. 'And the titles read *High Priest of the Aten at the Temple of Akhet-Aten.*'

I felt a shiver snake down my spine. 'And the next bit? Can you read it?'

Ted was silent for a very long time. His lips moved, but no sound came out. Eventually he sat back heavily. It was just as well he was sitting down on the hard stone floor. I've a feeling he might have fallen over otherwise. His expression was of almost mystical awe, as if he'd just had a vision of some sort.

'It reads as a sort of message from Meryre to Akhenaten his king. It's in the form of a promise, or a pledge if you prefer. Meryre, the High Priest of the Aten, is swearing a solemn oath to lead Akhenaten's people out of Egypt, to keep his teachings alive, and to keep the treasures of the temple safe.'

I felt my mouth fall open and stared at him agog. 'You mean Meryre led the Exodus? *He* was Moses?'

Ted stared back at me, and I felt all the little hairs on the nape of my neck and along my forearms stand on end. 'Your interpretation would appear to be a distinct possibility, my dear.'

'So, when Panehesy inscribed the box containing his golden collar to say he would follow *his Lord* on every step of his journey to lead their people out of Egypt, it was Meryre he was referring to, not Akhenaten.'

'I think that must be right,' Walid replied. 'Meryre was the senior priest at the temple. Panehesy served under him. So it seems perfectly reasonable to suppose he might refer to Meryre as *my Lord*.'

It was almost too much to take in. 'Maybe Nabil won't be quite so disappointed after all,' Adam remarked benignly. 'Even if Moses was a priest at Akhenaten's temple rather than the pharaoh himself, it still proves it was Akhenaten's religion he was intent on preserving, and that formed the foundations of the major religions of the world today. I should say that's a very real victory for our friend the author.'

THE END

Author's Note

Many writers and historians have sought out the identity of Biblical Moses among the royal families of ancient Egypt. The Bible makes it clear he was closely linked to the royal household. Sigmund Freud, the Jewish father of psychoanalysis, was the first to suggest a link between the apparently monotheistic beliefs of the pharaoh Akhenaten and the great monotheistic religions of the world. In his book *Moses and Monotheism,* published in English in 1939, he suggested Moses was an Egyptian. He postulated that Moses might have been a follower of the pharaoh Akhenaten, who may have served at his court. Other writers have gone further, notably Ahmed Osman. In his book *Moses and Akhenaten: The Secret History of Egypt at the Time of the Exodus*, the author sets out an extensive body of evidence to build the case that Moses was the heretic pharaoh himself.

This identification of Moses as Akhenaten appeared to be debunked when DNA testing on the skeleton found by Theodore Davies in tomb KV55 in the Valley of the Kings seemed to suggest the body was 'probably' that of Akhenaten. But other scholars have hotly contested this conclusion. They argue the STR analysis shows the KV55 mummy is highly unlikely to be Akhenaten. They suggest the ephemeral pharaoh Smenkhkare is a better fit with the genetic findings. So, many believe the body of Akhenaten has never been found. Most historians believe Akhenaten died and was originally buried, as intended in his rock-cut tomb at Akhet-Aten. His empty sarcophagus was found there, smashed to pieces. It has since been reconstructed and now sits on the forecourt of the Egyptian Museum in Cairo.

The links between the Biblical writings and historical research are fascinating and highly suggestive. It is impossible to make any absolute claims, which provides a wonderful canvas on which a writer of fiction can create a story.

What we know about the Exodus comes mostly from the Old Testament of the Bible, from the Talmud, which is a compilation of Hebrew laws and legends, regarded as second only to the Old Testament as an authoritative source of the early history of the Jews; and also from Manetho, a 3rd Century BC native Egyptian historian. Manetho's account of the Exodus was derived from Egyptian folklore. His work was subsequently transmitted by the Jewish historian Flavius Josephus.

It must be expected that the Old Testament and Talmudic stories contain many distortions, arising from the fact that they were transmitted orally for a long time before being finally set down in writing. Even so, one can sense there must have been genuine historical events behind the folklore, myths and legends that had perhaps been suppressed from the official accounts of both Egypt and Israel, but had survived in the memories of generations.

When Howard Carter discovered the intact royal burial of Tutankhamun in his tomb in the Valley of the Kings in 1922, many hoped to gain an insight into the possible links between Biblical mythology and historical fact. Just as gripping as Tutankhamun's history and treasures was the possibility of his religious connections. Given ancient Egypt's prominent role in the Old Testament, with figures such as Joseph and Moses described as close to the royal family, Tutankhamun was seen as a route to greater knowledge about the events recounted in the Bible. Sadly, little textual material was found in Tutankhamun's tomb, so these questions remained unanswered.

Certain factions raised concerns over the DNA testing of Tutankhamun's mummy, lest the results might strengthen an association between the family of Tutankhamun and Biblical Moses. In short, there was a fear it would be said the Amarnan pharaohs were Jewish. It is fair to say, DNA testing has not ruled this out. Once again, this provides intriguing fodder for a fiction writer.

The Copper Scroll exists and is a unique type of document among the Dead Sea Scrolls found in the caves near Qumran. The Copper Scroll is mysterious and there is a considerable variety of opinion on how it should be translated.

One of the mysteries is the Greek characters inserted into the text that seem to have very little to do with the content of the Copper Scroll itself. But if those Greek letters are read in the sequence in which they appear in the scroll, they clearly spell out a reference to the ancient Egyptian pharaoh Akhenaten.

The Copper Scroll is certainly an inventory of a large quantity of treasure, and appears also to contain a record of where this treasure was buried to keep it safe. The Copper Scroll text suggests that it incorporates a code and that the code is also contained in a document hidden in a specific place, near some of the treasure listed in the scroll. Many believe this place to be among the tombs of the nobles in Amarna, ancient Akhet-Aten.

As I write, these remain troubled times in Egypt politically. The coup d'état that removed President Morsi from power was as described in this novel, although I have taken some liberties with the exact timing of events where it suited the action in my story. Thankfully, the British Foreign and Commonwealth Office did not issue a repatriation order. For many months it advised against all but essential travel to Egypt. It lifted these restrictions in November 2013. I'm pleased to say this means Merry and Adam are free to continue their adventures, although it does not bode well for the success of their business offering Nile cruises to discerning travellers. Now the military is back in control I can only hope for a period of stability and a return of tourists to this unique and ancient land. One thing is for sure. Egypt has seen it all before.

I hope you've enjoyed this fifth book following Meredith Pink's Adventures in Egypt. If so I'd very much appreciate a review on Amazon. I also read and respond to all comments on my website https://fionadeal.com

Fiona Deal
July 2014

If you enjoyed Akhenaten's Alibi you may also enjoy Seti's Secret – Book 6 of Meredith Pink's Adventures in Egypt, available from Amazon.

Here is Chapter One …

Chapter 1

Summertime 2013

Of all the people I might have expected to find standing on the gangplank of our dahabeeyah at daybreak, my ex-boyfriend was not one of them. But there he was, in the flesh, arms folded, feet planted apart, and with a deep scowl on his face.

'Dan!'

His expression may have had something to do with the fact that I myself was not actually inside the *Queen Ahmes*, but approaching it from the riverbank. Judging by the look of him, he'd been there for some considerable time waiting for me – us, I should say, for I wasn't alone – to return. He must have heard us pull up in Ahmed's car, now parked under the knot of palm trees behind us.

'At last!' he barked, confirming my assessment of his long wait.

I quickened my pace as I negotiated the steep stone steps leading down to the crumbling causeway where our dahabeeyah is moored. This wasn't a good move. The steps are treacherous at the best of times; and with Dan now striding angrily towards me, this didn't seem likely to be one of them. I lost my balance and let out a yelp. Thankfully, Adam was right behind me and shot out a steadying hand.

I recovered my voice along with my footing. 'Dan! What on earth …?'

'I've been waiting here for *hours!*' he growled. I use the terms *barked* and *growled* advisedly. Dan's ability when annoyed to sound a little less than human is second to none. 'Where the hell have you been for half the night?' Then he ran an appraising glance over the small party of whom I was just one. His raking gaze took in the dusty, dishevelled and sweat-stained appearance not just of me, but also of Adam, Ahmed, Ted and Walid, clustering protectively around me as we made it without further mishap to the foot of the stone steps. I daresay the vexation in Dan's expression was as clear to them as it was to me as the sky lightened with the breaking dawn.

My ex-boyfriend's sweeping glance didn't miss the linen wrappings clutched protectively against the professor's narrow chest. 'No, don't tell me,' he swept on. 'It's stark staringly obvious where you lot have been; as if I hadn't already guessed it!' His tone became downright accusatory. 'You've been inside that bloody tomb again!' He glared at each of us in turn. 'Haven't you?'

There was no point in attempting to deny it of course. I'm sure our guilty expressions were a dead giveaway, if further proof were necessary.

The strange part, if that's what it could be called, was that for the first time in all our experiences with it, we'd locked up and left the tomb without any trouble. Nobody had come to confront, incarcerate, or attempt to kill us. It had been an odd feeling to pick up the Aten disc from the floor inside the Hathor Chapel in Hatshepsut's Temple and watch the stone panel grind back into place wondering how long it might be before we next opened it, and in what circumstances that might be.

We'd piled back into Ahmed's police car, thinking only to come back to the *Queen Ahmes* for some much needed sleep, before gathering again to exclaim over the night's discoveries, and wonder what to do about them.

But we'd reckoned without the sudden, unexpected and, I have to say, unlooked-for appearance of the ex-boyfriend I'd thought was happily – or resignedly at least – up to his neck in wedding preparations back home in England. I had no idea what he was doing here. But I felt sure I was about to find out.

'Dan!' Adam exclaimed in rather more welcoming tones than mine. 'What a surprise! You should've let us know you were coming! Please; come on in.' He ushered us along the causeway and onto the gangplank as he spoke. Pulling a key from his pocket, he set about unlocking the door that opened into the little wood panelled reception area on board our dahabeeyah.

Dan allowed himself to be swept along by Adam's bonhomie. But I wasn't fooled. This was no social visit. I could only imagine the difficulty he'd had getting here.

'I thought international tourist flights into Luxor had been suspended since the Foreign Office imposed a ban on all but essential travel to Egypt,' I blurted my thoughts aloud.

Dan looked daggers at me. 'Damn right, and a devil's own job I've had to get here, I don't mind telling you! I had to take a scheduled flight from Heathrow into Cairo, since the commercial charter flights from Gatwick were cancelled. On arrival I suffered an impertinent interrogation at the immigration desk from some jobs-worth official who spoke the worst English of any Egyptian I've ever encountered!' He broke off briefly at this point and cast a quick and, I have to say, rather disparaging glance at Ahmed. 'Well,' he amended. 'Maybe with one or two exceptions… Anyway, after much to-ing and fro-ing I managed to get the halfwit to understand that I needed to travel because I had family out here. Once he finally condescended to let me on my way, I hailed a taxi to the station only to find I'd just missed the sleeper train down here to Luxor. So I had to wait for the ordinary passenger one, and then travel third class in a packed carriage without air conditioning. I've been travelling for *hours*. And then to turn up here late last night only to find you weren't here ...' He left this hanging. There was no need for him to spell it out. Dan was quite clearly not a happy man.

But none of this was what made me stare at him in consternation. '*What* family?' I challenged. I knew for a cast iron fact that there was not one solitary person on Egyptian soil to whom Dan could claim to be related.

He let out a puff of impatience and glared at me. '*You*, Meredith!'

This was another bad sign. When Dan calls me my full name, rather than the abbreviated version or a nickname, it's a clear-cut indication of bad temper.

'But I'm not... I mean, we're not...' I trailed off in confusion.

'We were together for ten years,' he announced as if I needed reminding. 'I think that entitles me to sta – er – state some connection.' I had no doubt he'd been about to say '*stake a claim*' but with a quick glance at Adam he performed a neat verbal swerve at the last moment. 'Besides which, your mother...'

My mother?!' I cut across him. 'What does my mother have to do with this?'

But I wasn't the only one who'd spotted his quick rethink mid-sentence. Despite Dan's split second glance at

Adam, and his lightning recovery, there was someone else who had cause to question the claim or *connection* Dan seemed to be staking to me.

Ted coughed, interrupting my demand to know where my mother fitted in. He was far too polite to cut across me in the same way I'd done to Dan. 'Eh hum,' the professor started. 'Is my daughter here in Egypt, Dan? Is Jessica with you?'

Dan cast a somewhat uneasy glance at his future father-in-law. It's fair to say their relationship hadn't got off to the best of starts last year. But since Dan – for all his bluster – was so far superior to Jessica's first husband (about whom the less said the better), Ted had decided to overlook his character flaws and welcome him to the family. I thought this was to Ted's great credit. Dan can take some getting used to. As he'd just pointed out, I'd had a full decade to come to terms with his quick temper and tendency to lecture. And, if my current raised blood pressure was anything to judge by, I still wasn't sure I'd completely cracked it.

'Er, no,' Dan shook his head. 'Jessica stayed at home. I considered it was potentially too dangerous for her to come. All the News reports have been describing Egypt as a war-zone since President Morsi was toppled.'

'These News reports are grossly exaggerated.' Ahmed cut in, using pure and faultless English, and flashing his beautiful new white teeth. He'd been practising his 'th's' since his teeth were fixed, with some success. I was quite sure his flawless pronunciation was intended to put Dan firmly back in his place.

Dan ignored him. 'When I turned up to find you weren't here, it did occur to me you might have been sensible and gone away for a while. But then I saw you'd left one of the windows on the latch, so I knew you couldn't be far away. You'd never lock up and leave for any length of time without making sure the dahabeeyah was secure. Besides…' he treated me to another accusatory glare, '…when did you ever do the sensible thing, Meredith?'

Ted subsided now he knew his daughter was safely at home, and that his prospective son-in-law had shown a modicum of care for her wellbeing. I was grateful for Ted's forbearance since I didn't appreciate Dan's hectoring tone and had every intention of telling him so.

I opened my mouth to retaliate but Adam forestalled me. 'Why don't we make some coffee and toast and head up onto the sundeck, so we can all say hello properly?'

Lovely Adam. Always the voice of reason. I bit back my angry retort, contenting myself with a fulminating glare at my former boyfriend. Then I allowed Adam to take my hand and lead me down the narrow corridor towards the back of the boat, where the kitchen is situated.

'What the hell is he doing here?' I muttered once we were alone, putting thick slices of bread in the toaster while Adam busied himself with the coffee machine.

'I imagine your mother sent him,' Adam said equably. 'You can't blame them for being worried about you, Merry. It's because they care.'

'Yes, well, his timing stinks,' I complained, getting butter out of the fridge and banging down jars of marmalade, honey and jam on a tray. I didn't want to be reminded that people I loved were concerned about me. I wanted to get on with the excitement of the discovery we'd made overnight.

I felt sure Adam equally could do without the interruption and the distraction of my ex turning up unannounced like this. But Adam and Dan had formed an unlikely friendship of sorts – thanks, I think, to Adam's never-to-be-forgotten rescue of Dan from a dice with death on a clifftop not so long ago. And Adam suffers less with impatience than I do. Whatever, he didn't comment further while we finished preparing the breakfast things.

As we reached the top of the spiral staircase that leads up onto the sundeck, it was to find Dan frowning as he contemplated the charred furniture and stripped back floorboards. 'What in God's name happened up here?' He turned towards us, sounding shocked.

'The small matter of a fire,' Adam said grimly, setting down the tray with the coffee things on it.

Dan gazed about him, his frown deepening. 'That much I can see for myself! But how...? Surely you're not stupid enough to allow people to smoke up here?' He must have caught something in the brief look Adam and I exchanged. He sat down with a thump, swinging his gaze between us. 'It wasn't an accident, was it? Someone set the *Queen Ahmes* alight on purpose. Oh God, it's worse than I thought. Who have you made an enemy of this time?' This was said with a kind of weary resignation, as if it were almost boringly predictable that we'd be up to our necks in some sort of trouble.

I shifted uncomfortably under his critical gaze. 'Before we start on all that, I want you to answer my questions,' I demanded. 'What are you doing here in Egypt? And where does my mother fit in?' I was quite keen to deflect Dan's interrogation. I decided I'd much prefer to give an accounting of our recent activities once I had some reinforcements to back me up. And since Walid, Ted and Ahmed were taking their time about joining us up on deck (discretion being perhaps the better part of valour), I felt it was in my best interests to stall for time. Besides, I'd asked my questions first.

'We want you home, Pinkie.'

I stared at him in dismay, shocked into overlooking his casual use of my nickname.

'That goes for you too of course, Adam,' Dan added quickly, clearing his throat. 'Look, we all know how much this business venture means to you both. But you knew from the start what a huge risk you were taking given Egypt's dodgy political situation and its impact on tourism.'

'Hang on –' I started to interrupt.

But Dan was not to be diverted now he'd started. 'The fact is, none of us could have foreseen this second revolution coming so quickly on the heels of the first one. And now the News reports are of running battles in the streets and rivers of blood. Put simply guys, it's just not safe for you to be here anymore. It's time to call it a day and come home.'

'But –' I tried again, shooting Adam a look of appeal.

Dan steam-rollered verbally over the top of me, yet again. 'Your parents are worried sick, Merry. The very fact that your mother picked up the phone to *me* of all people should show you just how frantic she and your dad are. She said she's left you voicemail messages, but you haven't returned her calls. You sent just one short text message last week to let her know you were ok. Nothing beyond that. Can't you understand how concerned they are?'

I bit my lip, feeling like a balloon that had been burst. All my indignation deflated in a heartbeat. I hated to admit it but Dan was right. I'd been so caught up in everything else going on, I really hadn't given my family back in England more than a passing thought. But, even so, going home? No. Going home was the very last thing I wanted to do.

'I'm sorry.' I looked directly into Dan's eyes, wanting him to see I meant it. 'I've been horribly thoughtless. Of course I should have phoned Mum back. It's just –'

I broke off at the sound of a heavy footfall on the wooden planks behind me. Ahmed was the first one brave enough to join us up on deck. Walid followed. And, bringing up the rear, Ted came up the spiral staircase just a few paces behind them. I had the strongest impression they'd arrived together to have strength in numbers.

Adam poured the coffee while our friends pulled up a selection of chairs and recliners that had fared best in the fire and were still sturdy enough to sit on.

'I can't even think about coming home right now,' I started. 'It's not just that we need to give Khaled time to finish his repairs of the *Queen Ahmes*. You see...' I broke off, not really sure how to begin to tell Dan everything that had been happening.

'You've made another blasted discovery!' Dan finished for me. 'Credit me with a bit of intelligence, Meredith! I do have eyes in my head. I saw those wrappings the professor was carrying when you got back. You've been back inside the tomb, and you've found something else to rock the world, as if the damned tomb itself wasn't enough! And you no doubt have a whole host of criminals chasing after you, baying for your blood like a pack of hungry wolves. Am I getting close?'

The professor cleared his throat. 'Closer than you may think, my boy.' He leaned forward and stirred milk into his coffee. 'Except they're not criminals. And they're not chasing after us. At least, not anymore. One of them, the one who attempted to blackmail poor Walid here, was killed in the rioting in Cairo. The other, who so cavalierly set alight to this dahabeeyah, is missing, presumed drowned.'

'Both individuals worked for the ministry for the preservation of ancient monuments here in Luxor,' Walid added. 'They found out about the tomb because a copy of that letter we all signed turned up in Mustafa Mushhawrar's bank box when his possessions were cleared after his death.'

'So, the tomb is now an open secret.' Dan concluded.

'Not quite,' Adam put in. 'We have no reason to believe that anyone outside of these two young men knows about the tomb.'

'But surely the one attempting blackmail must have made copies of Mustafa's letter. He'd have wanted an insurance policy to back him up for sure. How do you know he didn't lodge a photocopy of it with everybody he knew?'

'We don't.' Walid said baldly. 'We just have to hope it is not so. As it is, the one copy of the letter we know my blackmailer had in his possession has disappeared. It was not found among his paltry belongings after his death.'

'And the man you presume to have drowned?'

'Gamal Abdel-Maqsoud.' Adam supplied. 'He jumped into the Nile in Cairo after setting light to the *Queen Ahmes*. He didn't resurface. We waited and scanned the riverbanks on both sides. There was no sign of him. We presume he may not have been able to swim and might have been caught up in reeds under water. He certainly knew of the tomb and its location. But we don't believe he had a copy of the letter.'

'So, you have no idea where the letter is now. Anyone could have got their hands on it.'

'That's about the size of it,' I agreed flatly.

'Well, it's a right old soup, that's all I can say.' Dan made this pronouncement as if delivering a verdict.

'It's potentially a ticking time bomb,' Adam agreed. 'That's why we knew we had not a minute to waste in getting back inside the tomb to see if we could find the evidence to debunk Nabil Zaal's latest theory.'

'Nabil Zaal?' Dan queried, 'Ah yes, I recollect him now. He's the author you hooked up with earlier in the year. You sent us that lovely newsy email about him, Pinkie; remember? He claims some of the key figures of the Old Testament were in actual fact Egyptian pharaohs, isn't that the one?'[4]

I nodded, recalling the glee with which I'd written to tell Dan and Jessica the story of how we'd come to be acquainted with the writer, and as a by-the-by, the claim to fame our

---

[4] Farouk's Fancies – Book 4 of Meredith Pink's Adventures in Egypt

dahabeeyah could boast, having once played host to Egypt's last reigning monarch, King Farouk.

'Well, we all know the Old Testament is a tissue of lies from start to finish,' Dan declared bluntly and, quite possibly, blasphemously. 'So, what preposterous theory is he peddling to the gullible this time?'

It was Ahmed, however unlikely that may sound, who paused in the action of liberally buttering a slice of toast to respond. Perhaps he saw an opportunity to practise his newly perfected English and prove Dan wrong in his earlier insulting denigration of his command of our language. He sat up straighter in his chair, thrust out his feet and looked Dan full in the face. 'He claims that the father of the Jewish faith, and the forefather of both Christianity and Islam, the man we know from religious teachings as Moses, was, in actual fact, the pharaoh Akhenaten. He believes Akhenaten was the one who led the Israelites out of Egypt towards the Promised Land in the Exodus.'

I nearly jumped up and applauded. Every 'th' was enunciated to perfection. Allowing for the Arabic accent it was impossible for him to disguise, Ahmed had delivered this speech, no matter how pompously, as if English was a language he'd been speaking all his life. It was only a matter of a couple of weeks since our friend, Selim, had fixed his dental implants in place. But aside from the startling physical improvement, something in his new dentistry seemed also to have untangled Ahmed's tongue from his teeth.

Sadly, Dan seemed to notice neither Ahmed's transformed appearance nor his flawless pronunciation. 'Akhenaten? He was the one who uprooted everyone from Thebes to Amarna when he decided he'd had enough of Egyptian tradition and wanted to go his own way, right? And now your writer-chum would have us believe he uprooted everyone all over again, well, some of them at any rate, and led them off into the sunset of the Sinai? Sounds like a damn fool theory to me! Besides, I thought Akhenaten was one of the fossilized occupants of that gold-stuffed tomb you found. How's it possible for a man to be leading his previously enslaved people through the waters of the Red Sea and trooping up Mount Sinai to collect the Ten Commandments, or whatever the hell it was he's supposed to have done, while simultaneously lying safely mummified inside a secret tomb only a stone's throw from here?'

I heard a choking sound to my left and realised Adam was swallowing down hard on a bubble of amusement. 'See, Merry; some of your knowledge rubbed off on him afterall,' he murmured quietly out of the corner of his mouth. Then he nodded his head at Dan to show his agreement and addressed him in his more everyday tones. 'You're quite right, of course. But I'll admit some of Nabil's arguments were quite compelling. He got us doubting ourselves. We took it into our heads to check, just to be sure.'

'So, you broke back into the tomb and, what? Lifted the lid on the sarcophagus?'

'Yes,' Ted confirmed. 'That's exactly what we did.' Somehow, it sounded better coming from him. As an Egyptologist of the most unimpeachable scholarly credentials, his involvement lent a tenuous kind of credibility to our activities. Under his watchful eye, we could convince ourselves our actions were less about adventure hunting, and more about the search for historical truth.

Walid too, with his senior ranking position at the Egyptian Museum in Cairo, and his contacts in the Ministry of Antiquities, added the weight of authenticity to our trespass into this throwback to antiquity. It was Walid who spoke up now. 'And, thankfully, we were able to satisfy ourselves that Akhenaten, or, more accurately, his mummy, is indeed one of the occupants of the tomb. I am perfectly convinced the other is Nefertiti. Nabil Zaal's hypothesis has indeed proved to be wide of the mark on this occasion. Sadly for him.'

Dan stared round at us. 'Why am I sensing a "*but*"?'

We exchanged glances. Telling Dan everything we had so far was perfectly reasonable. Dan knew all about the tomb. He'd been inside it. More than that, he was one of the small band of what we might call co-conspirators who'd signed their names to the letter Walid had insisted upon. The letter that had subsequently proved so troublesome and ill judged. There had been a time, very recently, when I'd been worried Dan himself might fall prey to our blackmailer's malicious threats. I'd even toyed briefly with the idea of warning him. I'll admit it was *very* briefly. I'd been put off by the prospect of Dan hotfooting it out here to Egypt to throw his weight around. But now he was here anyway. The spanner was well and truly in the works. Even so, I wasn't sure it was necessarily sensible to share the rest of the story with him. Dan could be hot tempered, unpredictable and occasionally irrational. There was no telling how he might react. Besides, we'd barely had a chance to draw breath ourselves. It was still only a scanty few hours since we'd made our latest discovery. Dan's precipitate arrival had denied us the opportunity to talk it through and decide what to do next.

'There's more you're not telling me,' Dan pressed, watching our faces. 'Isn't there?'

I felt rather than observed the long breath, almost a sigh, the professor let out and knew he'd made the decision to come clean. As Dan's future father-in-law, perhaps he felt he had no choice but to trust him. And since Ted was something of an elder statesman amongst us, I knew we'd all defer to his judgement and take our lead from him. So I decided to sit back with my coffee and my toast and hear the story told, rather than attempt to be the one to tell it myself. The warmth of early morning was stealing across the deck as the sun lifted higher in the sky. The pinkish light of dawn was giving way to the golden tones of daytime. I watched an egret flapping its wings against the stretching sky, pale blue and endless above the dahabeeyah. The Nile lapped gently against the hull below us at the waterline and I could hear the slinky feral cats mewling on the causeway. Settling comfortably against my sadly scorched cushion, I looked across at the professor, interested to hear how he would put it all into words.

Ted placed his coffee cup on the table, adjusted his glasses and looked through them at Dan. 'Yes,' he admitted. 'There's more.'

Dan crunched on a square of toast and waited politely for him to continue. If he was impatient he managed not to show it as Ted allowed a long pause to draw out before he went on.

'As Adam rightly said, the proof of Akhenaten lying mummified inside his sarcophagus enabled us to debunk Nabil's assertion that the heretic pharaoh was also Moses. But, hidden inside the sarcophagus, we found evidence to suggest another candidate for the role.'

'You're saying Akhenaten wasn't Moses, but you think you know who was?'

'Quite so; my boy. Quite so. Although I'm still not sure I can believe the evidence of my own eyes.'

Stillness seemed to settle over our small party as we waited for the professor to continue. I'm not sure any of us could quite believe it either. Yet we'd all been there and witnessed the discovery.

'What we found suggests in the strongest possible terms that the man who led the Israelites out of Egypt in what the Bible calls the Exodus was the high priest who served at the temple of the Aten in ancient Akhet-Aten. His name was Meryre.'

'And what exactly did you find?' Dan asked, narrowing his gaze on his future father-in-law's face.

Ted cleared his throat. 'We found a set of clay tablets wrapped in linen secreted inside Akhenaten's outer coffin. The first of them reads as a kind of promise made by Meryre to the dead Pharaoh.'

'Oh God,' Dan groaned, rolling his eyes upwards. 'It sounds just like the dratted papyrus all over again!'

I stared at him. I simply couldn't understand why he wasn't transfixed with wonder. But then, the Egyptology bug had never bitten Dan in the way it had the rest of us. He stared back, and I could see his inability to grasp our excitement was every bit as strong as my own failure to comprehend how it could leave him so cold. The trouble was, to Dan's way of thinking, since the life had gone out of these ancient relics several millennia ago, he just couldn't see the relevance of them to the modern world. And he'd made his opinion on the Old Testament of the Bible abundantly clear already.

Ted managed not to react to the rudeness his daughter's fiancé exhibited with this less than enthusiastic response. Instead he chose to carry on as if Dan hadn't spoken at all. 'On the tablet Meryre promises to lead Akhenaten's people out of Egypt, to keep his teachings alive, and to keep the treasures of the temple safe.'

I'd noticed Ahmed had been fidgeting and twitching in his chair as the conversation progressed. As such a big man, his fidgeting and twitching was hard to ignore. I'd swear I could feel the tremor he was sending through the charred floorboards underneath our feet. Since it was impossible to take no notice of him, I sent him a questioning glance.

His dark eyes snapped and flashed back at me. 'I wondered how long it would take for someone to get around to mentioning the treasure,' he announced. And then, forgetting his newly perfected English in his excited agitation, he added, 'Tell to him about de treasure map, professor.'

About the Author

Fiona Deal fell in love with Egypt as a teenager, and has travelled extensively up and down the Nile, spending time in both Cairo and Luxor in particular. She lives in Kent, England with her two Burmese cats. Her professional life has been spent in human resources and organisational development for various companies. Writing his her passion and an absorbing hobby. Other books in the series following Meredith Pink's adventures in Egypt are available, with more planned. You can find out more about Fiona, the books and her love of Egypt by checking out her website and following her blog at www.fionadeal.com

Other books by this author

Please visit your favourite ebook retailer to discover other books by Fiona Deal.

Meredith Pink's Adventures in Egypt

Carter's Conundrums – Book 1
Tutankhamun's Triumph – Book 2
Hatshepsut's Hideaway – Book 3
Farouk's Fancies – Book 4
Akhenaten's Alibi – Book 5
Seti's Secret – Book 6
Belzoni's Bequest – Book 7
Nefertri's Narrative – Book 8
Ramses' Riches – Book 9

More in the series are planned.

Also available: Shades of Gray, a romantic family saga, written under the name Fiona Wilson.

Connect with me

Thank you for reading my book. Here are my social media coordinates:

Visit my website: http://www.fionadeal.com
Like my author page: http://facebook.com/fionadealauthor
Friend me on Facebook: http://facebook.com/fjdeal
Follow me on Twitter: http://twitter.com/dealfiona
Subscribe to my blog: http://www.fionadeal.com

Printed in Great Britain
by Amazon